Final Solution

A Novel

Lawrence L. Graham

iUniverse, Inc.
New York Lincoln Shanghai

Final Solution

iUniverse books may be ordered through booksellers or by contacting:

iUniverse
2021 Pine Lake Road, Suite 100
·   Lincoln, NE 68512
www.iuniverse.com
1-800-Authors (1-800-288-4677)

Because of the dynamic nature of the Internet, any Web addresses or links contained in this book may have changed since publication and may no longer be valid.

This is a work of fiction. All of the characters, names, incidents, organizations, and dialogue in this novel are either the products of the author's imagination or are used fictitiously.

ISBN: 978-0-595-45190-6 (pbk)
ISBN: 978-0-595-89497-0 (ebk)

Printed in the United States of America

Final Solution

For Rick

Acknowledgements

The author extends his grateful appreciation to Wilfrid R. Koponen for his invaluable help in the preparation of the final manuscript.

Author's Note

Even though some of the names and places in this book are real, this is a work of fiction.

To quote W. S. Gilbert, these references are *"merely corroborative detail, intended to give artistic verisimilitude to an otherwise bald and unconvincing narrative."*

Might some of the events portrayed have actually happened? Some did. Some have been altered to fit the author's purposes. Others did not happen at all.

Is it possible that such things might be happening even now?

History has a strange way of repeating itself.

Prologue

Germany, 1945

It was time. Heinrich Himmler was about to steal the Third Reich's hoard of gold. Operation Aurum was dangerous. It required careful timing, daring and great secrecy. It was also brilliant: billions of Reichsmark's worth of gold that would keep Hitler's dream alive.

Himmler had been an early supporter of Adolph Hitler. He had promised to bring order out of the chaos of the time and engender patriotism in every citizen. Himmler believed in Hitler's promises: work for the unemployed, prosperity to business people, profits to industry, expansion to the military, social harmony and the restoration of Germany's former glory. The Third Reich would make Germany strong again; the payments of World War One reparations to the Allies would cease. Greater Germany would tear up the odious treaty of Versailles that oppressed the German people. Under Hitler's leadership they would stamp out government corruption, oppose Communism, and deal firmly with perfidious machinations of Jewry.

The highest moral standards would guide the superior Aryan people of greater Germany. Out of this would come the purification of their race, a process that would also end the moral decay caused by non-Christians, homosexuals, inferior races, and the intellectual elite.

Ultimately, these enemies of the State would be disposed of in The Final Solution devised by Himmler himself. Yes, Himmler was a true believer. And he was not alone.

The officers of the Schutzstaffel (the S.S.) also took oaths of loyalty to their Fürher. They dressed in medieval armor and paraded on horseback as the Teutonic knights their lives were supposed to emulate. It was be their honorable duty to set the example of German purity. It would also be their duty, and the duty of lesser citizens, to bring all Aryan peoples into the greater Germany. That, all agreed, must be accomplished by any means, including force of arms.

Himmler joined in the secret planning for Hitler's war of conquest. But their early planning revealed a serious flaw: Germany had very limited resources. Hitler and the generals of the Vermacht realized that they would lose a conventional war. Because resources were limited, the strategy of a *blitzkrieg* or 'lightening war' was devised. A *blitzkrieg*, properly executed, would give Germany control over oil fields, mineral deposits, manufacturing plants, and the wealth of its neighbor states. The concept was simple: move fast enough to get what was needed before the Fatherland ran out.

The new Reich expected every true German to give all for the Fatherland. The *Lebensborn* (Source of Life) program was intended to ensure the pure racial heredity of the German people. Young girls had the patriotic duty to contribute Aryan children for this purpose. Boys joined the Hitler Youth, in which physical and military training took precedence over academic and scientific education. The objective of this organization was training 'Aryan supermen,' future soldiers who would serve the Third Reich faithfully. Hitler himself explained the objective in 1933:

> *"My program for educating youth is hard. Weakness must be hammered away. In my castles of the Teutonic Order a youth will grow up before which the world will tremble. I want a brutal, domineering, fearless, cruel youth. Youth must be all that. It must bear pain. There must be nothing weak and gentle about it. The free, splendid beast of prey must once again flash from its eyes.... That is how I will eradicate thousands of years of human domestication.... That is how I will create the New Order."*

When Hammer's Final Solution was put into action, even those convicted of various 'crimes' against the Third Reich were made to contribute towards its ultimate victory. 'Work makes Free' was the motto above the gate of the concentration camp at Auschwitz. The irony was not lost on Auschwitz's inmates. First, all belongings of any value was taken from them. Gold-framed glasses, wedding rings, and the change in their pockets were taken upon their arrival. Then, their slowing starving bodies were put to work to extract every possible calorie of energy. When fatigue and starvation brought the freedom that only death can give, gold fillings were removed from their teeth before the corpses went to the furnaces. Others, who were unable to work anymore, were buried alive. An experiment was conducted to see if fat could be rendered from the bodies to make soap, but this proved to be inefficient. Truly, work freed prisoners from the pain and toil of this world. It killed them.

But now, in the spring of 1945, it was clear that however clever the blitzkrieg strategy had been, it had failed. Directed to their targets by newly invented radar, the few to whom "so many owed so much" had ended the blitz over Britain. There was no opportunity to cross the Channel and invade England without control of the air.

Germany had been unable to achieve that. It was, as Churchill said, "not the end. It is not even the beginning of the end. But it is the end of the beginning."

That had not been the only failure. Germany's intelligence service predicted that the United States would not enter the war. But it did in 1941. Furthermore, Intelligence was woefully low in estimating of how much military matériel the U. S. could produce. And, finally, Hitler's ill-fated second front ended in disaster in the Russian winter.

Germany had done the one thing that it could not do and win. It had become bogged down in a defensive war on two fronts. It had run out of manpower and matériel and there was no more to be had. Himmler knew now that it was only a matter of time. He realized that for Hitler's dream to survive the collapse of the Third Reich, it would be up to him and other loyal Nazis to perpetuate it.

A group of SS officers, headed by Himmler and Martin Bormann set up the Organization of Former SS-Members (ODESSA) It was then, and is now an international Nazi network. Its purpose was to help Nazi leaders escape to other countries. There they would perpetuate the dream of Aryan world domination.

The ODESSA had collaborators Argentina, Egypt, Germany, Italy, Switzerland, and even the Vatican. Argentina had supported the Axis powers throughout the war. From there German submarines made forays into the Gulf of Mexico and the Atlantic coastal waters of the United States. And, by secret agreement with the Argentinean government, the ODESSA had already established an expatriate headquarters in Buenos Aires.

Now it was time for Himmler's Operation Aurum to be put into action. It had three objectives. First, it had to gain them as much time as possible. Second, it had to ensure the escape of the party's leaders. Third, it had to have money to support ODESSA's objectives.

At war's end, the street-to-street fighting in Berlin was fierce. Finally, the Russians were only a quarter of a mile away from the Führerbunker, where Hitler madly presided over the rapid disintegration of his Third Reich. Shortly after midnight on April 30, 1945, he married Eva Braun in a small civil ceremony. They committed suicide together the next day and their bodies were first burned and then buried in the ruins of the chancellery garden.

Grand Admiral Karl Dönitz was never a true believer in the Reich. He had loyally remained at his post as head of the German navy anyway. Hitler designated the Admiral as his successor as Head of State. Given this mandate, the Admiral established a new German government at Flensburg, near the Danish border. Dönitz named himself Reichspräsident, a post Hitler had abolished years earlier. Significantly, Dönitz was not Führer, but rather President, an indication of his determination to return Germany to a democratic state.

At the same time Himmler contacted Count Folke Bernadotte of Sweden at Lübeck, near the Danish border, and began negotiations for surrender in the West. Himmler said he hoped the British and Americans would turn against the Soviets. The objective would be to defeat Communism before it could spread. The Count was promised the remains of the German Army would fight with the Allies in this cause.

But these gestures were mere sham, a small part of Himmler's Operation Aurum. Even as Dönitz and Himmler carried out their part of the Plan, their fellow officers of ODESSA were hard at work on the third part of the deceptive task: moving the gold. There was a lot of it. Taken from the gold reserves of conquered lands, stripped from the convicted criminals in the concentration camps, and added to Germany's own, there were tons of it; enough to keep the Nazi dream alive for generations.

Like most of the Third Reich's leaders, Himmler had a double. In this case, his doppelganger was a Nazi fanatic, whose sole purpose in life had become protecting his leader. When Himmler was scheduled to appear in public, his double appeared briefly first, in order to take any sniper's shot that might be waiting for Himmler himself. Now the time had come for him die.

"Hans, my good friend," Himmler said, "Now I must ask of you the supreme sacrifice." And he explained to him what was to be done. Thus it was that Himmler's doppelganger turned himself in to the Americans as a defector. He contacted the headquarters of General Dwight Eisenhower and said that he would surrender all of Germany to the Allies if he could be spared prosecution. Eisenhower refused to have anything to do with the supposed Himmler. Instead Himmler's double was arrested on May 22 as a major war criminal. Hans committed suicide in Lüneburg prison by swallowing a potassium cyanide capsule before interrogation could begin. His last words were, "I am Heinrich Himmler!"

Leaving Dönitz to deal with Bernadotte and the Allies, Himmler made one last trip to Berlin to supervise the last part of Operation Aurum himself.

Working in strictest secrecy, a group of slave laborers constructed two identical sets of heavy wooden crates. Each set was painted dark green, numbered on four sides and stenciled on top with the German eagle.

One set of crates was loaded with gold ingots, laid between layers of lead foil. The crates were then sealed and set aside. The other set of crates were similarly treated. But they contained only lead weights and scrap metal. One set of crates was loaded onto a convoy of trucks. Then the second set was loaded onto a second convoy.

When the slave laborers' work was finished, Himmler ordered them shot. He looked around the workshop for a last time, stepped over the still bleeding bodies of the dead workers, and gave his next orders.

In the dark of night, the two truck convoys set out through the ruined streets of Berlin. The blackout hoods over each truck's headlights gave barely enough illumination to navigate through the rubble of the once proud and beautiful city.

The convoy bearing the second set of crates, divided into two groups. The larger one headed for Austria and Lake Toplitz. There, with the help of local labor, the crates were dumped into the 350-foot depths of the dark water.

The smaller group of trucks was bound for West Bohemia. At the Zbiroh Chateau, workers had already prepared a false bottom for a huge abandoned well. More of the crates were placed there, using a large crane. Then the false bottom was put in place and the well was filled with earth.

While the work was going on in both locations, the solders took advantage of the opportunity to bury their weapons and other gear, change into civilian clothes, and escape.

But the real gold convoy headed in the opposite direction, to Falkensee. Despite repeated heavy Allied bombing, some of the tracks at this rail center had been kept open. Now, two trains waited on a siding. The gold crates went into the second train. And, when the trucks had been relieved of that burden, they were fully fueled and loaded on flatbed cars behind the gold-laden boxcars.

Simultaneously, the first train was being loaded with small amounts of gold, jewels, silver, china, 3,000 Oriental rugs, and 1,200 paintings. The Pro-Nazi Hungarian solders who were in charge of this shipment were told that it was of great importance to ODESSA. In fact, the train was a decoy. And that decoy was of the utmost importance to the success of Operation Aurum. Tipped by a double agent that the train was en route, it was captured by U.S. forces in May 1945.

While the Allies were celebrating their good fortune, and the Hungarians were nursing their injuries and wounded pride, the second train slipped through by another route, unnoticed. Everything was going according to Himmler's clever plan.

The journey of the gold train took almost all of the night, but it arrived without incident just outside Lubeck, where the gold was transferred back to the trucks for the trip to Kiel and the submarine pens there.

U-Boats 56, 103 and 235 had all been sunk during Allied raids on the shipyard and submarine pens in Kiel. However, German ingenuity had been brought to bear, and all three of these supposedly destroyed vessels had been raised, repaired and hidden away in specially constructed and artfully camouflaged pens at the inlet to the Kiel Canal.

A small, carefully selected crew manned each U-boat. All had served honorably in the Kreigsmarine, and more importantly, each crewmember was a dedicated member of the Nazi Party. Three by three, the trucks lined up to have their crates picked up by the overhead gantry cranes and then lowered in to the holds of the submarines.

With this work completed, the soldiers were ordered on board the decks of the submarines. They were told they would be ferried to neutral Denmark, only a few miles away. In the deep water of the Kattegut, the subs submerged, leaving the solders to either swim the twenty miles to shore or drown. None of them made it.

The submarines sailed on, submerged, taking in air and exhausting fumes through their recently invented snorkels. If ships were sighted in the distance, the submarines reverted to battery power and withdrew the snorkels below the waves. They surfaced rarely, only three times during the 108-day voyage. The vessels were fueled for a 12,000-mile voyage, well under their maximum range of 15,500. To save from loading even more fuel, the diesel allotment was calculated for consumption at 10 knots per hour, their most efficient speed. To further reduce weight, the smallest possible crew manned the subs. The weight of an average human body was worth about $100,000 in gold, and a gallon of fuel was worth $5,000. By operating as it did, this small flotilla was able to carry an additional $300,000,000 in bullion. Overall, it carried over five billion dollars in fine gold to the coastal waters of Argentina. It cannot be said to have been an easy voyage, but Operation Aurum was successful thus far.

Plans for unloading the gold at the port of La Plata had been organized less well. However, certain sympathetic Argentinean banking officials were more than happy to supply trucks and drivers to ferry the gold from the sheltered pier to the banks' deep underground vaults. However, the boats' crews had to manhandle it from the subs to the trucks. That part of the operation took eight long nights of heavy sweating labor.

Finally, the last of the gold was safely stowed in the vaults, and most of the crew went ashore for a well-earned, if very discreet, period of rest and relaxation. Six former Kreigsmarine officers stayed behind. Helpful explosives experts from the Argentinean navy verified that scuttling charges were properly set and operative. On the next moonless night, the flotilla set sail on its final journey. Led out of the inlet by an Argentinean frigate, the subs trailed along through rarely traveled waters, showing no lights. By the time dawn broke, they were well out of sight of land, sailing a Southeasterly course towards the Argentine Basin. Twenty-four hours after leaving, in the evening twilight, the charges were armed. The officers were taken off by a ship's boat. They stood, hats off, on the deck of the little frigate, watching the subs rolling in the gentle swells of the southern mid-Atlantic. Like three solemn cannon salutes, three muffled explosions rumbled through the night sky as their unterseeboots disappeared from sight.

The Argentinean captain offered them a toast of Champaign to celebrate their victory. They returned his toast with two of their own, one to the faithful ships just lost and a second to their new Fatherland.

Ashore, the bankers gradually transformed the gold into bearer bonds, stocks, and other safe investments. Each member of the crew was given a nest egg for investment in a venture of his choice. These ventures would allow each of them to support themselves in comfort for the rest of their lives.

The huge balance of the corpus was invested as safely as possible until the time was ripe for the second phase of Operation Aurum: the rise of the Fourth Reich.

Chapter One

Mark Taylor was tired—bone tired, but traveling to his new home, the first of his own, was the first exciting step in a whole new life. This one last hurried trip to New York had cleared up everything. Most people, looking at his overall appearance, would think of "the boy next door." In his jeans and jeans jacket, they might have mistaken him for an athlete or perhaps a construction worker.

He settled back in the business-class seat of the airplane, stretched out his longish frame, buckled up and ignored the flight attendant's pre-flight briefing. Once they were airborne, Mark reclined his seat to full back and relaxed into the headrest. He ordered a scotch on the rocks as soon as he could and savored the smoky tang of the Glenlivit.

After a few minutes, the pretty flight attendant brought him a second scotch and another little bag of munchies to go with it. She took in his good looks: dark blond hair, broad shoulders and slender waist. She smiled warmly at Mark and he returned the smile automatically, then thought, "Too bad."

Outside the plane window, the fall evening was darkening into night. Lights in the towns and villages below were beginning to come on. Here, at altitude, the setting sun was still visible, tingeing the fluffy clouds with rosy pinks, reds and—farther around the horizon to the East—deep purples and blues.

He was glad to be leaving New York and moving to a quieter and gentler life in Atlanta. In a couple of hours, he would be back in his new, little, sparely furnished Midtown apartment. There, he hoped he could really be himself for the first time by losing himself in the anonymity of the city. He could dress in jogging clothes and go to Piedmont Park, like any other guy, or go to one of the Midtown bars dressed in a pair of jeans, very little else, and show off his physique a little. His rosy thoughts blended with the rosy sunset clouds outside the plane's window. He drifted off to sleep warmed by the Glenlivit and dreams about a new life in Atlanta.

The pretty stewardess woke him just before landing and asked him to raise his seat and tray table. She lingered for a moment, smiling, and then moved down the aisle after he gave her only a nod and began to collect himself.

Mark had brought only his carry-on bag, with a couple of changes of clothes, including the new, carefully packed black suit that he had just picked up at the outfitters in New York. So, he was able to hurry up the jet way as soon as the door opened, with the intention of taking a MARTA subway train to the Midtown station.

Hartsfield International Airport was busy as the huge terminal always is, filled with hustle and bustle. It was even busier now, at the end of the business travel day. Then, above the other airport sounds, came the announcement: "Arriving passenger Mark Taylor meet your party at the Inter-Denominational Chapel. Arriving passenger Mark Taylor: meet your party at the Inter-Denominational Chapel."

"Very strange," Mark thought, startled, "who would want to meet me there?" He sought out a police officer and asked where the chapel was.

When he got to the little cubicle that served at a spiritual oasis at Hartsfield-Jackson, he opened the door and stepped inside. A man in black was there, facing away from the door, kneeling in prayer. Not wanting to interrupt, Mark closed the door softly. "Come in, Mark," said the Bishop of Atlanta, as he stood and turned around, "I have a little assignment for you. Your background and previous work as a policeman are just what I need at the moment."

"What?" he gasped. "Police work?"

"That's right, Mark. Police savvy, anyway. Newly ordained Episcopal deacons don't often get this kind of first assignment. But I have a problem, and I think you're just the man to handle it." Mark could only stare with complete puzzlement at his new boss. "Now," his bishop said, continuing, "do you have a collar with you?"

"Yes, sir, I do," he answered, more puzzled than ever.

"That's fortunate. If you had to go into town to change, that would be wasting time. Go find a rest-room stall and change there. I realize that you've been traveling all day, but you can't go around representing the Bishop of Atlanta in blue jeans. I'll wait for you here."

Mark could only manage a faint "Yes, sir," as he hurried towards the door.

Mark went out of the tiny chapel, and closed the door softly behind him. There was a men's room not too far down the corridor. In he went, washed his face and hands and combed his unruly hair. Then he commandeered the handicapped toilet stall to change. It took only a couple of minutes to transform himself from an anonymous, jeans-clad traveler to a black-clad member of the Anglican clergy. As he emerged from the stall, Mark garnered a couple of odd looks. But he pretended that he changed in and out of his clerical collar in bathroom stalls all the time and headed back towards the Chapel.

"So much for dinner and a good night's sleep," he thought to himself. "I wonder what the bishop wants."

When they had seated themselves, facing each other from opposite ends of one of the tiny pews, the bishop began by consulting his watch. "We have only a few minutes before your plane leaves for Fort Lauderdale, Mark, so I'll be brief."

"Fort Lauderdale, sir?"

"Yes. You'll be representing me in Fort Lauderdale. Your plane leaves in just over an hour, and you still have to clear security, again, so please don't interrupt until I've briefed you."

"Yes, sir. I mean, no, sir; I won't, sir."

"This matter concerns the death of Paul Thomas. Our new Dean had only recently appointed him Organist and Master of the Choirs at the cathedral. Paul was a highly respected musician and composer. In Anglican circles, he is very well known; one might even say famous. And he was a long-time, close personal friend of mine, as well.

"Paul died under rather peculiar circumstances, in Fort Lauderdale, sometime last night or early this morning. He had never married and has no family. The police called me a few hours ago, after they had identified him. I want you to go to Fort Lauderdale and make all of the necessary arrangements to bring his ashes back to Atlanta for burial. Long ago, he had appointed me executor of his estate, so I have the authority to deal with all of that."

The bishop reached into the inner pocket of his suit coat and handed Mark a bundle of papers. "Here are your plane ticket and the necessary documents authorizing you to act on my behalf. I have also included a fairly recent photograph in case you need to identify the body. You may need money as well, so I am handing you a credit card that can be used to draw against my discretionary funds. Use what you need, but be frugal.

"You will be met in Fort Lauderdale by an old lawyer friend of mine, Mr. Talbot Smith. He will have made arrangements for your stay in a hotel there. And you will need to rent a car to use while you are there. I suggest you rent one before you leave the airport. If you need any legal assistance while there, consult Mr. Smith first. Please be as discreet and as inconspicuous as possible. Now, do you have any questions, Mark?"

"Well, yes and no, sir. I mean, the assignment is pretty straightforward. I claim the body and his belongings on your behalf, find an undertaker and arrange for the body to be cremated. Then I bring the ashes back to Atlanta. What I don't understand is your use of the phrase, "peculiar circumstances."

The Bishop frowned for a moment while he considered Mark's question. Mark had seen that look before, and it didn't look any different above a purple shirtfront and clerical collar. His Grace, the Bishop of Atlanta was hiding something, and he wasn't doing a very good job of it.

If police savvy was what he wanted, then investigative technique was what he was going to get. Mark simply waited a moment, and looked the bishop straight in the eye. "Sir?" he said, as firmly as he could.

The bishop thought for a moment longer while he considered Mark's question. Then his face cleared. "Right," he said, decisively, "Paul Thomas's body was found nude, in a swimming pool, at a rather seedy motel. I would prefer that this curious circumstance did not become a subject for gossip. Idle gossip never does anybody any good and often does harm. I'd like Paul to be remembered for all of the good he did in his life, not for this odd circumstance of his death."

The bishop paused, wondering whether he had left out anything. "Well, don't miss your plane," he instructed, then added, "Keep me informed." He rose, indicating that the conversation was at an end.

Mark could only respond, "I'll do my best, sir," and started to open the chapel door open for his superior.

"Just one more thing," the Bishop said. Then he laid his hand on Mark's head and gave him his apostolic blessing.

Mark sprinted for security screening, hoping that he wouldn't miss his plane. Another sprint down the escalator got him to the underground train, which got him to his concourse, where he sprinted again for the gate. He just made it.

For the second time that day, he settled into an airplane seat, this time in coach, as befitted a member of the clergy using church funds to travel on church business. The relaxed, pleasant dream of his new life had abruptly evaporated with this puzzling new assignment. More unhappily, it brought back old memories of a life that he had hoped was behind him.

He had been a policeman in what he now thought of as his previous life. But he had changed vocation in a big way. He was now a newly ordained Episcopal deacon, one day to be a priest.

When he was little, policemen had often come to his mother's cheap apartment. They were real-life action heroes to him. As a child, he had experienced physical and emotional abuse up close and personal, repeatedly and with regularity at the hands of one or another of his mother's many boyfriends. It was the police who came to stop the drunken brawls and the beatings. And he wanted to be one of them. He wanted to purify the world to make it a safe place, a good place for everybody, especially for kids.

As soon as he turned sixteen, he moved out to begin his own life. It had been rough. In spite of his unpromising start, Mark managed to graduate from high school. Then he worked his way through the police academy by earning money doing odd jobs. He saved on living expenses by sleeping in the basement of the store where he was the janitor. And he saved on his food bills by waiting tables, eating staff meals, and taking home leftovers. He was a real loner in those days with no friends, no family and no time for a love life.

Finally, he graduated from the academy, got his uniforms, got sworn in, and went to work. That's when all of his idealism began to evaporate.

He had wanted to be a hero. But he wasn't a hero to most of the people he had to deal with. He was just another cop, a guy they tried to get around or away from or if they couldn't do that, through. After a couple of years he had a stomach full of domestic disturbances, bar fights, and high-speed car chases going the wrong way on one-way streets, not to mention scrapes, bruises, contusions, a broken wrist, and a bullet hole.

He watched, increasingly dismayed, as some older officers cut corners, skirted regulations, covered for each other, made fag jokes and concentrated on safely getting by until retirement. He didn't want to end up like them: disillusioned and bitter. Or like some of the younger ones: badly wounded or killed on duty. And he swore he would not.

He realized that he had to choose: either stay a cop or use being a cop to become something else. So his police work became a means to an end. The police department offered assistance with getting a college degree, and he took the chance. More than a little afraid of the prospect, he started at a two-year college.

At first, he was surprised that he enjoyed school. He took courses in criminal justice and began to play the academic games that the faculty and students played. Being street-smart, he was a pretty good game-player himself, once he got the hang of the rules. As it turned out, Mark was also a quick study and made good grades. Still, what with going only part-time, it took six years in two schools to get his bachelor's degree. He was plenty pleased with himself when he finally graduated, but he still wondered, "what next?"

His salvation from the danger and drudgery of police work came about in an odd way, as salvation almost always does. It began when he took a job moonlighting as a security guard at a very large and very prestigious Episcopal church.

The job turned out to be easy. He kept the alcoholics and bums off the property when the congregation was around. He opened doors for dowagers. He learned who people were and let them know it when they left their headlights on. If somebody parked too close to a fire hydrant, or no-parking zone, his own police badge ensured that his brother officers would issue no citations. Then, he would gently reprimand the miscreant himself, and everybody was happy.

It was through this connection that he got to know the clergy of the parish. He came to respect them, too. They seemed to understand his still unquenched desire to make the world a better place. Their ways of going about that were different, though, even strange, compared with police work. They used an odd combination of intelligence, guile, and love as their weapons. Somehow they managed to navigate the treacherous waters of serving the rich and helping the poor, without compromising principle. It was something that he had rarely seen his police buddies do successfully. Ever so quietly, the clergy went about ministering to "all sorts and conditions of men."

Mark recognized his calling. Or at least he thought he did. He discussed it first with the rector and then with the bishop. Both of them counseled him to think very carefully about what a life long commitment to the Church would entail. They didn't encourage his ambitions. But they didn't discourage them either.

So, there followed the Church's set and orderly series of events: inquirer's class; confirmation; another, longer conference with the rector, and a statement from the vestry to the bishop attesting to his "sober and Christian life for the three years past."

Even so, it was a difficult time for him. He wanted to say "yes" to himself, but he knew that he could not change his orientation. Nor could he believe that he was called to a life of celibacy. As much as he wanted this career, he also decided that he would not lie to get it. Finally, he called and made an appointment to see his bishop.

When that decisive day came, Mark sat nervously down in an armchair in the bishop's comfortable wood-paneled office. His bishop took the one on the opposite side of the fireplace. A small fire crackled on the gleaming marble hearth. The atmosphere was cozy, warm and relaxing. But Mark was anything but relaxed.

The bishop spoke first. "You have something on your mind, do you not?" he asked.

"Yes, sir, I do." Mark responded.

"If something is troubling you, we should discuss it," his superior said. "I hope you can trust me with whatever it may be." There was a short pause while Mark said nothing. The bishop continued, "I have been in ministry for more than forty years, now. I've already heard and seen almost everything there is to see and hear. Whatever it may be, it's not likely to shock me." He smiled with encouragement in his eyes.

Mark took a deep breath and said it as simply as he could. "I'm gay."

"Ah." There was another thoughtful pause. "So that's what you wanted to tell me. Before you say more, let me tell you that I'm glad you did. I am honored by your trust."

"Thank you. I want very much to pursue ordination. But I had to tell you because I won't start down that road with a lie."

The bishop nodded his approval, then said, "We have always had gay clergy in the Church. And, in the past, we have always expected them to be celibate. Period. But we know now that being gay isn't a choice; it's a given. So we find ourselves in new theological and moral territory. The crux of the matter is this: do you think you can be honest to your own being and also live as a Christian priest?"

Mark stared into the fire, and into the depths of his own soul. Finally he said, "I believe I can, with God's help."

"It will mean either celibacy or finding a life partner, you know," his bishop said, quietly. "That's nothing more than what is expected of all our clergy."

"Yes, sir, I understand that."

"It will likely mean fewer opportunities for employment, too. There are parishes that simply would not want you."

"Yes, sir. I know that, too. But, I believe that will change in time."

"From your lips to God's ears," the bishop said, and smiled. "I can see no reason why you should not enter seminary. I believe you will make a good scholar and a good priest. Underdogs often do. After all, Moses was a slave and a murderer, and he led the people of Israel out of bondage. Jesus was born to an unmarried teenage mother. Gay people are the underdogs of America."

Soon, Mark moved to New York and entered General Theological Seminary. It proved to be the most challenging and exciting time of his life. He was astonished to find that, unlike many of his contemporaries, he even enjoyed learning Greek. On schedule, he completed his studies and graduated.

Right after graduation, Mark had moved his very meager belongings from the seminary to his tiny one-bedroom apartment in Atlanta. After that had come the pre-ordination Ember Days, with fasting and prayer. And then the awe-inspiring rite itself: the Bishop, resplendent in cope and mitre, laying his hands on Mark's head and praying,

> *"Give your Holy Spirit to Mark, fill him with grace and power, and make him a Deacon in your Church."*

Mark had been prepared to be completely unimpressed by it all, just the first rung on the clerical ladder. Instead, he had choked up and brushed a couple of tears from his cheeks.

Now, after the long hard work of seminary, he was, if just barely, one of the Episcopal clergy. "The almost Reverend Mr. Taylor," his Bishop had joked to him.

He was supposed to have put on his collar tomorrow and go to St. Phillip's Cathedral, to see his bishop for the third time since graduating from seminary. There, he should have finalized the details of his first parish assignment and begin his new life: respectable Anglican cleric by day, gay blade by night. At least that's how Mark had fantasized it would work out.

Instead, he was staring out of the plane window into the dark night, wondering how on earth a certain well-known musician, named Paul Thomas had turned up nude and dead in a seedy motel swimming pool. Mark was worried, too, about the many pitfalls that could lie ahead while he dealt with delicate matter for his bishop.

Chapter Two

Ardmore, Oklahoma, 1956

The old brick church had very thick walls. Even in the intense heat of this August afternoon, the still interior remained relatively cool. It smelled of old hymnals, furniture polish, and of dust recently disturbed by the passage of a vacuum cleaner down the carpeted aisles.

The building did have stained glass windows, but it didn't have 'Catholic' pews. Instead, it had hard-backed theater seats. The seats radiated out from the focal point of the building: the pulpit that was raised high in the center of the podium at the front of the church. On either side were arranged imposing chairs for the minister and the leaders of the congregation. Below the pulpit, and clearly subordinated to it, was a spare oak table with the words "In Remembrance of Me" carved into its frame.

Behind the ecclesiastical furniture were theater seats arranged in rows for the church's choir. Behind them rose the building's most impressive ornamentation, the pipes of a large and imposing organ.

At the beginning, the organ had been a matter of some controversy. Most of the deacons had opposed its installation, because organs are not mentioned in the Bible. However, Reverend Thomas pointed out that the church used electric lighting and that wasn't mentioned in the Bible either. Besides, a prominent and wealthy merchant, who was a member of the congregation, had offered the organ to the congregation, to be installed in time for his daughter's wedding. The only other nearby church that had a real pipe organ were the Presbyterians, and they were thinking of getting a bigger one.

Reverend Thomas certainly didn't want the merchant and his gift to go there. The Presbyterians, he knew, sent their pastors off to seminaries, where they learned how to pervert the Bible's very clear teachings into the warped and sinful things Presbyterians taught. He didn't trust them. And he had other, more ulterior motives, too. His son, Paul, was interested in music and was starting to take organ lessons. The organ Paul practiced on was the one at the Presbyterian Church. Reverend Thomas felt vaguely uneasy about his son's even setting foot in such a questionable place.

Reverend Thomas's own education had consisted of public high school and two years at a Bible institute. After that, the elders in his home church had ordained him and he set out to serve the Lord. At the institute, he had been inculcated with the dogma that "the Bible says what it means and means what it says." Furthermore, the only true Bible was the 1611 King James Version. More modern translations were highly suspect and perhaps even the work of the Devil. During his two years at the institute, he was drilled on what the books of the Bible were, and what the "clear and only meaning" of them was. He found reassurance in what his teachers told to believe. When he began preaching, he reassured his congregation in the same way.

But on this hot August afternoon, the church was empty, except for six-teen-year-old Paul, who was practicing. Practicing, Paul Thomas told himself, for something that he really didn't like doing at all. He knew that his feelings were dis-loyal to his preacher father, who insisted on loyalty from his only son. He didn't mind playing for church, too much, but he hated playing for revivals. And that was what he was being made to do eight whole days: it was revival time again.

When the stifling heat of August came, folks left on vacations, weekend trips to the lake, or spend Saturday nights at air-conditioned movie theaters, any place to find some relief from the heat and boredom. So, quite naturally, church attendance began to lag. And every year, Paul's father was able to convince the Board of Deacons that the congregation was backsliding. To prevent losing their members to Satan com-pletely, Paul's father always brought in some hell-fire-and-damnation preacher to compete with the town's sinful attractions, like the newly constructed bowling alley. This evangelist's job was to call the congregation back from these worldly attractions, lest they (and their offerings) be lost.

It was fairly easy to convince his board to agree. The annual revival was another form of summer entertainment, although the senior Thomas would never admit that, even to himself. In a small town, whose inhabitants were starved for diversion, any change brought out the bored, the curious and the emotionally unstable. The church building always filled up with people for the revival services. Usually, revivals were a financial success, too, with the church splitting the "take" with the visiting preacher. With one service every night, and two on Saturday and Sunday, the coffers were often full by the time the evangelist took his half and left for his next gig.

But when the church filled with people in August, it became sweltering. Men took off their suit coats and women fanned themselves with paper fans supplied by one of the local funeral homes. Last year, Paul smirked; there had been a real flap over the fans. Somebody at the funeral home had slipped up. When the boxes of fans were opened, it was discovered that the pictures on the fans were "The Sacred Heart of Jesus," "The Blessed Virgin Mary," and "The Infant of Prague." His father had been furious about the 'Catholic' paper fans and had burned them. A competing funeral home was invited to provide proper "Protestant" paper fans, which it did with alacrity.

Those fans had really been needed, too, with temperatures inside the church in the nineties. The preaching was heated, too. After forty-five minutes or so of listening to the almost hypnotic cadences of the preacher's booming voice, the congregation could almost feel the fire and smell the brimstone. Teenagers who had not been saved, and others in the congregation who, they now felt, had fallen from grace, teetered on the brink of a momentous decision. Should they give their lives to Christ? Leave the temptations of the world behind? Make a public acknowledgment and answer the altar call?

That's where Paul's playing came in; that was the moment he was practicing for. The hymn would be played and sung, perhaps over and over again, at the end of the visiting evangelist's sermon. Paul launched into his rehearsal for the last verse by adding a powerful bass stop and switching on the "Tremolo," a mechanism that caused the organ's sound to tremble. Led by organ and choir, the congregation would sing the familiar words:

> *Just as I am without one plea,*
> *but, that thy blood was shed for me,*
> *and that thou bidd'st me come to thee,*
> *Oh Lamb of God, I come, I come.*

And come they did, walking down the aisles to the front of the church, crying, falling to their knees on the carpeted concrete floor. His father and the evangelist would raise them up, embrace them, and turn them to face the congregation. And get their names (if his father didn't already know them) and get them to come back the next night to be baptized (if they hadn't already been). And everybody would have a grand time.

Then, the working-class men and the farmers would go home, glad that they had taken their wives and children. And the women would gossip the next day about who had been saved for the first, or second, or third time.

And Paul would feel less than satisfied with his part in producing an emotion-filled moment that had, for him, no lasting effect and no real meaning.

Paul eased the crescendo pedal forward to Full Organ for the last four measures to produce a thunderous climax. As he did so, he felt a hand come to rest lightly on his right shoulder.

When he stopped playing, a voice said, "You play so beautifully."

He turned on the organ bench to face the speaker, the young and attractive evangelist Jack Johns.

"Thank you," Paul said.

Johns faced him squarely, placed his hands on both of Paul's shoulders and said, "Your playing means so much to me. I don't know quite how to express it, but I am very moved by you."

"Thank you," Paul said again, feeling a bit uncertain.

Jack Johns was a tall and charismatic man. His education was even more scant than Paul's fathers. Jack's father was a revivalist, so his family was always on the road. For that reason, he was home schooled, thereby sheltered from the temptations of worldly things. He was just twenty, Paul knew, but already had a wife and two small children, a boy and a girl.

What Paul didn't know was that Johns had started out as a child preacher, a phenomenon like child actors or baby beauty contestants. He was, in fundamentalist circles, an attraction that drew the crowds. After a suitable warm-up period of hymn singing, Bible reading, and prayers, his father would cry out little Jack's cue: "A little child shall lead them!" Then little Jack would appear. Dressed entirely in white (shoes, suit, shirt and tie), he was a knockout with his beautiful blond hair and deep blue eyes.

But little Jack was no "spirit-filled miracle." He was just a cute, charming child that his preacher father and doting mother had trained like a circus animal. He parroted what he was taught to say and performed the gestures that went with the memorized script. He was a great success on the revival circuit. His parents profited hugely.

His performances continued into his teenage years, and he developed a following of his own. Young people his age liked him; at least most of them did. He attracted them to youth camps and young people's meetings. Some of the girls fell for him, and a couple of the boys did, too. One of the girls was Martha. She was a couple of years older than Jack and had just lost her virginity to the captain of the football team.

She missed her period at a youth camp where Jack was appearing. She figured her chances were better with Jack than with the brutal athlete who had practically raped her. When the opportunity offered, she cornered Jack in the camp's rustic chapel. There, she had her way with him in a closet filled with musty choir robes. A month later, she wrote to Jack to say she was pregnant. Marriage followed immediately for the two of them, and she delivered a baby girl. It was said to be "premature." In reality the girl was the football captain's. Jack didn't know that and Martha never told him. Jack was seventeen and Martha was nineteen. Two years later, they had a boy of their own.

By that time, "Reverend Jack" had set out on his own. His parents had been able to retire very comfortably to a lavish beach house on the Gulf coast. They never went back to church.

Most of his parents' money came from Jack's work as a child preacher. So his parents shared it with Jack's new family. Jack bought a station wagon and a trailer and set out on the revival circuit just as his father had done. Martha appeared to be the dutiful preacher's wife, caring for their family and supporting Jack in his work. In public, Martha was always modestly dressed, with her hair piled high, her face scrubbed and shiny. A smile of holy joy seemed to perpetually transfix her narrow mouth. She said little, in dutiful obedience to St. Paul's injunction "let the women keep silence." But Martha had ambitions. She soon became the business manager of the operation, and a very shrewd one at that.

Actually, Jack knew little more about Christianity, or the Bible, or church history than he did when he first started preaching as a child. He just parroted what he read or heard other preachers like him say. His natural acting ability, good looks, and innate charm accounted more for his success.

Jack stood there, behind the handsome Paul, waiting for him shut down the organ and close the console.

"I came over especially," Jack said to Paul, "to say thank you for all your hard work. But I think you've probably practiced enough for today, don't you?"

"As you see, I was just about to quit," Paul said, truthfully.

"My wife's very busy back at the trailer," the evangelist continued, "so I'm having lunch out. Would you like to join me? My treat."

Paul thought to himself, "I wonder where this is going?" Aloud, he said, "Sure. Thanks."

Although he lived almost continuously under his father's very watchful eye, Paul already knew how he felt about sex. He had been taught that it was a sin to "abuse himself" and that he should "save himself for the right woman," presumably a local girl of whom his dominant father and mousy mother would approve. But Paul already knew that he wasn't interested in girls. Once he realized he was attracted to men, he had thought a lot about his feelings.

Certainly, his father had warned him about the perverts who lurked in bus stations to kidnap boys and do unspeakable things to them. And he had heard his father preach about the sin of Sodom and the downfall of civilizations because of the "sin that dare not speak its name." When his father suggested he escort one or another of the girls in the congregation to a church supper or to a youth meeting, Paul obliged, hiding his dark secret under a cloak of heterosexual piety.

Even so, by age sixteen, Paul had already availed himself of more than one opportunity to experiment with sex. The first time was at regional church youth meeting, where the young people stayed with local families. At his first such meeting, Paul was in the church fellowship hall waiting to be assigned a host family, when another guy came into the room. He was about Paul's age, and Paul fell for him instantly. The young man's eyes locked with Paul's, and he came across the room to shake hands.

"Hi," he had said, "my name's Andy. You want to be roomies?"

Paul had said "yes," and they had stood in line together. After an evening church service and dinner in the church basement, their hosts had taken them home They had been given the guest room, with its double bed, in a remote part of the house. They fell into bed and into each other's arms at the same moment.

From that moment onwards, Paul knew that he was destined to be one those "queers" that his classmates made fun of and that his father said God abominated. And he didn't care. But, he also realized that he had to keep his feelings a deep dark secret in Ardmore, just to be safe. That same year, the high school football coach had been fired for "doing things" with a member of his football squad. And the teenager who had been the object of the coach's misplaced affections had been sent to a hospital for psychiatric therapy and electric shock treatments.

For straight-acting Paul, however, there were other out-of-town excursions, with similar opportunities for sex. He furtively took advantage of those when he could. And he longed to escape from his father's narrow-minded domination, escape the stifling Oklahoma heat and the small-town restrictions that were the norm in Ardmore. Until he did that, he knew that he could never be who he really was. Escape he would, he told himself, as soon as any reasonable opportunity came along. As it turned out, escape came in the form and person of Jack Johns.

The two of them walked out of the church into the brightness of the noonday sun. They got into Jack's station wagon and headed north, out of town towards the Arbuckle Mountains.

"Where are we going to eat?" Paul asked.

"Oh," Jack replied, "I got us a picnic. It's in that box in the back seat. Fried chicken, potato salad; you know."

"Great," Paul responded, turning to glance at the box. "I'm really hungry."

"I'm sure you are," Jack said, laughing and patting him on the thigh, "You've been working very hard on your music."

They drove along in silence for a while. Then Jack turned the station wagon off the main road and down a dirt trail that led towards Arbuckle Lake. He seemed to know exactly where he was going. Paul decided that Jack had scouted the area earlier and became more convinced than ever of the real purpose for the afternoon's excursion. They stopped in a secluded spot near the water.

"It looks nice and quiet here, don't you think?" Jack asked.

"Yes," Paul replied, as they got out of the car. "A great place for a picnic."

"You get the box," Jack instructed, "and I'll get a blanket for us to sit on."

Paul helped Jack spread an old army blanket out in the shade of some trees near the shore of the lake. They put the box in the center of the blanket, and began to unpack it. Paul was astonished to find some bottles of cold beer along with the chicken and potato salad.

"Want one?" Jack asked.

"I've never tasted beer," Paul said, quite truthfully. "I don't suppose I really ought to. Dad says that drinking's a sin." Paul wanted to know how Jack would justify drinking.

"I think you've probably misunderstood that," Jack said in reply. "It's getting drunk that's a sin. Even St. Paul says to "take a little wine for your health's sake." Beer's a lot like wine, except it's made from grain instead of grapes."

So, Paul had his first taste of beer. He had walked past Ardmore's only pool hall many times, and he knew that beer was sold there. This tasted a lot like how the air from the pool hall door smelled, kind of sour, and bitter, and rich all at once. He sipped along on his bottle while they ate chicken and potato salad. Pretty soon, his head was feeling a little muzzy.

"This is so relaxing," Jack said. "Why don't we just throw everything back in the box and take an afternoon nap under the trees?"

"Fine," said Paul, wondering whether Jack would make a move.

It didn't take Jack long. As soon as they were stretched out beside each other, his hand brushed up against the side of Paul's leg. "You know," he said, "my wife is a wonderful woman and I love her and the children very much. But she works so hard most of the time that she doesn't always want to have sex when I need it."

Paul didn't know quite what to say to this revelation, so he said, "I always thought married people had sex whenever they wanted to."

"Well," Jack said, laughing again, "not really. They only have sex when both of them really want to. Sometimes that's not very often. Certainly not nearly as often as I'd like."

"So, I guess you're kinda horny most of the time?" Paul asked.

"Yeah," Jack said. "I'm glad you understand about that." He squeezed Paul's thigh. It's something we men can talk about with each other. Sometimes some guys even help each other out."

"Do they really?" Paul said, trying to sound innocent.

"Yeah. You know, it's more fun than just taking care of it yourself."

Paul knew his cue when he heard it. "Exactly what can guys do with each other?" he asked.

So, Jack began to show Paul. Up to that point, Paul's experiences had been furtive, something done in the dark under sheets and blankets. Jack opened up a whole new catalogue of sexual experience for Paul. Paul was eager, and Jack was more than a little experienced. They had an exhausting and thoroughly satisfying time of it.

Afterwards, they did take a nap before loading the box and blanket back in the car. On the way back, Jack said, "I'd really like to keep what happened just between us, OK?"

"Sure," Paul said obediently, "I wouldn't want my dad to find out. I don't think he'd like either the beer drinking or what we did afterwards. He's pretty strait-laced."

"You're right about that," Jack said, "And this business of being very strait-laced is one reason I've been thinking a lot about my calling"

Paul said he didn't understand.

"The world is changing," Jack said, "and what I preach has got change with it. I need to broaden my message and reach more people who are in need of other kinds of ministry. Preaching at revivals is all right as far as it goes. I make a fair living from doing revivals, but I think I could do better. I'd like to find a way to preach full-time, but I don't want to have a church like your dad does."

"Why not?" Paul asked, defensively, "What's wrong with that?"

"There's nothing wrong with it," Jack responded, "It's just that you have to constantly try to please all of the deacons, and their wives, and all of the major contributors. If you don't you're likely to lose favor, or your income will suffer from lack of donations, or you might even get fired. And you're always poor. I don't want to live like that. I want to be independent and have money. I think having money is a sign of God's approval."

"How are you going to do that and still be a preacher?" Paul asked, genuinely intrigued.

"Healing." Jack said.

"Healing?" Paul replied. "What do you mean?"

"I mean, I want to start a healing ministry. I can get a tent and travel the country, set up wherever I like, and operate independently."

"And heal people?" Paul said, somewhat astonished.

"Exactly; a preaching and healing ministry. My kids are little and my wife wants to settle down to care for them. With the kind of income I could generate from an independent ministry, I could let her do that, make plenty of money and still keep my independence. Right now I have to give half of what I generate to the church where I preach. If I was independent, I could keep it all and send most of it home."

"But with your wife gone all the time, wouldn't you get awfully lonely?" Paul asked.

"You know," Jack said in reply, "I'm going to need a minister of music to help me, and you just might be the guy for that—now that we really understand each other. We could keep each other from getting lonely."

"You know," Paul replied, "That might just work out fine."

When they got back to the church, Paul's father was waiting for them. "What have you two been up to?" he inquired, smiling benignly.

"We went out to Lake Arbuckle," Paul replied. "We had a picnic, and Reverend Johns has been teaching me about Saint Paul. We had a great time."

"You have such a fine, talented son," Jack Johns said as he patted Paul's shoulder.

Chapter Three

Austria, 1928

Nicholas Alexander von Hutton was an aristocrat of the old school. But he recognized that the winds of change were blowing in Germany. His family had owned the same land and occupied the same schloss for more than six hundred years. They had achieved that long-lived stability by knowing which way the political winds were blowing—and they had often held onto it by having a foot in each camp.

Von Hutton had been brought up to understand his first duty was not to his wife and children, but to the family name and those who would come after them. Perpetuation of the family and its right of inheritance came first. He was quite sure that God himself wanted things to be this way. His was an orderly and unchanging way of life, and God was orderly and unchanging, too.

The democratic ravings of that upstart Austrian called Hitler annoyed von Hutton. What did Hitler know? His family was nothing. He had been merely a corporal in the Great War, while von Hutton had led an entire regiment. But, this Hitler— just out of prison—had written a book, *My Cause*, that was catching people's attention. And, von Hutton had to admit that the man was a spellbinder of a public speaker.

The wind, von Hutton decided, was probably blowing in Hitler's direction. He thought it brought a decided stench with it. But then, one couldn't help which way the wind blew. He would wait a while. But, he would put his first son out of harm's way. After all, it would be he who would inherit.

His offspring, young Nicholas Alexander von Hutton II, was bored. Alex, as he was called in the family, was not looking forward to another long summer day at his father's schloss. The military regularity of life there, the awful sameness of every day, was simply too dull. He wished for excitement, adventure, and new experiences in new places. Even his university days had been more exciting, with study, drinking and the pursuit of women. And there were those all-too-brief trips to Berlin and Paris, where everybody seemed to be carefree and happy. Compared to that, summers at the schloss were dull indeed.

Alex had bathed, as he did every morning, in a tub filled for him to the exact temperature he liked by one of the footmen. Now, Alex toweled himself dry, as he did every morning. He looked out of the small window at the tops of the pine trees beyond, but the view was the same. Same trees. Same sky; nothing new to be seen. He sighed. Next, he looked down at his lean, muscular body. Nothing for him to be unhappy about there, not an ounce of fat, just good solid muscle. He ran his hands over his smooth chest, his hardened belly, and his firm thighs. It felt good to be young, manly, and strong.

Alex turned to the mirror above the shaving stand and admired his unshaven face reflected there. It was an almost perfect Teutonic face: angular, high cheekbones, shapely nose, and blue eyes surmounted by blond hair so light and fine that it was almost white.

Leaning forward, he carefully removed the gauze bandage that covered the wound on the left side of his chin. It was coming along well, he thought. He pulled gently at the edges of the cut until a few drops of blood appeared. Then, wincing slightly (as nobody was watching), he reached into a nearby container for the salt. He rubbed it into the cut each morning. The unhealed wound stung and turned an angry red. Smiling with satisfaction, he again admired the progress of his new dueling scar.

Such scars were seen by upper class Austrians and Germans as a mark of their social status and their honor. These scars were usually acquired in university dueling societies, where the idea was not to wound, but to allow oneself to be wounded as an exhibition of personal courage. The true winner of a duel was he who walked away with a nice juicy scar, to show that he'd stood the test. The scars showed everyone that the wearer had courage and education.

Students too afraid to actually duel would make other arrangements. Alex had not feared the actual duel with razor sharp sabers. He was prepared for that. What he had feared was his opponent's lack of skill. He wanted to improve his facial appearance with exactly the right scar. He wasn't at all interested in having his handsome looks disfigured for life in the process. One could not realistically leave that to the chance of swordplay. So, near the end of his last term at university, he had made the cut himself, in the privacy of his own room, with a straight razor. Now, he was irritating the wound with salt to ensure a proper scar resulted. It was very important for his wound to be prominent; it was evidence that he could fulfill his destiny as a member of Germany's ruling class.

Alex's father had his own, definite ideas about Alex's destiny. He knew his son to be the kind of man he wanted to succeed him. However, the proud, handsome young man was also idealistic and impetuous. He didn't smell the stench in the political wind that his father so keenly sensed. They had argued about it often enough and the old Graf had gotten nowhere.

Alex poured hot water from the pitcher into the shaving basin, lathered his face, and shaved it carefully with the same gleaming straight razor that he had used to wound himself. Then he put on a fresh bandage, dressed for the day, combed his beautiful blond locks perfectly, and went down to breakfast.

His father was waiting for him with plans that were to change the whole direction of young Alex's life. During their meal, the Graf said only that there was something of importance to discuss. Afterwards, their faithful Josef brought them coffee in the library and closed the tall double doors as he withdrew.

"My boy," his father began, "you have grown into a very fine young man. I am proud of you and I want to be sure you to understand that. Do you?"

"Yes, Father."

"Good. Very good. I have enjoyed our recent political debates. I think that I have not changed your mind. You certainly have not changed mine. I do not trust this Herr Hitler. I believe that there will be another war."

"But that would be a good thing, Father!" young Alex exclaimed. "We would recover our honor, would we not? We would show them who the superior race is!"

"If we won, Alex. Only if we won. War should be made only when there is not any other option, and then only when the outcome is certain victory."

"But we are strong! The others are weak and dissolute; they cannot prevail against us."

"Perhaps. Perhaps not," the Graf said gently. "But any further political debate is not the reason for us to be sitting here letting our coffee get cold. I have more urgent matters to discuss with you. Time will tell which of us is right. In the meanwhile, we must prepare ourselves for either eventuality."

"You are thinking of the good of the family, Father?"

"I am. No matter what the outcome, the family must continue. You and I already find ourselves on opposite sides of the political fence. Sooner or later, each of us must show where we stand. I stand for the old order. You, my son, stand for the new. So, for the sake of the family, we must now quarrel and go our separate ways."

"Quarrel, sir? I have no quarrel with you." Alex was at once appalled and frightened.

"Of course not, nor I with you," his father said reassuringly. "But we must make it appear so. The servants must see that we have grown cold towards each other. You will leave the schloss today in a quietly controlled fury. You will stay at the inn in the village. And, in a few days, you will go to America. There, you will experience democracy for yourself. And you will study democratic law and the capitalist business system. Everything has been arranged. You will embrace this new thing for the sake of the family. There will be no further communication between us, but our New York bankers will provide you with any funds that you need. And, in an emergency, you can contact me through them."

Alex sat silent for a long time, staring into the log fire.

"I know that this is a hard thing," his father said gently. "If it is too hard, you must tell me so at once."

Alex sighed deeply. "It will be as you wish, father. I do it in obedience to you and for the sake of our family."

Alex took one last look around the room. He knelt before his father, took his old hands in his young ones and kissed them both. Then Alex stood, squared his shoulders and strode manfully from the room, slamming the doors behind him. Upstairs, in his own room, he cried silently, the salty tears wetting the bandage on his chin and making the wound sting yet again. Then he bathed his eyes, dried them on a crisp linen towel, and rang for Josef.

"I am leaving, Josef," he said stiffly when the butler appeared. "I do not plan to return. Please have my belongings packed for me, and send them to the inn in the village. I will stay there until my plans have been completed. And send for the car."

Five minutes later the Graf's own 1926 "K" Daimler-Benz drove Alex into the village and dropped him at the inn. After he had been waiting for two days, a telegram arrived from the United States. It was from his father's bankers there, announcing that his travel arrangements had been made and that plans had been completed with Harvard for Alex to study there.

His trans-Atlantic reservations on Norddeutscher-Lloyd's Columbus were for a first-class suite. Planned before the Great War, but completed afterwards, Columbus was among the best that an impoverished Germany had to offer. Other nations' passenger liners were much larger, faster and far more opulent than the outdated Columbus. Even her original name, Bismark, had been changed to something less provocative. Such things shamed Germany, and Alex's pride as well. "Someday," Alex said to himself, "we will get our own back. Even the Blue Riband for the fastest Atlantic crossing will be ours again."

The voyage was uneventful. So was Alex's train trip to Cambridge, Massachusetts. His entrance into the campus life at Harvard caused barely a ripple. Other German students noticed, of course, and made him welcome. Already tutored in British English, he quickly adopted the American version of the language and excelled in his studies.

From time to time Alex visited New York to see his father's bankers, replenish his funds, and—over a quiet luncheon—report on how he was doing in school. As Alex was still supposedly on the "outs" with his father, the senior von Hutton was never mentioned. But it was clear that Alex's reports were passed along to him. And on suitable occasions, there were expensive gifts. These were supposedly from the trustee who oversaw his personal accounts. But Alex knew from the character of the gifts themselves that his father had ordered them.

Then, in September 1930, the Nazi Party became the second largest political party in Germany. When Alex made his next regular trip to New York, his trustee had a surprise for him.

After dealing with their financial business, Alex and the trustee had gone out to lunch. They were half way through their soup when Mr. Aldridge said, "Alex, I am so pleased that you are going to be able to visit Berlin during your Christmas vacation from school."

Alex, who had just taken a mouthful of very hot New England clam chowder, almost choked on it. He managed to swallow the scalding stuff instead, cleared his throat, and took a sip of ice water. "Yes," he said, "I am, too. I just haven't decided on the best way to travel. I hate the idea of crossing the North Atlantic in a ship at this time of year."

"Why not take the Graf Zeppelin?" Charles Aldridge replied, conversationally. "I understand that it's quite comfortable and reliable."

"Oh," Alex replied, apparently intrigued. "Fly across the ocean in a German dirigible? What an excellent idea! Thank you for the suggestion, Mr. Aldridge."

"Not at all, Mr. von Hutton. I'm glad to be of help. My office can make all of the arrangements for you, if you like."

Dutifully, Alex said that this would be fine. Deep inside, though, Alex wasn't at all sure that it would be fine. He had never flown in anything, let alone a giant gasbag filled with explosive hydrogen. He knew, of course, that Dr. Hugo Eckner, the chairman of the Zeppelin Company, had wanted to use nonflammable helium to lift his fleet of airships. But the United States was the only place in the world to obtain it. Congress distrusted Hitler's increasing influence and passed a law that prohibited sales of helium to Germany. Alex steeled himself to the danger and went anyway. As he said to himself, "After all, orders are orders, are they not?"

Alex was pleasantly surprised. The famous dirigible was huge, of course. And majestic, too, tethered to its mooring mast, moving gently as the wind shifted slightly. There was a big crowd at the landing field, just to see it take off. Even though this German trans-Atlantic air service was a regular thing, people still came to the landing field or stepped out of their houses to watch whenever the ship arrived or departed.

Alex left his small traveling bag with an attendant and followed the other passengers up the circular stairs inside the mast. He stepped gingerly across the gangway into the lower part of the airship and found his way to his cabin. It was a superior one with a window. Soon, the airship lifted gently away from the ground, the engines started, and it flew with effortless grace over New York and towards the Atlantic beyond.

The day salon and the smoking room were luxurious. The dining room served excellent food and drink. With a ratio of one crewmember per passenger, the service was unparalled by any other means of travel. It was a wonderful trip for Alex. The Germans had excelled. They had the newest and best means of international travel and the rest of the world was hustling to catch up. Alex was delighted.

But when the Graf Zeppelin landed, Alex had to come back to earth, too. He disembarked, had his passport stamped, picked up his bag, and headed into Berlin. His hotel reservation was for a small and undistinguished hostelry near the city center. He was accustomed to better, but he supposed there was some important reason for him to stay there. The manager himself greeted Alex with considerable deference, ordered the bellboy to bring his bag, and escorted him to the best suite of rooms. Alex pronounced himself satisfied, tipped the bellboy and thanked the manager.

Alone, he explored his surroundings. There was a sitting room, with a small balcony overlooking the street below. The two bedrooms shared a bathroom between them. There was a serving pantry, and a small dining table. It was serviceable and clean, but pedestrian.

Alex showered and shaved. Once again, he admired the now healed, perfect dueling scar that his labors had painstakingly produced. It had excited comment in America and had certainly made an impression on his traveling companions and the hotel manager. It had been more than worth the pain and trouble. He smiled at his handsome reflection in the mirror and then stretched out naked on the bed for a nap.

He awoke in the early evening and decided to check out the nightlife. But Berlin had changed. Swastika flags were prominently displayed in many places. The previously risqué nightclub reviews now had a decidedly muted tone. There was an odd tension in the air: a mixture of excitement and worry. He returned to his hotel early, disappointed, went to bed, and slept deeply.

He was awakened by muted voices early the next morning. He donned his dressing gown and went into the next room to discover that his father had arrived sometime during the night. The elder von Hutton was just dismissing the waiter with his breakfast order.

"Ah, Alex," his father said conversationally, "You're up. Do you want breakfast, too?"

"Yes, sir, please," Alex said, settled quickly with the waiter what it would be, and made sure that the door was firmly closed behind him.

"Surprised?" the senior von Hutton wanted to know.

"Very."

"I'm sorry to spring this on you, but it was the only way I could think of to meet discreetly. Officially, we're still not speaking. Unofficially, I am very glad to see you. You're looking good. And I hear that your studies are going well."

"Yes, father. Harvard isn't particularly difficult."

"And how do you like America?"

"It's all right, I suppose. But I find it disorderly and the people very undisciplined. And the economic conditions are very bad just now. The government seems incapable of acting. Perhaps it's just me, coming home from abroad, but Germany seems to have changed."

"Yes, Alex, you're right. Germany has changed. And not for the better, I fear. It is our Herr Hitler that I have come to talk to you about."

"Our Herr Hitler?" Alex asked. "Have you become convinced at last?"

"I have become convinced that Hitler will become Germany's new leader, and that the future of Austria is tied to Germany. I fear that he will bring disaster in his wake. Although I have no real knowledge of such things, I believe that Germany may already be secretly arming for another war."

"But you said our Herr Hitler. You don't support him, then?"

"Outwardly, I must. I distrust his leadership, but for the sake of the family, I must support it. And I must ask you to do so, too."

"But father," Alex laughed, "I already do!"

"And, my boy, that is well-known in certain circles where it does both of us credit. So, I have been asked to enlist you in the service of the German Fatherland."

"Am I to come home, then?"

"Unfortunately for us personally, the answer must be no." von Hutton replied. "I wish you could return and live peacefully at the schloss with me. But that cannot be, at least for now."

"Then what am I being asked to do?" Alex wanted to know.

"Remain in America. Hitler will come to power soon, and you, like other Germans abroad, will have to choose whether to stay or return to your homeland. You will stay in America. You will find a lovely American girl and marry her. You will renounce Hitler and your German citizenship and become an American citizen. In this, there will be much personal danger for you."

"What?"

As though he had not heard Alex's interruption, the old Graf went on. "You will find employment in an occupation of your choosing. The money in your trust fund has been converted to American dollars, and an additional sum has been added to it. I will become yours absolutely upon your return to America. There should be enough to ensure your financial success."

"That doesn't sound like serving the Fatherland to me," Alex said sourly. "Not at all."

Von Hutton went on. "And you will wait. At some time in the future, someone will contact you. This person will mention the word wolf and a conveyance, such as an automobile, in the same sentence. You will meet him. He will be your handler and he have instructions for you."

"So my American life is to be a sham?"

"Oh, no, Alex. It must be very, very convincing. To be so, it must be exceedingly real. Several years will probably go by before you hear anything at all. You are to be what is called a sleeper agent. The code I have given you will awaken you to duty."

"Ah," Alex said, pleased and excited by the prospect. "A spy." He rubbed his dueling scar reflexively and smiled.

Chapter Four

The Natahala Valley, South Carolina, 1950

The farm lay in a small valley between two ridges of mountains. The cluster of farm buildings included the family house, a tobacco-curing shed, a smokehouse, a spring-house, a corncrib, hen house, woodshed and some other smaller structures. To these original nineteenth-century buildings, others had been added as needed. A second house had been built just after the Second World War and a couple of trailers added even more recently.

Over the years, the family had expanded, and now three generations, with more and more mouths to feed, were toiling to wrest a living from the same amount of land and its increasingly depleted soil.

Even in the 1950s, subsistence farming of this sort was still common enough in the rural South. Families still grew the traditional cash crops of tobacco and cotton. They augmented their base income by growing and canning their own vegetables and fruits, by curing hams and making sausage from their own hogs. Cows produced milk, cream and butter. A hillside spring supplied their drinking water. The animals and chickens were watered from a well. The chicken yard produced eggs and fresh meat as well. The nearby forests and fields supplied ample wild game, wild Muscatine grapes and blackberries for jellies, hickory logs for smoke-curing meats, oak wood for heating and cooking, pine for buildings, and split cedar shakes for shingles. Store-bought yard goods were sewn into dresses and shirts on the Singer sewing machine, work made easier now that it had been electrified. Cloth scraps and pieces from worn-out garments were cut into fancy shapes and hand-sewn into quilts. Old rags were braided together and then hand-sewn into rag rugs. Everything was used; nothing was wasted.

But the post World War II era had also brought changes. Electrification of rural areas increased dramatically during the Great Depression. In 1929, the Natahala River had begun to power hydroelectric plants. Defense projects for World War II and the Korean War prompted a series of new hydroelectric dams that brought "the electricity" to remote rural areas like this mountain valley.

There were better schools, electric lights and electric power to operate home and farm equipment. The need for animal and human labor had been reduced immeasurably. What wasn't operated by electricity could now be run by gasoline. Tractors and trucks replaced mules and wagons. A corner of the barn now housed a tractor and other mechanized farming machinery. The old horses and mules that were once the barn's only residents were put out to pasture to enjoy a tranquil retirement.

It seemed as if World War II was just over when an "iron curtain descended from the Adriatic to the Baltic," as Churchill put it. Next, China became a client state of the Soviet Union and turned Communist. Senator Joseph McCarthy stirred up fear at home, while the threat of Communism crept over the globe. The next country under threat was Korea. It was not long before war broke out there, too.

The family took counsel together. Jeb, the grandfather of the clan, presided as he always did. "Tarnation," he said, "I never heard of sech places. Korea and the like—ain't never heard of 'em. Git down that old atlas."

They got the atlas down from a high kitchen shelf. They poured over it, sitting around the dining room table. Puzzling over the unfamiliar words and searching the maps, they finally found the far off place where yet another part of the world was threatened with Godless Communism.

"Well," old Jeb said, "That there draft is still goin' on. I reckon Shrimp's draft age, so he might jest as well go and git it over."

He looked sadly at his two grandsons. The youngest was Stuart, still called "Junior." He had been named after his deceased father. Everybody called his older brother, Alan, "Shrimp" because of his small stature. Their cousin Jeb was the middle child and had been named for his grandfather and father, so his nickname was "Third."

"Tarnation," grandfather Jeb said again, sadly shaking his old gray head.

The next day the family gathered early at the old farmhouse to see Shrimp off. Their grandmother had cooked a hearty breakfast for the whole clan: fried eggs, hickory-smoked ham with red-eye gravy, grits, and buttermilk biscuits with sweet butter and Muscatine jelly. Mostly, they ate in silence. Four men would be left behind, grandfather Jeb, Jeb II, Third, and Junior. More of the work of farming would now be borne by the women. They all knew that, but neither duty nor hard work was new to any of them.

After breakfast, farewells were said at the farm. There were chores to be done and the others' time could not be wasted on sentiment. Shrimp threw his small bag into the back of the pickup truck and climbed in beside his grandfather for the drive into town.

"Town" was Wests Mill, where the weekly paper was printed, where the post office was, and the store where the family did most of its trading. "Waller's Store," the sign said, "Always a Warm Welcome." Jeb and his grandson marched inside, out of the cold December mountain air, to warm themselves by the glowing, pot-bellied stove.

"You hear about this here war in Korea?" Jeb asked the proprietor, by way of opening the conversation.

"Yep," Mr. Waller said, "I guess it's official. We're at war with them Commie Chinks or whatever they're called."

"Tarnation." old Jeb said. "When's that bus due fer Greenville?"

"You goin' in to Greenville?" Mr. Waller asked, surprised.

"No," Jeb said, shaking his head, "but Shrimp is. He's goin' to sign up fer the Army. I need a bus ticket." So saying, he opened his leather pocket purse and drew out the necessary folding money.

The money was exchanged for the bus ticket in silence. Then, Mr. Waller handed the money back. "Damn and blast," he said, "I ain't gonna take your money. If you can send your boy off to war, at least I can pay the bus fare."

Jeb started to object, but Mr. Waller cut him off. "Nope," he said, "no use to argue. Your money's no good for bus tickets today."

Jeb nodded stoically in acknowledgment of this kind gesture.

Shrimp had never traveled to the city or been out of the valley much. Yet, when the bus came, he shoved his meager possessions, packed into a cheap cardboard suitcase, into the luggage bin and climbed resolutely on board. The two men waved a stolid goodbye to each other as the bus pulled out. No emotion showed at their parting; emotion was not manly.

The family occasionally got short notes and post cards from Shrimp. He was sent to Fort Benning, Georgia, for basic training. Afterwards, Shrimp stayed on for the more difficult and rigorous parachute school of the Army's Airborne Division. Then he shipped out for Korea.

What the family didn't know about were the personal demons Shrimp was fighting. Shrimp had grown up in the country, where farmers make their income, in part, by the copulation and breeding of animals. On summer nights, he and his kin had sometimes heard the sounds of human copulation, too, above the cries of owls, the sounds of crickets, and the deep bass of the bullfrogs at the distant pond.

But neither Shrimp, Third nor Junior had never had a woman. He had been brought up to respect women. Until they found the right woman, Shrimp, Third and Junior had always taken care of themselves, or helped each other out.

So, it came as a real shock to Shrimp when he found out that the horsing around they had been doing back home not only was frowned upon by the United States Army, but was actually a crime, one for which people went to prison. Even worse, it was queer stuff that no real man would ever do. The enemy was described as "cock-sucking chinks" and "butt-fucking commies." Sex between men was simply wrong. It was done only by the degenerate enemies of the God-fearing United States. Shrimp kept his dreadful secret to himself.

The Army had done its work well. Shrimp's Army education had instilled self-loathing. He had volunteered for Airborne's hard training and dangerous work to prove his manhood. In his last letter he wrote, he said that now that he was a man, he had "put away childish things." He hoped they had, too, he said.

He carried his shame and self-loathing to an early grave. In the bitter Korean winter of 1951 he was shot during a retreat. No one saw him fall. He lay there unable to move, watching his blood congeal in the snow. The sins of his previous life bore heavily on his heart. He despaired of reaching Heaven. Presently, he not longer felt the cold. A curious warmth enveloped him as the final healing of death bore his soul away.

The telegram was delivered a few days later:

> *"The Secretary of the Army regrets to inform you that your service member, PFC*
> *Alan J. White is missing in action. No further information is available at this time. We*
> *will inform you of any change in his status."*

Third had loved his cousin deeply. It was, as was the love of David for Jonathan, "a love surpassing the love of women." Grieved and angry, Third vowed revenge and set off for Greenville to enlist.

Other young men had volunteered too, before the draft could catch up with them. In Greenville, they found the recruiting office, stood in endless lines, stripped for their physicals, filled out forms, answered questions and finally stepped forward at the recruiting sergeant's command, raised their right hands, and swore their oath.

Like Shrimp and hundreds of others before and after him, Third checked the "no" box next to "homosexual tendencies" on his medical form.

Third's short bus trip from the Natahala to Greenville was to become the first of many journeys. Some, like his next, was a physical journey by train to Fort Benning, Georgia. Other journeys were of the mind: seeing and trying to understand new places and new ideas that were completely foreign to their previous lives.

The recruits' arrival at Fort Benning was a real shock to them. Shoved into formation, they tried to march, but mostly shambled along, to be issued uniforms, duffel bags, and boots. They walked on in the warm winter sunlight to the barber, where they were shorn of all of their hair, and then to the hospital for shots. They were quartered in open-bay barracks, shown how to arrange their clothing and make their bunks. Finally, they were fed at the mess hall and fell gratefully into exhausted sleep, only to be startled awake by the boom of the morning cannon salute, the trumpeted sound of reveille, and their sergeant's urgent shouting.

The physical training was hard and seemingly endless. They ate huge amounts of food, put on weight and muscle, ran for miles with heavy packs, learned how to handle the M-1 standard-issue rifle, how to kill with a bayonet, how to kill silently with knife and hands. They drilled and learned how to respond to voice and hand commands.

And they learned about other things, too. About gambling, although it was forbidden. On their first weekend pass, they crossed the river to Phoenix City, Alabama. In places that were "off limits," they joined other American boys to learn about drinking. Third saw his fellow soldiers going off with women. "Whoring around," Third said to himself. It was something he had been brought up not to do.

They had all seen the Army's instructional films about venereal diseases including gonorrhea and syphilis, and they took the information seriously. They had been issued rubbers and watched a demonstration about using them. Third thought it was disgusting and embarrassing.

Some of the boys decided to have a little farewell party of their own. They rented a few rooms at a cheap motel, bought some bottles of whiskey, gathered in one of the rooms and began to pass the bottles around.

Some of them got tipsy before going out in search of female company. Others of them, less accustomed to drinking, got stinking drunk and retired to their respective rooms to sleep it off. Third was one of these. He was sharing his two-bed room with three other guys, two of whom had already fallen asleep.

Third tumbled into one of the beds and fell asleep, too. Later, he was awakened by his bedmate, who had snuggled up against him.

Third shoved him away. "Stay on your side of the bed," he said quietly, "I ain't no queer."

"Aw, c'mon, Third," the young man whispered.

Next morning, they rose silently, as if nothing had happened. They shit-showered-shaved like the Army had taught them, put on their civvies, checked out, and headed back to Fort Benning. They were the only ones in their sweltering barracks that second night, lying in their narrow bunks, wearing only their Army-issue khaki boxer shorts.

Each arose and went into the latrine alone.
Each despised themselves for their weakness.

Chapter Five

Fort Lauderdale, 1997

Mark stared out the plane window into the darkness until sleep overcame him and slept most of the way to Fort Lauderdale, in spite of the odd turn that his new life had taken. He was still very tired after only his brief nap on his way to Atlanta. He had consumed two Glenlivits on the previous flight, but hadn't eaten anything since breakfast in New York. They weren't serving any food on the Fort Lauderdale flight either. When he finally landed for the second time that day, he was tired and concerned about his first assignment. And he was famished.

True to his promise to the bishop, Talbot Smith was there to meet him. Mark wasn't at all sure how he would recognize Mr. Smith, but Smith spotted Mark right away, the young blond guy in black clericals. Mark wasn't used to being that easy to pick out of a crowd.

"Father Taylor, I presume," was how Talbot Smith greeted Mark.

It was the first time Mark had ever been called "Father," and it stroked his ego.

Mark merely replied, "Dr. Smith, I presume," and Smith grinned back at Mark's acknowledgment of his *Juris Doctor*.

Smith was a dapper elderly gentleman who was dressed in light grey suit, cream shirt and conservative tie. He was clean-shaven, but had a huge shock of completely white hair. A lavender silk hankie peeped coyly out of the breast pocket of his jacket.

"I hope you don't mind," Mark continued, "but I'm famished. I haven't eaten since breakfast."

"Then by all means, let us dine," Smith responded. "You can pick up your rental car and follow me. I know where all the good restaurants are."

Mark was more than agreeable to that, so a few minutes later they were headed towards the waterfront and food. Drink, too, as it turned out. The little restaurant faced the beach across A1A. Even at this late hour, the beach was crowded, Mark immediately noticed, by well-built and scantily clad men who were obviously enjoying being close to each other.

Mark pretended not to notice, while his lawyer host perused the menu and the wine list, but Smith caught him glancing at the beach.

"I hope you don't mind," Talbot Smith said, "but I've brought you to what might be called the more festive part of the beach. This place really does serve very good food, and I must admit that I personally enjoy the view."

Mark said he didn't mind and changed the subject by saying that he was ready to order if Smith was. Mark blushed, and Talbot Smith saw it. Nothing more was said about their surroundings.

Mark's host ordered a bottle of very good Pinot Grisio. They had a crisp salad, fettuccini with shrimp and bay scallops in an excellent sauce, and crème caramel for dessert. Mark did credit to it all and felt much better afterwards. Talbot Smith picked up the check, saying, "my town, my treat," and they walked back to the parking lot together.

As they walked, Smith suggested, "just follow me to your hotel. I'll just see you into the lobby to say good night."

The hotel was one of those cheap, anonymous beachfront things that turn into instant slums if they aren't painted every year or two. This one was clean and presentable, but certainly on the inexpensive side. It was exactly what the Bishop had told Smith to arrange for Mark. It stood in stark contrast to Smith's taste in restaurants. After seeing the bishop's choice of hotel, Mark was even more appreciative of Talbot Smith's hospitality.

"Shall I call on you for breakfast?" Smith asked.

Mark thanked him for his kindness, but said that he was certain that Smith had his own schedule to keep. He assured Smith that he would be fine on his own. The fact was that Mark didn't want him hanging around. The bishop had wanted discretion, and discretion was what he was going to get. But Mark did have one question. "Do you happen to know exactly where Paul Thomas's body was found?" he asked.

"Yes," Smith said, "As it happens, I do. The Roosevelt House Motel." He didn't offer to explain how he knew this and Mark didn't ask.

"Well, thank you, Mr. Smith, for a very kind reception and an excellent dinner. I hope I may call on you for assistance if I need it."

Smith assured Mark that he could and handed Mark his business card. Talbot Smith took his leave. Mark looked after Smith as he went, more puzzled and concerned than ever.

Then, Mark turned to the desk to complete his registration form. The skinny, pimply-faced teenager behind the desk handed him an electronic key card and said,

"Enjoy your stay, Father." Fatherhood twice in one day! Mark was rising in the world.

Mark said, "I hope to have a very pleasant stay." But he had a suspicion that he wanted to check out. And it was anything but pleasant.

As soon as Mark got to his room, he shed his coat and collar, opened the sliding door onto the porch, which overlooked the beach, and let in the warm sea air. The pleasant tang of the fresh salt breeze soon dispelled the stale deodorized motel smell.

He fished around in his bag and found his copy of Damron ("the little black book of gay travel"). That ever-helpful compendium lists every gay establishment, attraction, and cruising place, city by city, for the entire United States. He looked up Fort Lauderdale. Under the heading "Accommodations," Mark found what he was looking but dreaded to find:

"Roosevelt House Motel [MO,SW,N]"

Which translated, meant Men Only, Swimming, Nudity in some areas. Which, translated again, meant that Paul Thomas's body was found at a motel that was just a cut above a gay bathhouse. It was quite clear to Mark that if these "peculiar circumstances" became public, there would be a scandal, and he didn't want that to happen. More importantly, much more importantly, The Bishop of Atlanta didn't want that to happen.

"Seedy motel" is what the bishop had said. Mark wondered how much his bishop suspected and how much the bishop really knew about his old friend's private life. Mark decided to find out about who knew what. The place to start asking those questions was the place where Paul Thomas had died.

Mark phoned the Roosevelt and found out it had a room. Then, using his own credit card, he guaranteed the reservation. Figuring that he could hardly ask for directions from another motel without arousing the reservation clerk's curiosity, he asked for directions from the airport. Neither did he plan to show up at the Roosevelt House in his black suit and clerical collar.

He took a quick shower and changed back into his jeans. He added a tight-fitting T-shirt that showed off his pecs and six-pack abs. He didn't want to distort how his jeans fit over his shapely butt, so he put his wallet, keys and, motel key card in the pocket of his jeans jacket. Finally, he closed and locked the sliding glass door, drew the drapes, shut the room door behind him, and headed for the lobby.

The skinny kid on desk duty took in Mark's transformation in a single glance. His look said it all, "Oh, yeah, right, some kinda preacher you are!" Mark just grinned a friendly grin at him, waved, and went out to his rental car. His responsibility to keep the lid on the situation meant that he would be better off knowing what was under the lid. Now he was prepared to do a little discreet detecting.

Mark drove around a little on the unfamiliar streets until he finally got his bearings and found the place. It wasn't quite the dump he had expected, at least from the outside. The walls had been painted recently, and it sported a new-looking electric sign: "The Roosevelt House Motel." The words twinkled across a neon rainbow. He saw, too, the smaller sign that said, "Sorry, No Vacancy."

Mark wondered whether it always said that, just in case a straight couple wandered in. But, that was one question to which he would never know the answer. He had more important questions to ask.

When he stepped into the plant-infested jungle that passed for a lobby, a heated argument was in progress. The middle-aged, paunchy man behind the desk, in T-shirt and leather jeans, was talking to a short, puny blond guy who was alternately yelling at him in a shrill voice and crying.

"Look," the tired desk clerk said, "I've tried to be nice to you because that's the way I am. I let you stay on today because I felt sorry for you."

"I don't care!" the little guy fairly screamed back, "We had a reservation for a week, and I need to stay a night or two more at least. I gotta earn some money so I can get outta here."

The desk clerk again: "Look, I already explained it to you a dozen times ..."

Then he saw Mark.

"Sorry, Mac, no vacancy," he said, glancing at him before he turned back to his small blond problem.

"Sorry, Mac," Mark shot back, "I've got a reservation."

"Oh, you must be the guy that just called. You got here fast enough." He shoved a registration card in Mark's general direction and turned again to the little blond, who didn't look more than eighteen or nineteen.

"... At least a dozen times," he resumed. "Your date signed for the room; you didn't. It was his credit card, not yours. You don't have a credit card and you don't have any cash, so you can't pay for the room, and you can't sign for his card, either. That's fraud, and that means police, and I'm having none of that."

The kid started to open his mouth again, but the desk clerk got there first. "I'm really sorry," he said again, with exasperation in his voice, "but the guy's dead, they've taken his stuff and the body away, and now you've gotta go, too."

There was a pause while they looked defiantly at each other.

"So, go!"

The little blonde's shoulders fell. He sighed and picked up his cheap little backpack, shrugged with resignation, and turned towards the door, tears still on his cheeks. Anger? Frustration? Probably not sorrow.

Mark had wanted to know more. The decision was a no-brainer. As the kid turned towards the door, Mark said quietly, "Wait outside," and gave him a knowing look.

The kid's eyes sparkled just like the motel sign. "Cool," he mouthed.

Mark finished filling out the registration card and handed it back. If the clerk heard or saw anything, it didn't show in his face or manner, but then he'd probably seen plenty of pick-ups like that before.

"You want the phone turned on?" the clerk asked.

"Sure," Mark said.

"That'll be an extra twenty-five for the phone deposit and another five for the keys. Cash. I'll give you a receipt, and you can get it back when you check out."

"Right," Mark said, and shelled out a twenty and two fives. The clerk took them and wrote a receipt, which Mark pocketed.

"There's a safety deposit box in the room," the clerk said, "and you've got a key to it. It's the little one on the key ring. Use it. We ain't responsible for theft."

The clerk had thus established his level of trust, and the general caliber of the place; perhaps also delivered a warning. He turned away and began going over a list. Mark went outside. The kid was waiting as Mark had told him to.

"Follow me," the kid said eagerly, "I know right where our room is."

He led the way past the secluded swimming pool, where several well-built, naked men were lounging and playing in the water. They didn't pay much attention to Mark and the kid, just another couple of guys going up to a room to trick. Mark followed the kid's little bubble butt up the outside staircase and around to the back of the motel. He hadn't realized that buns that small could wiggle that much. They stopped outside a second floor room that faced the pond behind the motel.

"It's very cruisy back here," the kid said, smiling.

Mark opened the door onto more stale motel smell, and they both went inside. Mark turned on the noisy air conditioner under the window and switched on a dim table lamp. The kid, with studied nonchalance, began to shed his clothes, obviously preparing to earn his bed for the night. Mark waited, appreciating the performance.

When the kid turned around, he revealed a compact, smooth, tight and nicely muscled body. He said, "I really appreciate your help and I want to show you how much." He stepped up close and brushed Mark's chest with his fingers before he asked, softly, "What'll it be?"

"First, I want to know your name."

"Jason," Jason said.

"Mine's Mark," Mark replied. "So, Jason, when did you eat last?"

"What?"

"Aren't you hungry?"

"Oh! No, not now, but I know I will be later." He smiled coyly and pressed closer.

"OK, then," Mark said, "you'd better get ready for bed. Why don't you go take a shower?"

Jason looked a little puzzled, but did as Mark asked.

While he was in the shower, Mark did as the desk clerk had suggested. The little room safe was in the alcove under the clothes rack. It stood on four stubby legs that were bolted to the floor. They showed signs of prying, but had obviously held fast. That was reassuring. Particularly since he was putting the bishop's debit card inside along with his own valuables. He locked the safe, detached the little key, and hid it under the stout leg of the bedside table. Mark stripped down to his shorts and hung up his clothes. Then he purposefully put his shoes next to the leg of bedside table where the key was hidden. He stretched out flat on the bed, put his hands behind his head, sighed deeply, closed he eyes, and waited. "Real undercover police work, this is," he said to himself, smiling.

Jason's shower didn't take long. He emerged swathed only in a flimsy towel. It was supposed to be a bath towel, but Mark had seen bigger hand towels. Still, it covered the kid's little butt and actually wrapped around his slender waist.

Jason came over to the bed, lay down beside Mark, rolled over to him, and said softly, "Please. I want to make you feel good. What do you want me to do?" His hands were on Mark's chest again, moving lightly over the hair.

It was a delicate situation. Mark wanted information, but he was pretty sure that, if he asked Jason direct questions, he would either play dumb or want money. And, if Mark paid him, he suspected, the kid would probably say whatever he thought Mark wanted to hear. For the kid, Mark suspected, truth was negotiable.

So, hanging on to his cool as best he could, Mark said, "What happened?"

"What?"

"You know. Why did the old guy on the desk kick you out? I couldn't figure out what was going on."

"Oh, that," Jason said, dismissing the subject. "I don't want to talk about it."

"Oh, but I do," Mark said, expressing eagerness to hear about the kid's adventure. "It sounded like somebody died. Did you see it?"

"No, really, I didn't see a thing."

It was said, Mark noted, with undue emphasis. His instincts told him the kid was lying. He had certainly seen something. Perhaps he was afraid. That would account for his reluctance to leave the safety of the motel and eagerness to hide in a room.

"Oh," Mark said, disappointed.

Jason moved against Mark again, trying to focus his interest on sex. "Anyway, I'm a lot more interested in you."

"Who was he?" Mark persisted.

"Just a guy I know—knew," he corrected himself. "Paul used to take me places sometimes."

"You're not from around here, then?"

"How'd you know that?"

"You don't sound like you're from around here, and you're staying in a hotel. Tennessee, maybe?"

"You're pretty sharp," Jason said. "I used to live in Tennessee, but when I came out, my folks got rid of me. Now I live in Atlanta. I'm an exotic dancer, and I model some, too. But I really liked Paul, so I kept him company sometimes."

"That was kind of you," Mark said. "People get lonely. What did he do? Do you know?"

"He said he worked at a church," the kid said, "But, we'd drink together sometimes, and that's a sin. So, I don't think he took it very serious. And you know, preachers say gays go to hell, and yet here he was." His gesture took in more than the room. "Do you believe that?" he asked.

"What?"

"About gays going to hell?"

"No, I don't," Mark said firmly. "I think God loves everybody."

"That's cool," Jason said.

"So, what happened this time?"

"Nothing much to tell, really. I mean, we got here and went to bed and got off. Then, later, Paul said he wanted to take a swim. I didn't, so I waited for him here. I fell asleep, and when I woke up, he still wasn't back. I was worried, so I went to look for him, and there he was, face down in the pool. He wasn't moving, so I knew he was dead."

"How awful," Mark said, not needing to feign interest this time. "So, what time was that?

"About 2:00 yesterday morning, I guess" Jason said. "I ran to the office and told the night clerk. He told me to clear out of the room and put my stuff in the back office. That way, the cops wouldn't make trouble for either of us. I stayed in there while he called the cops. When they came, he told them the guy was alone. So they packed up Paul's stuff and took his body away. They even came into the back office to copy his registration card. I hid under the desk while they did that. Then they started asking lots of questions, like did the manager know how to get a hold of his wife. Stuff like that."

"Was he married?" Mark asked, wanting to know what Jason would say.

"Oh, he wasn't married," the kid said, "I got standards. I don't play around with no married men. They're just trouble. They asked how Paul paid, too, but the manager said cash. Say, I wonder if I could get that deposit back."

Jason was practical to a fault. Mark was glad he'd followed the desk clerk's advice and used the safe.

"Well," Mark said, "that was really something, wasn't it? So, the manager let you back into the room afterwards?"

"The night clerk did. He said he didn't want no trouble, so he wouldn't tell the cops nothing, if I wouldn't. I said I needed to stay, so he said, 'OK' when the new guy came on late this afternoon, he didn't like it. He wanted me outta here. You heard him, didn't you?"

"Yeah, I sure did. So what are you going to do now?"

"Whatever you want," Jason said.

Chapter Six

Tulsa, Oklahoma, 1957

When Jack and Paul had first hit the road that first summer, with their tent revival, they had parked Jack and Martha's mobile home at a trailer park in Tulsa. Jack's wife and the two children stayed behind when Jack and Paul went on the road. It was to the trailer that they returned at summer's end, when Jack returned to guest preaching. The trailer was crowded then, before Paul returned to Ardmore to finish high school. Jack and Martha slept in one bedroom, the children in the other, and Paul slept on the sofa bed in the living room.

Martha had agreed to let Jack sink their meager savings into a truck, a tent, folding chairs, public address system, and a small Hammond organ for Paul to play. "Jack Johns World Wide Ministry," it said on the side of the truck. But in reality, it was just Jack, Paul, and the locals they hired to help out. Paul was always glad to be on the road with Jack. He had Jack to himself then, and he enjoyed that. He wasn't really in love with Jack, but he enjoyed being with him, on stage and off. They always shared a room, to save money, Jack explained to Martha. But, of course, it was always for more than that.

Jack John's grand plans didn't turn out to be so grand. For one thing, the operation was a lot more complicated than he had envisioned. Most municipalities required them to get permits. Often, they had to pay ground rent to set up their tent. People didn't always show up for the services. Some link to, as well as a financial arrangement with, one or more local congregations was still necessary. And there were the expenses of gas, insurance, housing, and food.

Yet another reason was that people's attitudes were changing. Tent revivals were becoming passé. Modern Americans traveled more, listened to the radio, and watched television. People developed a different view of the world. That view didn't square up with the old-time preaching of the tent revivalist.

So, Jack Johns' dream of having independence and an affair with Paul worked out, but the idea of plenty of money faded quickly in the light of reality. And Martha, if she was anything at all, was realistic. She made it perfectly clear that she didn't want Jack gallivanting all over the country when he could be at home helping her with the house and kids and bringing home a regular pay check.

In spite of these difficulties, Paul figured that things had still turned out pretty well for him. Jack borrowed Paul from his father the next summer, with the promise that he would take good care of him and give him the opportunity to find out what evangelistic preaching was all about. Paul's father was delighted that his son was going to have such a great opportunity to see Christian love in action. So he gave Jack and Paul his blessing. For Paul, it was a way out of Ardmore and his first real sexual affair. For Jack, Paul was essentially free help and an outlet for his deeply hidden homosexuality.

Martha didn't particularly like Paul. She had an odd feeling about him, but couldn't admit to herself that there might be something fishy going on between Paul and her husband. She was too proud. On the other hand, she wasn't much concerned, either. She was one of those odd women who grow cold after they have children. She was content so long as Jack brought home money and left her alone in bed.

When Paul finished high school and moved in with Jack and Martha permanently. That's when things came to a head. The revival circuit had paid less well each year, and Martha saw financial disaster looming. It was also Martha who came up with the solution to the problem of how to make a better living.

The three of them were sitting around the kitchen table going over finances and planning Jack's next tour, when Martha said, "I don't know why you don't just preach on the radio and stay home."

"What?" Jack said.

"You heard me." Martha retorted. "Why don't you just preach on the radio and stay home."

"And how, my dear, would I make money doing that?" Jack asked, sarcastically.

"I don't know what difference that makes," Martha said, "you're not making any real money now. At least you'd be here where you're needed."

Paul saw yet another family squabble looming, and he wanted to forestall that. He hated it when Jack and Martha quarreled in front of him. And lately, they had been doing that a lot. "Look" he said, "you could sell something, too, couldn't you?"

"Sell something?" Jack said, laughing, "like used cars?"

"No," Paul said, wanting to be taken seriously, "something religious. Like bibles or something."

"Maybe Paul's onto something," Martha said, slowly, thinking it through. "What you need to do is find a way to get people to send you offerings. They could mail them in."

"Why would they do that?" Jack asked, unconvinced.

Martha thought a moment, and then said, "Because you would pray for them to be healed."

"I do that anyway," Jack said. "I don't think the idea of buying my prayers would work very well."

Paul said, "But you really do all of that already. We don't charge people admission to get into the tent, we just pass the plate. It's your preaching they come to hear. A lot more people would hear you on the radio. And you could just ask them to send in their offerings to keep your ministry going."

"And," Martha added, "You could send them a little token back."

"Like what?" Jack asked, finally intrigued by the idea.

"Your picture, maybe," Paul said, "like a movie star."

"How about a picture of Jesus?" Jack said.

"Yes," Martha replied, "and you could autograph it."

"That's a pretty good pitch," Jack said, "Just write to us, let us know about your illness so we can pray for you, help us continue our healing ministry, and we will send you your very own picture of Jesus. I'll even autograph if for you."

"There's a downside." Martha said. "Airtime costs money and we don't have it."

"Actually," Paul said, "I don't think it does."

Both Jack and Martha focused their undivided attention on him. "What?" they said in unison.

"I don't think air time has to cost money." Paul repeated. "I don't know exactly how it works, but I think radio stations have to give away some free time."

"That's my department," Martha said immediately. "I'll find out."

She was the undoubted business manager of the operation. And there was no question that she would follow up on getting anything free that she could get. So Martha researched Federal Communications Commission regulations. She found out that, yes, indeed, a certain amount of airtime had to be given away in the public interest. She compiled a list of radio stations and found out about traffic and programming and which stations wanted free, high-quality programs that would be simple and inexpensive for them to air.

They found a cheap studio apartment for Paul that had enough room for the Hammond organ. For the very first time in his life, Paul had a place of his own. He could practice whenever he wanted to, without disturbing the others, something that pleased Martha a great deal. And, of course, it was also the perfect place for Paul and Jack to continue their secret affair.

They sold the truck, the tent and the folding chairs for what they could get, and spent the money on Jack's new radio ministry. They rented a post office box, and began to tape programs using a good tape recorder and a couple of expensive microphones set up in Paul's apartment.

It turned out that producing a half-hour radio program every week took a lot of ingenuity. Instead of repeating the same sermons to new crowds, Jack had to come up with a new idea every week. Fortunately, he was good at that. And it also took a lot of effort. But, as Martha pointed out, it didn't take any more effort than traveling from town to town did, and it was a hell of a lot cheaper.

So, the three of them toiled away. Jack learned to tone down his bombast for the microphone, and Paul learned how to handle the background music for broadcast. The small radio station at the nearby university was only on the air for a few hours each day. They paid the school, which was strapped for money, to duplicate their tapes on its professional copying equipment.

Martha kept calling station managers, and they kept mailing out their tapes every Monday. Pretty soon stations began to pick them up. About six months later, when they were almost completely broke, the checks that were coming in began to exceed their expenses, and the bank account began to grow. That's when the trouble started, although it didn't seem like trouble at first.

They had all done without so many things for so long that all of them wanted everything all at once. Martha wanted a bigger trailer, and they all wanted new clothes. But it was also Martha who put her foot down about these expenditures.

"We have to invest our extra money in the business," she insisted. "The programs we are producing are fine for the small stations that will air them. But larger stations, ones with the really big audiences, won't take our tapes because the production quality's too poor. We need to invest in having our programs professionally recorded. We have to grow our business, first, and then spend real money later on."

"And, another thing," she told them, "we have to start recording what people want to hear."

"Whoa, there, Martha," Jack said, "I don't want to be told what to preach. I preach the Word."

"Jack, dear," Martha said, using her most brilliant smile, "I understand that. And I know that people are hungry for the Word. But I have been puzzled by something odd. Sometimes your sermons bring in a lot of money, while other times they don't."

"Really?" Jack said. He didn't pay much attention to the books and relied on Martha to pay the bills.

"Yes," she said. "See, I've made a little chart. In this column is the subject of the sermon, and in the next column how much money came in from that tape."

"Interesting," Jack said, intrigued. "You mean that people seem to respond more to some subjects than to others?"

"That's right," she said, still smiling. She knew her husband, and she knew she had him hooked.

Paul said nothing, but listened more intently than ever.

"Here's how it works," she continued. "The people our programs reach seem to respond best when your sermons condemn the sinfulness of the world. You really get their attention when you attack the sin of the cities: things like prostitution, abortion, drinking, gambling, and homosexuality. Your Sodom and Gomorrah sermon really paid off."

Martha had probably never heard of market research, and she wouldn't have known what it was if she had heard of it. But market research was what she was doing. Martha had found the broad outline of what would work for their broadcasts: playing on people's fear of change and the unknown.

In the weeks and months to come, she would add a program number to each tape, and have Jack say, "When you write to us, please be sure to mention Program number ___." That way, she could track exactly how much money each tape at each station brought in. All she had to do was compare the postmarks on the letters with the program numbers inside.

After a while, she began to use profits to buy time on stations that were particularly productive. The better time slots brought even more money. Jack responded to Martha's management skills by preaching on topics that were financially rewarding to them. As he did so, his messages became more fundamentalist in character and increasingly conservative politically.

It was at this point that Jack John's World Wide Ministry attracted the attention of The Foundation for Religious Truth in America. It provided generous funding to religious organizations that shared its conservative aims. Founded originally by a few members of the Conservative party, its support came chiefly from one person. That individual had ties to Pan-American Oil and Gas, and other financial resources in Argentina. Sensing big money, Martha encouraged this connection and urged Jack on in his conservative, fundamentalist thinking.

Paul, meanwhile, grew more and more disenchanted. He often had doubts about the narrow religion his father preached, but he knew his father to be an honest man, one who believed in what he said. Although the elder Thomas was stern and narrow-minded, Paulo knew him to be loving and compassionate with the members of his congregation. Paul knew his father had made compromises, sometimes, to keep his job. But Paul also knew his father wasn't in it for the money. Now, it was starting to look as if Jack and Martha were.

Paul began to look for a way out. His opportunity to change his life was not long in presenting itself. He had been going to the weekly recording sessions at the campus radio station, arranging to move the little Hammond back and forth for each one in the back of a pickup truck. He found the campus atmosphere stimulating. There were a lot of young people around his own age, and they seemed to be having fun while applying. Paul had never had much fun, nor had he ever had any carefree friends. Having seen it from afar, he wanted to experience it firsthand.

So, when he was free one late summer afternoon, he left his little apartment and walked the few blocks to campus. He found the admissions office and asked about applying. The counselor was kind and friendly. He answered all of Paul's simple and sometimes ignorant questions about college without condescension. Paul said that he was interested in studying music, so the counselor walked him over to the music school. Paul was impressed with the old-fashioned stone buildings, leaded windows, and the recital hall, with its high, Tudor-style painted ceiling. There was a real pipe organ, which he was allowed to play for a few minutes. He was introduced to the dean, who was a kindly old gentleman. The meeting took place in the dean's office, with its pegged wood floor, Turkey carpets, fine old furniture, and Steinway grand piano. Paul had never experienced anything so grand. He fell in love with the place.

Of course, there were hurdles: the admission test, and money for tuition, books, housing, food, clothes. Paul had no idea how he was going to pay for any of that. "God will provide," his father always said. Paul hoped, and even prayed, that God would.

God's agents turned out to be Martha and Jack, although they probably would not have thought of it that way. Only a few days later, during their weekly program planning session, Martha said, "Paul, Jack and I have something to tell you."

Knowing from her tone of voice that it wasn't going to be good, Paul simply said, "What?"

"We'd like you to record a lot of your organ music, so we can program its use whenever we need it," Martha said. "That way you won't need to move the Hammond back and forth for our weekly recording sessions anymore; we'll have you on tape."

"Oh," Paul said. "In other words, I'm being fired."

"Now, now, Paul," Jack said, "We don't want you to take it that way."

"Of course you don't," Paul retorted, "but that's what you're doing. Now that the program's becoming a success, you want to kick me out and keep everything for yourselves. That's not fair."

"I don't know what's unfair about it," Martha chimed in, "we expect to pay you to record your music. Of course, after that, we'll own the recordings."

"OK," Paul replied, "just so long as it's fair. I'll give it some thought and let you know tomorrow."

"You'll let me know right now, young man," Martha practically shouted.

"No," Paul said, firmly and quietly, "I'll give it some thought and let you know tomorrow. Don't push me." His voice trembled slightly. He was close to tears. Returning to Ardmore was not an option. He walked to the door and out of the trailer. He decided to fight. Jack followed him.

"Paul," Jack said, stopping him, "please don't. I feel terrible about how you're taking this. You know I wouldn't hurt you for the whole world."

"Oh, wouldn't you?" Paul asked him. "Well, you already have, you know. If I'm going to give you recordings of my music and then move on, I need somewhere to go. And you're going to give it to me. You're going to pay my tuition and college expenses for the next four years."

"Oh," Jack said, astonished, "I don't think Martha would ever agree to that."

Paul gave him a wicked smile. "Make her understand, Jack. I'm sure you can find a way to do that. After all, I was only sixteen."

Chapter Seven

The Hamptons, 1939

The elegant old house was ablaze with light. Uniformed chauffeurs, who had driven their masters and mistresses to what promised to be one of the finest parties of the year, were gathered around the intimidating hood of the latest sixteen-cylinder Cadillac limousine.

The newest automotive development was always of interest, of course. But on this third Friday of March the talk was of war, not engines. The Anschluss, or forced inclusion of Austria into Greater Germany in 1938, was the first major step in Hitler's long-desired expansion of Germany. It was followed by the addition of the Sudetenland later that year. Now, Hitler's armies had just finished occupying Czechoslovakia.

Inside the house, the party was well under way. The only thing that cast the slightest pall over the proceedings was the news from Europe. It was fast becoming clear that there would probably be another war in Europe. Most Americans, including most of the Cordells' guests that evening, wanted the United States to stay out of it. The Great War had been enough. They did not want a World War II.

It was the seventeenth day of March: St. Patrick's Day. However, that was not the reason for celebration. The reception honored two-month-old Amanda Elizabeth Hutton, the second child of Mary Elisabeth Hutton, née Cordell, and her husband Nicholas Alexander (Alex) Hutton II. The child's private christening had taken place that very afternoon at Christ Episcopal Church. It was not only the Cordells' parish church, but also a very suitable place for such an important social event. The church, although rebuilt just fourteen years earlier, had been there since 1705. Older members could recall rubbing elbows with the likes of President Theodore Roosevelt and other important personages.

Amanda Elisabeth was off to a good start. Her godparents were among New York's most prominent people. The bishop himself had presided at the ceremony. That right reverend gentleman was now engaged in lively conversation with Amanda's brother, Nicholas (Nicky) Alexander Hutton III, who was already four.

"Do you know where Czechoslovakia is, Nicky?" the Bishop asked.

"Yes, sir. It's near where my grandpapa lives."

"And have you visited your grandpapa there?"

"No, sir. Grandpapa doesn't talk to papa other anymore."

"I see," the Bishop said, a bit embarrassed at this revelation. "And what did you think of the christening today."

"It was good. It was short."

That got a hearty laugh from His Grace.

His was not the only laughter in the room. One heard it above the chatter of the guests and the lively sounds of the five-piece orchestra. The latter was playing the latest dance tunes. The rugs and been removed from the largest of the drawing rooms. Afterwards, dance wax had been sprinkled on the parquet. A few of the younger couples essayed onto this impromptu dance floor to display their varying talents at doing the frenzied jitterbug movements of the Big Apple, the Shag, and the Susy-Q.

In the library, things were considerably more solemn, if not downright grim. The heavy library doors muted the sounds of the gaiety beyond while a discussion of the latest news from Europe took place within.

Alex, his father-in-law Oscar Cordell, and the family lawyer, Jeremiah Pinch, were deep in conversation. Mr. Cordell was speaking.

"Alex, your knowledge of the European market and the investments you have made for us in Germany have been very profitable for the family and the firm. I am deeply grateful to you for your hard work in this area."

Mr. Pinch cleared his throat gently before he spoke in his quiet, dry lawyer's voice. "However, Alex, it has been my duty to point out to your father-in-law that war may come. We can always hope that it will not, as indeed I do, but it is my duty to counsel prudence."

"Jeremiah has suggested to me that we should divest ourselves of our German investments, Alex. But I'd like to hear your thoughts, too."

"Frankly, sir, I agree with Mr. Pinch. There is, I think, a great deal of misplaced enthusiasm for Mr. Hitler, not only in Germany, but also here as well. The German American Bund, for example, has a lot of American followers because of their admiration for Adolf Hitler, his dislike for the Jews, and the recent military achievements of Nazi Germany. Nevertheless, I do not think we should let these temporary enthusiasms color our thinking."

"So you think that the Nazi movement in Germany will fail?"

"I have no way of knowing. However, Germany is still a poor country, with limited resources. It cannot sustain a long war successfully unless it expands its borders rapidly. The Great War was fought essentially to a stalemate. Germany lost. Unless Herr Hitler adopts some unforeseen and successful new strategy, Germany will lose again."

"Does your father agree with that?" Mr. Pinch asked.

"I doubt it," Alex lied. "I think he's been completely hoodwinked by that Austrian paperhanger. But the crux of the matter is this: if the United States does not remain neutral, our German assets may be impounded and made unavailable to us during a war. Even if the United States remains neutral, Germany's industrial complex could be destroyed or severely damaged. In that case, we will likely lose everything. I think we should quietly divest ourselves of our German holdings over the next several months."

Mr. Cordell summarized their meeting. "Thank you, gentlemen. At best, then, we would lose control of our investments; at worst they could become worthless. I will put your advice to the Directors on Monday and let you know what they decide. Mr. Pinch, I have a family matter to discuss with Alex. You are welcome to remain, of course, but you might get more enjoyment from some cold Champaign."

"Dom Perignon said he was 'drinking stars,' did he not?" Said the courtly Mr. Pinch, as he rose. "I shall withdraw with your kind permission and do the same."

"Sir?" Alex said, as soon as Jeremiah Pinch had closed the door, "You wanted to discuss something else?"

"Yes, Alex, I do. You've been a part of our family for over five years, now. I consider you my son. I hope that the recent events in Europe will not have an adverse effect on our relationship."

"If you are asking where my loyalties lie, they are with you and with America, which is my country now, too."

"Thank you. I knew in my heart that this was so, but I wanted to hear to say it. You continue to make me a very happy father-in-law. Now, let us rejoin the party."

Over the next five months, Alex's primary duty at Cordell and Company consisted of disposing of their German investments. As the world marched towards war, shares were sold and the money reinvested. As a secretly loyal German, Alex didn't like how the Directors were telling him to do the investing: buy shares in American companies with the capacity to produce arms and armaments. It made him feel disloyal that the proceeds from the sale of German stocks were being used in this way. He assuaged his feelings with the thought that in this sphere he could do only what he was told to do.

Things in Europe continued to heat up, so Alex supposed that it would be only a matter of weeks or months before he was called into the service of the Fatherland. It was pretty clear that Hitler's next target for expansion would be Poland. In an effort to forestall this, Britain and Poland signed a mutual assistance treaty in late August 1939. Scarcely two weeks later, the German invasion of Poland took place. It was a though Hitler had dared Great Britain to oppose him. But Britain lived up to its commitment. France, Australia and New Zealand quickly joined Britain in declaring war on Germany.

The world was again at war, but the United States stayed officially neutral. Unofficially, President Roosevelt was on the side of Britain and her allies. But the United States was not prepared for war. The end of the Great War had resulted in a rapid decline of support for the U. S. military. The Great Depression followed that. There was no money and no political will to change the status quo.

When it came to national loyalty, it was Alex's duty, as a sleeper agent, to deceive. However, he had almost none of that to do. His deception consisted only of not telling anyone, even his wife, about the assignment he had accepted. Months and months went by. Nobody called to use the word wolf and mention a means of transportation in the same sentence. He found the waiting difficult.

On December 7, 1941 America's neutrality bubble burst. Japan attacked the American Navy base at Pearl Harbor in Hawaii. Public indifference turned into public outrage overnight. Calling it a "day that will live in infamy," President Roosevelt asked Congress for, and got, a formal declaration of war against the Empire of Japan. Four days later, Japan's ally Germany declared war on the United States of America.

About a month after that, the war came to America's Atlantic coastal waters. Even before the institution of America's Lend-Lease program, the United States had been shipping war matériel to Britain with the impunity of a neutral nation. Then the tables turned as German U-boats began to sink American ships, with impunity, within sight of American shores. Almost immediately, a blackout was enforced all along the Eastern seaboard, lest the U-boats discover ships by night silhouetted against the glowing lights of the eastern shore.

Alex's coworkers were outraged. Secretly, Alex was delighted. He was eager to enter the fray on behalf of his Fatherland. But still no message came.

Then, in the spring of 1942, his secretary buzzed the intercom to say, "a Mr. Wolf on line three for you, sir."

"Alex Hutton," he said, picking up the receiver.

"Oh, hello, Alex," the unfamiliar voice said, "Long time no see. I'd like to get caught up. Can you join me for lunch today?"

Alex couldn't place the voice or the man. "I'll have to check my calendar," he said, buying time.

"C'mon, Alex, just hop in your car and join your old buddy Wolf at the Athletic Club."

"Great," Alex said, "My calendar's free. I could be there around 12:30, if that's alright." "Couldn't be better. See you then," Wolf said, and hung up.

Finally, the code words had been spoken that awakened him to duty. Alex felt a thrill that filled him with excitement.

About 12:15, Alex left his Wall Street office and took a taxi to Central Park South, the location of the famous club. Founded in 1864, it had become a haven for business leaders, as well as those interested in athletic endeavors. Known among its members as the City House, the Club's Manhattan address boasts panoramic views of Central Park, lavish guest suites and elegantly furnished meeting and dining facilities. Naturally, Alex was a member.

He paid for his taxi. The doorman touched his hat, opened the outer door to the Club, and said, "Good afternoon, Mr. Hutton. I believe Mr. Walters is waiting for you inside." Mr. Walters was.

"Hello, Alex, my boy," said the gray haired, portly gentleman in the exquisitely tailored suit. "It's good to see you. Let's go in, shall we?"

Alex had seen Charles Walters two or three times from a distance, but was hardly on the kind of friendly footing that Walters now appeared to feel for him. Walters, Alex knew, worked for a large construction company that currently had a lot of War Department contracts. He knew little else.

"Charles!" Alex said warmly, as they shook hands, "it has been far too long."

The maître d'hôtel seated them almost immediately, and he did so with considerable deference.

Charles suggested cocktails, but Alex demurred. He never drank during business hours and held a certain amount of distain for those who did.

"I think it would be a good idea if you did, Alex," Charles said seriously. "You may want it. I have some bad news."

They compromised on a bottle of wine to go with their luncheon. After the waiter had departed, Charles delivered his message as quietly and compassionately as he could.

"Alex, I am sorry to have to be the one to tell you. Your father is dead."

It struck Alex like a knife in the heart. He turned toward the window. The early greening of Central Park took on the Cezanne-like quality of an Impressionist painting. For a while he just sat and stared, saying nothing, waiting for the mists to clear. Charles waited in sympathetic silence. Finally Alex turned back to him.

"When and how?"

"Only a few days ago. I gather that he simply went off to bed and died quietly in his sleep. I believe it was your servant Josef who found him."

"He wasn't all that old. Just fifty-nine, I think. He was gassed during World War One, though, and his lungs were never strong after that. It was German mustard gas, too. That's the really sad part. The wind just suddenly changed direction and caught them."

"Still, you have your son to carry on the family name."

"We've dropped the "von," though."

"You can reclaim it after the war is won."

"And the schloss and land?"

"That, too. We will see to it until you return."

"We?"

"I can't say more for now. We probably shouldn't meet too often, either. We really have nothing that would cause us to do so, except a casual friendship. And I have my own work to do. It is work that you would not be at all interested in."

Alex understood immediately. Charles Walters was actively spying on his company. He was obviously making regular reports, too, or he would not have been asked to pass the message about the old Graf's death.

"It must be satisfying to be busy," Alex noted.

"It is. Still, a good long sleep is useful, too."

"So long as one does not become Rip van Winkle."

They laughed and then dropped the subject. An excellent salad had arrived, almost unnoticed, and was now in front of them. The rest of the luncheon was filled with banal conversation. As they were parting company outside the Club, Charles gave him his new code words.

"By the bye, Alex, it's 'umbrella and taxi,' next time. So long."

"Bye," Alex said, waving casually as he stepped into his waiting cab.

Alex now had a second secret to keep. He could not tell even his wife that his father was dead. It was a grief he would have to bear alone. As the months went by, grief changed to acceptance and then to the remembrance of good times past. And still Alex waited. May of 1944, with the D-Day landings in Normandy, came and went. In the Pacific, Douglas McArthur and Chester Nimitz island-hopped towards Japan. Soon Eisenhower was on the Rhine. Roosevelt died and the new President, Truman, ordered two atomic bombs dropped on Japan.

By the fall of 1945 it was all over. In twelve years, more than fifty-two million people had died as cities were bombed, armies decimated, aircraft destroyed and navies sunk. These casualties were not only combatants, but also civilians and ethnic or political undesirables who were worked to death, shot, gassed in transportation vans, suffocated in boxcars on rail sidings, inhaled Ziclon B gas in shower rooms, and went up concentration camp chimneys as smoke. These undesirables were simply guilty of being who they were: Jews, Jehovah's Witnesses, Gypsies, dissenting clergy, homosexuals and those who made critical remarks about the Nazi régime.

As the lights went on again all over the world, the Allies celebrated. Alex joined in these celebrations with a heavy heart. He had contributed nothing to the Fatherland's war effort. Worse still, the Fatherland had lost. Now, he reasoned, it was all over. He supposed that as an American citizen, he should just forget all about it and get on with his life. He found that hard to do.

That changed on a dreary spring day in 1947. The upper floors of Manhattan's skyscrapers of were swathed in mist. Intermittent rain, driven by fitful winds, beat against Alex's office windows. His secretary buzzed him to announce that Charles Walters was on the line.

Alex picked up the phone, "Hi, Charles," he said, "I haven't seen you in ages."

"Right you are, Alex. It's been far too long. I thought we ought to get together. Is the Club at 12:30 OK with you?"

"Sounds good to me."

"The weather's awful. Be sure to take and umbrella when you go out to get a taxi."

Alex laughed. "Yeah, it's raining over here, too." But his heart was beating fast.

It was almost an exact repeat of the meeting three years before. It began with the usual social chitchat. Then Charles said, "I've run across something that's more in your line than mine."

"Oh? What's that?"

"Hey, I'm a manufacturer, not an investment banker. So, what do I know? But this guy told me about a new venture that sounded like something you might like to look into."

"What is it?"

"Developing gas and oil reserves in Argentina. They're looking for venture capital, I'm told. The company is called Pan-American Oil and Gas. Here's the guy's card."

"Thanks, I'll check into it. I appreciate the tip. It looks like lunch is on Cordell, Hutton and Company today."

Charles abruptly changed the subject. "That boy of yours must be getting to be something of a grown-up, isn't he?"

"Nicky? Yes, he'll be eighteen in a couple of months."

"Why don't you wait until school is out and then take him along? Hell, why don't you take along the while family? A little vacation would do 'em good."

"Good idea, Charles," Alex said, picking up the hint, "I think I'll do just that."

When Alex got back to his office, his secretary told him that Mr. Cordell wanted to see him.

"Lunch at the Club, Alex? Important client, I take it."

"No, sir, just a tip. But it's probably a very good one. Oil and gas exploration in Argentina. An outfit called Pan-American Oil and Gas."

His father-in-law grinned and then broke into a hearty laugh. "I just had a call from Waite Phillips. Phillips Petroleum is family-owned, you know, and they're looking to expand production, too. What do you make of it? Coincidence or what?"

"I'd say not. Everybody wants a new car, now that the war is over. There will be a lot more of them on the road soon, and that means a higher demand for gas. But I think the real market expansion will be in petrochemicals: plastics and the like."

"I'd like you to take a good hard look at both of these opportunities and then prepare a detailed report for the Board. What do you want to do first? Oklahoma or Argentina?"

"Oklahoma," Alex said decisively. "I'd like to take Mary and the kids along to Argentina. If I wait 'til school's out, we can all go. We haven't had a vacation since the war began and I think it's time we did. So, it's Oklahoma first, if that's OK."

"Fine! Argentina can wait until all of you can have a good time down there."

A couple of days later the whole family piled into their new Cadillac and drove to the airport to see Alex off to Oklahoma. They got there early and had lunch in the observation dining room. Then Alex boarded the American Airlines DC-6 for the five and a half hour flight to Tulsa.

His meetings with Oklahoma's leading petroleum tycoon were uneventful and fruitful. He returned not only with an agreement in principle with Phillips Petroleum, but also with some good leads for other oil and gas related investments.

Almost immediately upon his return to New York, Alex and his excited family boarded a Pam American planes to fly to Miami. There, they changed to one of the Airline's famed Clippers for the trip to Buenos Aires. Service was luxurious aboard the plane, which was operated by the Pan Am subsidiary, Panair do Brasil. Cocktails were served prior to the elegant evening meal. During dinner, their seats were converted to private bunks for the night portion of the flight.

As Alex prepared himself for sleep, he reflected on how rapidly international politics could change when money and trade were involved. At the end of the war the American government knew perfectly well that the Germans had funded intervention in Argentine elections, subsidized the press for propaganda purposes, and purchased large quantities of strategic materials for the German war machine. But at war's end business interests wanted better diplomatic relations with Argentina. The American government found it convenient to conclude that German assets were not identifiable by the Argentine government and that no looted gold had reach Argentina. Any fears of a resurgent Nazism that might have existed were officially ignored.

Alex was about to find that the truth was somewhat different.

Chapter Eight

Fort Lauderdale, 1997

As it turned out, what Mark wanted from Jason that first night, was to be left alone so he could get some sleep. After hearing Jason's version of the past night's events, Mark turned out the light and got under the covers. Jason had only to shed his towel, which he quickly did. He curled up on Mark's left side. He just snuggled right up, put his left leg over Mark's and his head on Mark's chest. When Mark rested his arm across Jason's back, his hand reached all the way down to the kid's firm little butt.

Mark continued to control himself, but with some difficulty. Jason made a couple of half-hearted attempts to attract Mark's attention, but fatigue won out, as Mark had hoped it would. Soon, Jason relaxed and his breathing became deep and regular.

Mark needed information a lot worse that he wanted casual sex. He lay there on his back, in the darkness, eyes wide open, feeling sexually frustrated, and wanting badly to sleep. But he needed to make some careful decisions, too. He reviewed the long day's events, still puzzled by a lot of them. "This is one hell of a mess," he thought. "Handling this discreetly for the Bishop may become anything but easy."

First, there was the matter of the death itself. If the police decided that it had been a simple drowning, well and good. Then it would be equally simple to handle the whole episode. On the other hand, if they became suspicious, or if there was an autopsy, or if something else went wrong, the police already knew there was a connection to the bishop. Then, somebody was bound to talk to a reporter sooner or later.

Mark was also wondering, what he ought to do about his star witness, who was, at that moment, sleeping naked in his arms. Mark certainly didn't want some reporter getting wind of Jason and offering him five minutes of fame on the nightly news. Besides keeping the kid mum, there was also the issue of keeping him close. Mark was fairly certain that Jason knew more than he'd already reluctantly revealed. In fact, he might be the key to a lot of things that Mark hadn't yet found out. Mark decided he that didn't want Jason to disappear.

Although Mark wanted to hang onto Jason, Mark could hardly tell Jason why, lest Jason go after his five minutes of fame all by himself. Mark felt that he could hardly introduce him to Talbot Smith, gay or not, without seeing him raise at least one bushy white eyebrow. Mark supposed he could probably trust Smith, but at this point Smith had no need to know. For now, he decided, the fewer who knew, the better.

And Jason would probably be even harder to deal with when it came to the bishop. Not that Mark assumed that the bishop was innocent to the ways of the world. One doesn't spend a lifetime in the ministry without finding out a whole lot about human beings, much of it undesirable. But an explanation to Jason or any sort of introduction to the bishop could turn out badly if Jason had having a mercenary turn of mind.

"This is one hell of a mess," Mark repeated to himself. He thought things over a bit longer, made his decisions, and was then able to relax and drift off to sleep.

Mark had always been wakeful on those rare occasions in his solitary life when there had been somebody else in bed with him. But he was very tired and slept well that night. Even so, he was aware, when he shifted positions, that Jason moved easily in tandem with him. He never seemed to wake, just to respond to Mark's movements by readjusting his place in the bed, always managing to stay close. Mark didn't think that he was sleeping nearly as well as Jason, but when Mark finally woke in the morning, it was from a very deep sleep. And he was alone.

He looked around, but there was no sign of the kid. He jumped up and checked the bathroom. No Jason there, either. "Shit!" he said to himself. Next, he checked the safe, but it was still locked, and the key was still under the table leg. All of his other belongings were where he had left them.

He was not at all happy about Jason's disappearance. Pissed off was more like it, but Mark didn't see that there was much he could do about it. He needed to get back to his beachfront accommodations anyway. He had to make some calls and claim Paul Thomas's body. At this point, the lid was still on the situation, so the rest of his investigation could wait. He could dig further later, if he had to.

His thoughts returned to the absent Jason once more. "Well," he said to himself, "screw him." Mark was still fuming as he turned the shower on hot, grabbed his toilet kit, shed his shorts and closed the bathroom door on the air-conditioned coolness of the bedroom. He shaved in the shower, as he always did, scrubbed down, cut off the water, and toweled dry, using two of the motel's miniscule towels to do so. Then he stepped naked into the bedroom to find that he wasn't alone any longer.

There sat Jason, cross-legged on the bed, grinning.

"Hi," Jason said. "I got breakfast." He pointed to a large brown bag from Starbucks.

So Mark pulled on his shorts and sat down on the bed across from Jason, while he opened the bag. It contained two large café lattes, two large cups of orange juice, and two almond croissants.

Shame flooded Mark's soul. After he had awakened, the first thing he had suspected had been the worst: that he had been robbed. After he had checked the safe, he had thought Jason had run out on him after getting a free night's lodging. Mark hoped I didn't look as guilty as he felt.

"I hope breakfast's OK" Jason said, taking in Mark's somber face.

"It's a nice surprise," Mark replied, breaking into a genuine smile. "In more ways than one," he thought. Aloud, he asked, "Jason, how did you pay for it? I thought you didn't have any money."

"Oh, easy," Jason said. "I told the desk clerk that I'd loaned Paul the money for the deposit. He didn't know. He's the morning guy. He just let me have all thirty bucks. And I still got change, too."

"Clever," Mark thought. "Practical, too." The motel would probably have just kept the money if somebody hadn't asked for it. And that almost certainly would not have been Thomas's executor, His Grace, the Bishop of Atlanta. And there was a certain kind of justice in having Paul Thomas pay for their breakfast posthumously. The dead man already owed Mark plenty, and the day was yet young.

"Jason," Mark said, putting his previous night's decisions into action, "I have an idea. I have a room over near the beach. Why don't we move over there? I have a little business to attend to, and you could swim or sunbathe on the beach while I do that."

"Cool," Jason said. Then he looked a bit puzzled. "How come you got two rooms?" he asked.

"Well," Mark replied, "I had really wanted to stay here, but they told me they were full. When I got to town, I found out that there was a room after all. I'd already paid for the place at the beach, so I just kept it. But the beach is a lot nicer, and I suspect you'd like to get away from here. The manager's not all that friendly."

In reality, it was Mark who wanted to get Jason away from there, but Mark's explanation seemed to satisfy the kid. Jason just said, "OK" and then turned on the television. They finished their breakfast with CNN driveling in the background.

"What's that about," Jason asked.

"Something about global warming," Mark said. "I guess the two scientists CNN's interviewing can't agree. The German one says it's too early to tell anything. The one from the National Oceanic and Atmospheric Administration thinks it's already a serious problem."

"Is it? Serious, I mean," Jason asked.

"Who knows?" was Mark's reply.

They got dressed and Mark put his toilet kit in his bag and then sat down on the side of the bed to put on his shoes. While he did that, he slipped the safe key out from under the table leg.

Then he saw Jason. He was standing there watching. He looked solemn as Mark unlocked the safe and put its contents in his pocket, but Jason didn't say anything. They walked in silence to the motel office. Mark checked them out, picked up his thirty dollars, and hopped in the car with Jason. They headed for A1A. Jason turned on the radio, and they rode along in silence, except for the deep thump-thump-thump of the music from the station that Jason had picked.

Mark only made two wrong turns on the way back to the beach. While he was bumbling around on the wrong streets, he managed to find a discount store. "Just wait here," he said, "I won't be more than a couple of minutes."

Mark decided, on the spur of the moment, to run a little test. He said that he'd leave the engine running to keep the air-conditioner on. He went into the store, leaving Jason in the car, and bought a white dress shirt and a black and gold striped tie. When he got back to the parking lot, Jason and the car were still there. Jason was lying back against the upholstery, eyes closed, evidently enjoying the music and the cool air. "At least he isn't a car thief." Mark thought. And perhaps trust had been reestablished.

They parked in front of the beach motel and walked into through the lobby. Mark noticed that the skinny kid was still on the desk. "Don't you ever go home?" he said to himself.

The clerk's eyes held his reply, "Oh, yeah, right, you're some kinda preacher, and now with a trick, too."

"Alrighty, then," Mark thought, and aloud to the clerk, "Hello. Are you still on duty?"

"Yeah," the clerk replied, "my relief didn't show."

"Tough break," Mark said, all jovial, clerical, and good-natured, "I'd like you to meet my friend, Jason. He'll be staying with me for a couple of days."

"Yeah, right," the clerk replied, "whatever." He was completely unconvinced, Mark could see. Jason smiled and said nothing.

In the room, Jason stripped (again), opened his backpack, and took out the smallest thong bathing suit Mark had ever seen. Mark wasn't sure that it was legal to wear it in public, but Jason said it was. While he was dressing, if it could be called that, Mark checked the phone directory for the location of the police department. He dialed the number and asked for directions. He said, "to your office," for Jason's benefit. Mark was trying to establish trust between him and Jason, but he was far from ready to confide the nature of his business to the kid.

Jason went out onto the beach through the sliding glass door. "You'd better lock this, if you're going out. You don't want nobody stealing nothing," he said. "I'll sit out here on the porch if I get back before you do. And don't worry about me eating," he added with a grin. "I've still got change from breakfast."

"I've got two key cards for the room," Mark replied, satisfied that he could probably trust Jason with the few possessions left behind. "Why don't you take one of them?"

"Nah, it's better this way," was Jason's response. Mark could see that the business with the safe key had not set well with Jason. Apparently, there was more work to do in the trust department.

Jason bounced off towards the beach, and Mark drew the drapes closed to change clothes. He put on the cheap white shirt and striped tie that he had just bought to wear with his black clerical suit. When he checked his appearance in the mirror, he decided that he looked like an undertaker's assistant or maybe a Mormon missionary. But Mark figured that he would pass for an unimportant and anonymous nobody on a routine errand from a Prince of the Church. That was the effect he wanted, and Jason wouldn't see him in the collar and black shirt that he had carefully packed away. Mark wasn't yet ready to reveal his connection to Paul Thomas or the bishop.

Mark reflected on this. There was a lot of work to be done in the trust department. He liked Jason, but was reluctant to fully trust him. Yet. Mark decided it was his duty to work on his distrust.

Before leaving the room, Mark took out the picture of Paul Thomas that the Bishop had given him, along with the authorization papers. He studied the picture with care it to familiarize himself with Paul Thomas's face.

Then he set out for the Fort Lauderdale Police Department. But he had to pass the front desk first, in yet another costume. The tired looking, pimpled face looked up, took in Mark's latest change of clothes without a word, sighed, and went back to reading *Stereo Today*.

In complete contrast to the motel clerk, the bright young uniformed woman on duty at the police station was alert and helpful. Mark explained his errand and she told him where to find the detective in charge of the case.

She was waiting for Mark and introduced herself as Lieutenant Terry Collins. Mark was invited to take a seat in the visitor's chair. Mark presented the certified copy of the bishop's Letter Testamentary from the probate judge, his Power of Attorney from the bishop and his ID.

"I have come to claim the body of Paul Thomas," Mark said, formally.

Collins examined the papers for a moment before she spoke. "These are all in order," she said, "but I'm afraid we can't release body just yet."

"Why not?" Mark said, appearing to be somewhat miffed. This is what he had feared: complications.

"I'm sorry," Detective Collins said. "It was an unattended death, under somewhat unusual circumstances. And we do not yet have an official identification."

"Oh?" Mark said. "I thought that it was clear about whose body it is."

"We are pretty sure we know," Collins replied, "but we want to be as certain as possible. Although you are not the next of kin, can you identify him for us? I'm sorry to ask, but it really is necessary."

Mark said that he could and would. Collins telephoned ahead and then drove him over to the Coroner's office. When they got there, the body had been removed from its refrigerated drawer and placed on a gurney with a sheet over it. The coroner lifted the sheet from the face, and Mark looked down on the very dead face of Paul Thomas. Mark quickly took in everything he could see, and what he saw worried him. There were marks on the throat. He'd seen post-mortem marks like that before. They came from manual strangulation.

Mark nodded and turned away, apparently deeply upset. "That's him," he said, and hurried out of the room.

Detective Collins followed hurriedly. "Are you alright?" she asked.

"Yes, it's just that I haven't seen many dead people before," he said somewhat untruthfully. Actually, he didn't want to give Collins any opportunity to see the marks or ask the coroner about them.

"I'm afraid there's another complication as well," Collins said. "The coroner is unwilling to give a death certificate without an autopsy."

Is that really necessary?" Mark asked, with apparent innocence and distaste. "We would like to put this sorrowful business behind us." He tried to make the "we" sound as if he were speaking for somebody important, which, in truth, he was. But he knew that t his would be an uphill battle.

"I'm really sorry for your loss," Collins said with sincerity. "But I must ask you to understand that there are certain legal requirements that must be met."

As an ex-cop, he knew that to be true. And he also knew that he was beaten. Making a fuss would only would only make things worse. Now there would be a complete and thorough examination of the physical condition of the body. Mark could only hope and pray very hard that the M.E. would be hurried or sloppy and find nothing untoward.

"I understand," Mark said, accepting the inevitable with grace. "How long do you think this will take? We have to plan the funeral, you know."

"A couple of days. If you'll leave me your number, I'll let you know the results, and when you can claim the body. When we get back to the station, I can give you the gentleman's personal effects, though."

They drove back in Terry Collins' unmarked car and went straight to the property room. There, Collins asked for and got a plastic garment bag, a good black leather suitcase and a large brown envelope. Together, these contained all the worldly goods that Paul Thomas had apparently brought with him to Fort Lauderdale. With these was an inventory sheet.

"Would you like to check the contents against the inventory?" Collins asked.

"Thank you, but no," was Mark's reply. "I'm sure you folks are trustworthy." His best smile accompanied the words. Besides, he thought, "If anybody here is crooked, anything valuable would have disappeared before the inventory was taken."

Mark thanked the detective, who seemed to be thoroughly professional, as well as a very nice young lady. He signed the receipt showing that he had received everything. Detective Collins signed; the property room clerk signed.

"There's one more thing," Collins added. "His car is in the impound lot. Would you like to get it now?"

"I'm in a rental," Mark replied. "I'll have to come back for it."

"That's fine," Collins said. "Take your time. It'll still be there. Again, I'm sorry for your loss and for the inconvenience." See concluded, "I'll let them know you're coming for the car, and I'll keep you posted."

Mark thanked the detective for her help. Then he carried the luggage and envelope out to the car and put them in the trunk. Back to the motel, he decided. He wanted to look through everything.

When he got there, the same kid was still at the desk. This time, his hands were side by side on the desk, and his head was resting on them. He raised his head an inch and opened one sleepy eye. "Oh," he said, "it's you." He looked for a moment at the additional luggage, but said nothing, and put his head back down on his hands again. Mark was starting to feel sorry for him.

Mark was glad to be back in the privacy of the cool beachfront room. He opened the drapes and checked the patio, but Jason was not there. Mark drew the draperies closed again, and began to unpack Paul Thomas's things. There was a plastic garment bag with resort shirts and pants in it, but nothing in the pockets or anything that would have hinted at Thomas's church connection. The sealed brown clasp envelope contained a wallet, some credit cards, a couple of hundred dollars, a nice gold wristwatch and Paul Thomas's college ring. There were some keys: house, car, and a couple of others, one of them probably to a safety deposit box.

Mark kept digging. A nice black leather bag with lots of compartments contained a swimming suit, underwear, socks, and an expensive dressing gown. Another pocket opened to reveal his toilet kit. It contained all of the usual items, including a couple of prescription bottles, and some expensive brands of cologne. There were rubbers and personal lubricant in another section. A small pocket of the black leather bag held receipts for the Roosevelt House Motel, from an ATM, and the Thomas's gasoline credit card. Next to that pocket was another one with his appointment book in it.

Mark opened it, found the most recent dates, and began to read: "To FL with J at 8:00." Then, a blank day. In the back of the book was an address section. Mark looked through the extensive entries until he found "Rogers, Jason" and an Atlanta number. There were a couple of other "R" entries after it, so he had known Jason for a while. Apparently, they had been close friends, just as Jason had said.

There were other entries, too, with only initials and a word or two. More appointments for later in life, appointments that Paul Thomas would never keep.

Mark picked up the phone to call the bishop. The bad news was a delay in the proceedings caused by the autopsy. The good news was that he still had a lid on the situation.

Chapter Nine

Tulsa, Oklahoma, 1959

After leaving Martha and John, "to stew in their own juices," Paul set out for McFarlin Library at the university. The stacks were open, and nobody ever checked for a student ID. Officially, the library was for school personnel only. But, in fact, anybody could use it and lots of people did.

Paul found his way to the reference room, turned on his most dazzling smile, and asked the research librarian for help. Paul wanted to find out about writing contracts, he said. The librarian thought a minute and then referred him to a basic book on business that contained a chapter on the subject. Paul found the book and read it carefully. Then he went back and asked about contract forms. The helpful librarian referred him to a legal text on the subject. Paul read the relevant passages and copied some material out in longhand. Then he went back to his little apartment.

There, armed with his manual portable typewriter and some good bond paper, he proceeded to construct a contract. It was not a particularly long document and was written in simple clear English. It said that, in consideration of his previous contributions to the Johns ministry and in further consideration of his agreement to provide a series of recordings for that ministry, Jack and Martha Johns, together and separately agreed to pay his way through four years of college. "Paying his way" was defined as bearing "all expenses, including tuition, fees, room, board, books, and pocket money not to exceed one-hundred dollars per week per annum." Payments were to be made in advance of each fall term, provided only that he maintained a "C: average or better in the preceding term.

It was a stiff contract, and Paul knew Martha would have a conniption fit when it was presented. In 1960, one hundred dollars a week in spending money was a princely sum for a college student. He decided he'd demand high and negotiate down on that one point, if he had to.

He prepared signature blanks at the bottom of the last page, signed and dated his side of the contract, and set out for the Johns' trailer. When he got there, a steely-eyed and unsmiling Martha opened the door. "Oh, it's you," she said. "Have you come to your senses, yet?"

"Yes," Paul said, entering the trailer as Martha stepped aside for him. "I certainly have come to my senses. Where's Jack?"

"Jack is in the bedroom," Martha answered. "I'm handling this."

"Sorry," Paul said, "but I'll have to speak with both of you." Raising his voice slightly, he called, "Jack, would you join us, please."

A very browbeaten looking Jack emerged almost at once. "You really need to talk this over with Martha," Jack said, trying desperately to back out of the situation.

"Actually, there's little or nothing to talk about," Paul responded. "I just need both of your signatures. I have prepared an agreement, and I expect both of you to sign it."

Paul laid the contract on the kitchen table. To indicate that he wasn't going anywhere right away, he sat down. Martha picked the contract up as it might have been a bomb or a snake and began to read it. "Pretty fancy wording, young man," she said venomously.

"You're a good businesswoman, Martha," Paul retorted, still smiling. "I'll give you credit for that. You taught me everything about business that I know. As you are fond of saying, this is simply a business matter."

"Fine, then," said Martha, "we'll treat it like that. Your demands are outrageous and we refuse to have anything to do with them. Get out. And, by the way, the rent on your apartment is due next Tuesday. You can handle your own bills from now on."

Paul didn't move a muscle. "Jack," he said quietly, "I'm disappointed in you. I think I asked you to explain to Martha why it is important for me to have your support in my music education. Didn't you do that? I really hoped that you would."

Jack Johns turned pale. "Paul, I told Martha I thought we ought to help you out, but she's set on making a one-time cash payment to you."

"Oh? How much?" Paul asked.

"One thousand dollars," Martha said, triumphantly. "And that's all. And you quit your claim to any and all other interest in Jack Johns World Wide Ministry."

"Oh," Paul said to Jack, "then you really didn't explain, you just interceded with your business manager. I thought a complete explanation would be better coming from you, but I can handle that just as well, if you are unable or unwilling to."

Before Jack could stop him, Paul turned to Martha and continued, "Jack and I are lovers. He seduced me when I was sixteen. Homosexual sex is a crime in Oklahoma, and when an underage person is involved, it's also statutory rape."

Martha's mouth dropped open, and then it opened and shut several times, like a stranded fish gasping for oxygen. Jack slumped onto a kitchen chair and rested his head in his hands. He moaned slightly.

Martha recovered first. "I don't believe you," she screamed. "You lying son of a bitch! Get out of my house! I never want to see or talk to you again!"

"Now that I have your undivided attention," Paul said, still sitting quietly at the table, "let's get on with it, shall we? If this becomes public, Jack will go to prison and that'll be the end of Jack Johns World Wide Whatever. Martha, your dreams of fame and money will come to a fitting and abrupt end. Then, you can spend the rest of your miserable life cleaning toilets."

Martha was apoplectic with rage. She started toward Paul to slap him, but Jack, still pale and shaking, grabbed her arm and stopped her. "It's true," he said simply.

It was Martha's turn to sit down. She did so, weakly, finally recognizing the facts. "What?" she said defensively, "I don't believe it." Then her anger turned on her husband. "I always thought there was something wrong," she said, her eyes narrowing, "but I didn't want to think it of either of you." Another pause, then to Paul, "You'll never be able to prove any of this. So, you can still get out. This time before I murder you. And you'll get nothing, absolutely nothing, from either of us."

"Actually," Paul said, "I can prove it."

"Oh, really," Martha said with a sneer. "How?"

"Well," Paul said, conversationally, "I can describe Jack's hard dick in perfect detail. You'll remember, I'm sure, that when he gets a boner, his cock curves upwards and slightly to the right. He isn't circumcised, either. And there's that funny little mole right on the bottom of his left nut. Did you ever notice that when you were licking it? And how about the other one just inside his ass crack on his left cheek? You've probably never had your tongue there, so maybe you've never noticed that one."

"You little son of a bitch," Martha screamed again, "You little two-timing, black-mailing, faggot bastard!"

"Whatever you say, Martha. But please control your voice," Paul said. "You'll wake the children. Or the neighbors might call the police. What would you tell them?"

"Paul's right, Martha," Jack admonished. "I'm afraid that we're in a very bad position and we're going to have to agree to his terms. I don't like this situation any better than you do. But, you're only losing money. I'm losing money and a very good lay. Much better than you, by the way; you have no real interest or imagination."

Martha said nothing more. She grabbed the contract and signed it savagely at the bottom. Jack's signature followed.

"Now, you sneaky little blackmailer," Martha said, "where's my copy?"

"Oh," Paul said, "just sign this one, too, handing it to her. I'll perform my part of the bargain, you can bet on that. I'll prepare the music tapes for you and deliver them by the end of the month. I'll even show up for the next two taping sessions. You can keep the Hammond, too. You paid for that piece of junk and I don't want it anymore. I'll be playing a real pipe organ from now on."

"Just be sure to keep your end of the bargain," Paul continued. "I don't want you bringing lawyers into this. But if you do, I'll bring in the police. And don't forget to pay my rent and the utilities. See you at rehearsal," He added, smiling sweetly at the two of them as he went out the door.

He heard the door slam shut violently behind him, but he did not look back. He also heard Martha venting her fury on Jack, as he walked triumphantly away. By the time he reached the entrance to the trailer park, her voice had faded in the distance and his heart had stopped pounding in his chest. He had won! He had carried the day. No more Martha; no need to return to Ardmore and his family, and a free college education to boot. "Poor Jack," he said to himself as he strolled on. "He really should learn to stand up to her, but I don't suppose he ever will."

Paul was right about that. Far from standing up to Martha, it was she who stood up to the already compliant Jack. She laid down the law: no more seeing Paul privately, and no affairs with other men. And, she told him, "If you want sex, you can jerk off. I'm never sleeping with you again."

Within a year, the JJWWM radio program had generated enough money for Martha and Jack to buy a three-bedroom house: one for the children, one for Martha and one for Jack. When Jack complained about this arrangement, Martha retorted, "It's Jack's room so go jack in it."

From then on, Martha ran Jack Johns World Wide Ministry. She made the decisions and Jack carried them out. She might be the dutiful, subservient Christian wife in public, and Jack the center of public attention. But, behind the scenes, Martha was the boss. She was building a place in society for herself. She had children to raise and educate, and Jack was going to be her meal ticket to fame and fortune. She was quite determined about that.

This odd arrangement was to last the rest of their lives.

Chapter Ten

Buenos Aires, Argentina, 1947

Little Amanda Elizabeth Hutton (now 8) and her mother were obviously excited as they stepped off the Panair do Brasil seaplane and into the boat that would ferry them ashore. Amanda's father, Alex, and her brother Nicky (almost 18) were more reserved as befitted the men of the family. Nicky was just mimicking his father's outward appearance. Alex's bearing, on the other hand, was caused more by concern for his first real spy assignment than any desire to suppress emotion or appear macho.

The Huttons had left New York, and springtime, far behind them. Here, south of the Equator, fall was beginning. I seemed strange to change not only countries and languages, but also seasons so quickly. Thanks to the marvels of modern air travel, their entire trip, including a layover in Miami to change planes, had taken just over two days.

The livery service had provided driver and a limousine as promised. It whisked them easily through the traffic to their hotel. Afterwards, Mary commented placidly to her husband that she would have been happier if the driver had kept both hands on the wheel. The other, she had noted, had been vigorously employed in alternately blowing the horn and making what were assumed to be rude gestures.

Alex was in complete agreement about that.

Their suite at the Pan Americano Hotel was sumptuous. French doors opened onto a small balcony. Through them was a spectacular view of the city center. Almost directly opposite was the grandest of all, the Teatro Colón Opera House.

By the time they had settled into their three-bedroom suite, it was midday. They enjoyed a leisurely luncheon in the hotel's main dining room, and then retired for siesta, with the rest of the city's population. Although the trip in the giant clipper had been enjoyable, none of them had slept well on the plane. Siesta gave them all a chance to catch up.

They had the evening at leisure; Alex's appointment with his Argentinean banker was not until 10:00 the next morning. By local standards, they had an early dinner at 8:00 and then retired.

Next morning, while the rest of his family lazed in bed and then breakfasted in their suite, Alex dressed with care for his business appointment.

"Mary, I have no idea how long this is going to take, so please make plans for yourself and the children. I'll see you when I get back, whenever that might be."

Alex kissed his wife lightly on the cheek. Just then, the phone rang to announce that his car was waiting.

"Be careful, dear," Mary said, as she always did. "Remember that I love you."

"And I, you," Alex said as he went out and closed the door behind him. He whistled softly to himself as he walked down the long, heavily carpeted corridor.

It was the same car and driver that had taken the Huttons to the hotel the previous morning. The chauffeur's driving skills displayed no sudden, overnight improvement. Nevertheless, the driver deposited Alex at the front door of the bank at exactly 9:25. He then zoomed away, apparently without looking, leaving several hooting horns in his wake.

Alex shook his head slightly, straightened his already erect spine and walked into the imposing edifice to face the unknown challenge before him.

He was greeted warmly by the director's executive secretary, a fair-haired and blue-eyed gentlemen who spoke flawless English. He ushered Alex into the director's office almost at once and returned bearing a tray with a coffee service for two.

Señor Juan Cabandie, the director of the bank, entered a minute or so later. The director's English was flawless, too. "It is a pleasure to meet you at last, Mr. Hutton. I have heard a great deal about you, all of it good. I understand that you have had to be a very patient man."

"Yes," Alex replied, "investment banking does require patience. But it is also important to know when to act. It is a pleasure to meet you, Señor."

"I could not agree more. But before we get down to business, more coffee?"

"Yes, please, it's excellent."

"Thank you. I notice you have a scar on your chin and was wondering, if I am not being too personal, how you may have come by it?"

"It happened in college," Alex said, giving his standard and non-informative reply.

"Surely not at Harvard!"

Alex laughed. "No definitely not at Harvard. I got in while in Germany."

"Ah, yes. And that was before the War. A badge of courage, is it not?"

"That was the popular idea then, yes."

"You did not find it a hindrance of any sort during the War? I understand some German-Americans had theirs cosmetically removed."

"I chose not to."

"Then it still has some meaning for you?"

"Yes. It still means what it always has."

"That is good to hear. One should not let the old traditions or ideas die out. Civilization needs courage, honor and strong leadership."

"I agree."

"Let me speak more frankly, then, and in confidence."

"Certainly," Alex replied, "I shall hold our conversation in complete confidence."

"I believe that our mutual friend Señor Walters suggested this trip to you, and may have said something about taxis and umbrellas to you at the same time."

"Yes, he did," Alex replied.

"And would you have come otherwise?"

"Probably not. At least not until I found out more about any oil and gas development investments that might be in the offing."

"But knowing little about that, you are here anyway," Señor Cabandie observed.

"Yes. I am still interested in doing my patriotic duty, if that's what you're getting at."

"It is. You have, of course, become an American citizen, as directed. And you have done well in establishing yourself in the upper strata of society and in becoming successful in business. You have a lovely wife and charming children, I understand. So the question has to be asked: Are you happy as you are? Do you wish to continue as an agent, or do you want out? We will agree to whatever you desire."

Alex laughed again. "So far I haven't been much of an agent. Now that the War is over and the Allies have won, I don't see how I can be of much use. Whom would I serve? The Third Reich is dead as a post."

"All of what you have said is true, except the last thing. Believe me when I tell you that the Third Reich is not dead. It is only sleeping. At the right time it will awaken. If you agree, we want you to be a part of that awakening."

"Look," Alex replied earnestly, "I'm sorry that we lost. If there were any way to turn that around, I'd do it in an instant. But I'm not interested in signing on for some half-baked, harebrained scheme to do anything that's going to blow up in my face or in yours for that matter. If there's something afoot, I want to know a whole hell of a lot more than you've told me so far." Alex paused, then added, "Sorry. I realize I've been far too blunt, but there you have it."

Señor Cabandie studied Alex's earnest face for a moment. Then he said carefully, "Señor Hutton, I do not take your concern for rudeness. Sometimes it is best to speak plainly. It is now clear to me that this is one of those times."

"Fine. Speak plainly, then, and tell me what's going on."

"That is not for me to do. However, if you will return at the same time tomorrow, I will introduce you to my oil and gas development principal, and he will discuss this matter, as well as some investments with you."

Understanding that the interview had accomplished all that it could, Alex rose. "Thank you for your hospitality, Señor. I look forward to tomorrow."

"If tomorrow comes, Señor Hutton. Please think carefully tonight about what I have said. There is danger in going forward. If you want to withdraw your commitment, then all you need do is not appear here tomorrow. You may finish your vacation in peace. When you return to New York you can say merely that you found no investment that you could recommend."

"And what of our conversation, Señor?"

"What conversation is that, Señor? No, do not worry about that. We are both secure where things stand now. And either you will come tomorrow or you will not."

"Then I will simply thank you for your hospitality. I will give careful thought to what you have told me and we will see what tomorrow brings," Alex said.

The two gentlemen shook hands. The banker offered to summon Alex's car, but Alex said that he would prefer to walk back to the hotel. He found walking much more relaxing than being driven.

"How did it go?" Mary asked when he returned.

"Well enough, I suppose. I need more information before I can decide about it. I'll probably have to have another meeting or two."

They turned to planning an afternoon together with the children, had a quick lunch, and went out on a walking tour. Siesta overtook their plans, so they succumbed to the custom of the country. The evening was a repeat of the previous one as well, except that they dined later and the children were allowed to stay up well past their accustomed bedtime.

When they retired, Mary went to sleep almost at once. But Alex lay quietly awake for some time. "Dangerous" the banker had said. "How dangerous," Alex wondered. He decided to go and see.

Next morning the car did not appear. Alex took that to mean that he was not being pushed into a decision. He reconsidered his decision of the night before. It still looked fine in the clear light of day, so he walked over to the bank.

Señor Cabandie greeted him with the same courtesy, and the same excellent coffee, as on the day before.

"So," the banker said, "I take it that you have made your decision."

"I have."

"Excellent. As that is the case, let us go and see my principal." He used his telephone to order his car, and the two of them strolled to the front of the bank. Alex was relieved to see it was not the same car or driver. His relief changed to dismay as he discovered that this man's driving was even worse, if that was possible.

Their trip took them a short way into the countryside, to a large house enclosed by high plastered walls. The car stopped in front of a pair of high, solidly built gates. Two unsmiling men in dark suits opened them from inside. As they swept into the courtyard, the men closed the gates behind them.

At the door, another equally serious looking man looked them over carefully before leading them to a pleasant inner courtyard. A bald, elderly gentleman, who was casually and expensively dressed, rose to meet them.

"Señores," he said, "welcome. My English is not good. Is German alright?"

"It's been a long time for me," Alex said, "but I'll try to keep up."

"Good," the older man said, switching at once to what was obviously his native tongue. "I am known here by a Spanish name, which is a good thing, because in our Fatherland I am already dead." He laughed a thin laugh before he continued. "Señor Cabandie has told me that you have agreed to take the next step in fulfilling your promise to the Fatherland. I am grateful to you, von Hutton, very grateful." He held out his hand, "as my doppelganger said before he died, '*Ich bin Heinrich Himmler!*'"

"Good Lord!" Alex exclaimed, "Are you really?"

"Yes." Cabandie said. "Yes he is."

"I'm sorry, sir," Alex apologized, "I was very much taken by surprise."

"There is nothing to apologize for," Himmler reassured him. "Nothing at all. The bald head, the heavy black moustache, the horn-rimmed glasses; they make a difference, do they?"

"I would never have guessed. But now that you tell me and I see you, yes. It's really quite remarkable, sir."

"And now, Alex von Hutton, do you see why Señor Cabandie said that going the next step would be dangerous. There is no going back for you now. We cannot risk that."

"I pose no risk, sir. I never took the oath, but I will take it now, *"Meine Ehre heisst Treue.*"

"Thank you," Himmler said, truly moved. "I do not have an S.S. dagger to give you, so I give you my hand again."

The two of them shook hands again. Himmler gestured for them to join him at the table. Coffee appeared almost immediately and Alex sipped it gratefully. His heart was pounding and he needed to recover.

"Now," Himmler said, "first to business. It is easily disposed of. We have already funded a gas and oil exploration and development company. The world price for this commodity is going to continue to rise for many years to come. In order to further our real plans for you, we are going to cut Cordell, Hutton & Company in for a percentage. Cordell, Hutton & Company will invest and I think we will all probably all do very well out of it."

"Well," Alex said, smiling, "I certainly didn't have to negotiate very hard."

"No, this is a small part of a larger plan. We will ask you to become a director of the Pan-American Oil and Gas Company. With you, that will make two American directors. The other is a Mr. Peter Anderson."

"Even so, I have my due-diligence to do. You will understand that in America my company has a fiduciary duty to its shareholders."

"Of course. Señor Cabandie will answer your questions for you and provide you with the proper documents, certified by a chartered accountant and so on. The documents will be quite genuine and easily verified. You will have no problem with any of that."

"Will there be an overcall requirement?"

"I doubt that any additional funds will be required from any of the initial investors. However, we shall be prudent and include a small one in our agreement. It would make it more realistic, would it not?"

"Yes."

"Then, Señor Cabandie, you will know what to do?"

"Certainly, sir. It will be taken care of."

"Good. Now to the real reason for our meeting!"

Alex sat quietly giving Himmler his full attention.

"I think you told Señor Cabandie that the Third Reich was 'dead as a post,' did you not?"

"Yes, sir, I did. Perhaps I was wrong to think that."

"No, von Hutton, not at all. To all outward appearances, you are quite correct. But, as you can see, a few of us are still here. We represent its leadership. To that extent, it is very much alive. Have you heard of the *Organisation der ehemaligen SS-Angehörigen*?

"No, sir, I haven't."

"It is an organization of former SS members. We help each other in various ways, keep up ties to others in the Fatherland, and do our best to make sure that our former so-called crimes are not a subject for investigation. Some of us are here in Argentina and more in other sympathetic countries. Some are in the United States, and you have just become one of those."

"I certainly understand that you need to help each other and shield yourselves from the forces that now occupy the Fatherland," Alex replied. "But why recruit new members? I don't understand."

"Because there is to be a Fourth Reich," Himmler asserted. "We are waiting for the right time to launch it. I think that we are all agreed that Adolf Hitler was a great man, a visionary, one who saw the possibility of a great new, peaceful world, one that would be ruled by God's chosen race: the Aryan people."

Alex nodded.

"But Hitler was betrayed, in part by those who did not give him their complete and unquestioning loyalty, but even more by circumstances beyond anyone's control. Germany simply was not strong enough to carry out his will. It was a very close thing. But in the last months we ran out of men and matériel. The struggle became a defensive war and was un-winnable."

"I see. Yes, I agree."

"So we have now learned our lesson. We must have two things: an opportunity when the enemy is already weakened, and access to all of the manpower and military matériel that we need. We do not know when this will come about, be we know where. It will be in the United States of America."

Alex was more astonished than ever and began to wonder, again, whether this was some kind of madness on the part of a few fanatics.

"I see that you are astonished. I would be, too, if I were you. Let me assure you, then, that our plans are sound. We are not going to launch a war or do anything so stupid. We are going to take over peacefully and simply.

"Our plan is called Operation Aurum. 'Arum,' you know, means gold. Have you ever wondered what happened to all of the Reich's gold? Simple. We transported almost all of it here to Argentina. It is used to fund our activities, and investments such as Pan American Gas and Oil. And we make charitable contributions, too, when it suits our purposes.

"We would like you, and your son, to tale part in the next phase of Operation Aurum."

"My son? Nicky? How?"

"Von Hutton, you have established yourself well in America. You are, as they say, a solid citizen. Nothing could be more natural, now that you have been successful in business, than for your son to find a life in politics. Neither you nor he is alone in this venture. We had rather a large number of sleeper agents in America whom we had no cause to awaken until now. Most of them have children about Nicky's age. We have invited almost all of them to participate with us in achieving political influence during the next thirty years or so."

"What if the kids aren't interested?"

"That is where your schloss comes in. We would like to quietly open a private school there that would teach innocuous things such as German history and culture. It would meet in the summers only and would attract only the right sort of students. The occupation forces would have to agree, of course. But Austria is in the American zone of occupation and the Americans are already growing restless. Soon they will be gone, or have other worries; perhaps with the Russians. One way or another, they will not figure out what the real curriculum is."

"And when the time is ripe ..."

"When the time is ripe, these fine young men will have served America honorably in the armed forces. Some of them will have medals and other awards. They will take their natural places of leadership in the nation. And they will do it for the Fatherland."

"I'm certain that Nick will enjoy his schooling in his family's old schloss," Alex said.

Himmler rose from his chair and the other two stood as well. Himmler raised his arm in the old salute. "Seig heil," he said.

"To victory," the two echoed.

Chapter Eleven

Natahala, 1954

A second telegram came to the farm in the Natahala valley. Shrimp was no longer officially missing action. His frozen body had been found during the spring thaw and would be shipped home for burial as soon as the Army mortuary services had performed its duty.

When word reached Third, he was sick with grief. He went outside to be alone. "Oh, Shrimp, I'm so sorry. I hope you can hear me." He cried silently, until the tears would no longer come. Although barely eighteen, he went inside to announce to the family that he was going to finish what Shrimp had started. The war in Korea had become personal.

In 1951 President Truman had dismissed General Douglas MacArthur from his duties as Allied Commander. By the time Third was shipped to Korea, things had settled down to a stalemate. Hostilities continued, mostly along the 39th Parallel. In 1953 a truce was signed that would last for decades and permanently divide Korea into two countries, one free, one enslaved.

Third served out his enlistment in relative quiet and comfort. Then, it was time to go home. He'd been a good soldier, a man among men. He could hold his head up about that. But his secret longings for other men troubled him deeply. They were, he realized, something he had to deal with. He prayed for the temptations to go away, but these prayers did not receive the answer he wanted. Reluctantly, he came to realize that what he desired was not what God wanted for him. He would have to live as he was.

Finally, Third received his orders to ship out for the United States. He requested and got a delay en route so that he could visit Japan for the last time. On this, his last visit trip to Tokyo, he reluctantly joined some fellow soldiers who were going out in search of booze and broads.

They looked through the doors of several bars before entering a particularly dark one that had familiar American music coming from it. They looked around. There were few women in the place and only one hostess. The bar seemed to have a mostly male Japanese clientele, so they left in search of a more likely nightspot.

After considering the situation, Third told them a recent meal had not agreed with him, so they parted company. He returned to the first bar. He went inside, stepped up to the bar, ordered a beer, and cruised the place with his eyes. It wasn't long before the hostess joined him.

"All alone?" the slightly accented voice asked.

"Yes," Third said, "I decided to come back alone."

"Ah! You are here on R and R?"

"No, not exactly. What's called a delay in route. I'm taking a few days of vacation before returning to the States."

"Ah, yes. The United States. It is a great place, is it not? I have been to school there."

"Have you?" Third asked. "That explains your very good English."

"Perhaps you would like to come home with me, so that we can talk some more."

The approach had been very direct, and it startled Third. He didn't know quite how to answer. The bar was dark, but he was pretty certain that the person standing beside him wasn't really female. Then he thought, "what the hell," and said, "Actually, I left my friends because they were out looking for women and I'm not interested in that."

The response was a peal of bell-like, delighted laughter. "How discreet you are! Certainly, you have come to the right place. I hope I have not disappointed you in some way because I like to dress as a woman sometimes."

"No. You haven't turned me off, if that's what you mean," Third said, "But I've never met a man who liked to cross-dress, either."

"Then let us go to my apartment, and you can see everything about how it is done."

Intrigued, Third agreed to go.

With makeup and clothing removed, his companion turned out to be a slightly built but well-muscled young man about his own age. He called himself "Willan," because, he said, "It's as close as Americans can get to saying my Japanese name. It's impossible to for a Westerner to pronounce. And if you said it wrong it would sound like a word that is insulting and dirty."

"Both? I'll stick to Willan, then," Third said, as he shed the last of his clothing.

Willan suggested a long soak in the steaming water of the ofuro. Third thought it was scalding hot at first, but then began to relax and enjoy it. After a long soak, they emerged from the wooden tub and dried each other off.

In the next room, they lay down side by side on the futon. Dim light filtered in through the shoji as they moved close together and made love.

Third arose early, wanting to leave. But Willan insisted that Third should at least drink some tea. Third felt awkward. He had enjoyed being with Willan, but now he was feeling guilty about it.

"You look unhappy, Third san," Willan said. "Didn't I look after you properly last night? Should I do something else?"

Third smiled an embarrassed smile. "No. You were wonderful. I'm just worried that you'll think I took advantage of you. I'm leaving right away for the States."

"Oh! You Americans and your guilt! You have inherited these bad feelings from your puritan ancestors! Sex is healthy for you. It is necessary to relieve tensions to restore your inner tranquility. If you do not, you will become ill. It is even more important someone who is large like you. You must find release often to remain healthy."

"And what about you?"

"Oh, last night will keep me healthy for many days."

Third had hoped to catch a flight on an Army or Air Force plane from Tokyo to the States. But seats were hard to come by. It was easier to go on a Navy ship, so he resigned himself to a voyage home. It was very much like any Navy transport. The enlisted men were consigned to the lower decks where tiers of bunks provided crowded sleeping space with little privacy. "Officers' Country" was above, where commissioned officers had the comfort of staterooms that housed one or two people each. Even these spaces, while offering greater privacy, were cramped little rooms.

The weather in the south Pacific was calm and warm. Compared with the cramped living conditions inside, being on deck was always inviting. So, everybody on board tried to spend as much time as possible there, watching the endless waves roll past and feeling the gentle movement of the ship as it bore them homeward.

Late on one particularly sultry tropical night, Third went topside for a breath of fresh air and for some badly needed relative privacy. The moon was three-quarters full and shone on the placid sea, turning it to silver. Behind the ship, the wake glowed with its own phosphorescence. He strolled aft to take in this peculiar phenomenon at closer range.

There were others on deck, too, staring out across the moonlit sea. They stood apart from each other, each seeking the solitude that the ship otherwise denied them.

"Good evening, soldier," a quiet voice said.

Third turned towards the voice. Into the moonlight stepped a very sharp-looking Navy lieutenant.

"Good evening, sir," Third said, coming to attention.

"Stand at rest, soldier," the lieutenant said, "no need to be so formal when there's nobody else around and we're both here for the same reason."

"It is a beautiful evening, isn't, sir?"

"Yes, it is."

"I was wondering about the wake. It seems to be glowing by itself."

"It's doing exactly that," the lieutenant replied. "There are a lot of tiny sea creatures called plankton. When they are disturbed by the passage of the ship, they phosphoresce."

"So, the wake's really alive, then, sir?"

"Yes. Very much alive, just like you and me. Only I don't suppose that plankton have personal relationships." He laughed gently and moved a bit closer to Third.

Third didn't move away. He remained silent for a few seconds, thinking that he knew where this conversation was leading, but still unsure of himself.

"So," the lieutenant asked, "are you going to stay in the Army or go back to civilian life?"

"I'm ready to be a civilian, again, sir."

"Me, too. My name's Nick, by the way."

"My name's Alan, but everybody calls me Third."

"Oh?"

"You know, like some people are called 'Junior' so as not to be confused with their father. Only I'm named for my grandfather, so I'm Third."

"Got it, Third," Nick said. "I like it. It's original."

"That's me, sir," Third said, "definitely an original."

"I'm enjoying our conversation," the Nick said, making his move, "I've got a bottle of find old cognac that a buddy of mine liberated from the officer's club for me. What do you say we open it?"

"If you say so, sir," Third replied, his senses now fully alert and his anticipation growing.

"Then follow me, soldier," Nick said.

"Yes, sir," Third replied.

Nick moved back into the shadows, stepped over the base of the door opening and into the dimly lit companionway. The door to his stateroom was the first one on the right. They slipped silently inside and Nick turned the latch on the door. Then he turned on a dim light above the narrow bunk.

"Why don't you sit down," He invited.

Again, Third did as he was told. "It's going to get warm in here, isn't it, sir?" he asked.

Again the gentle laugh. "It may get downright hot, soldier," the lieutenant said. "What do you suggest we do about that?"

Third told him.

Afterwards, Third became anxious. "You know, Nick, I ain't supposed to be in Officer Country unless I got business here. I could get in a lot of trouble."

"Not any more than I could," Nick chuckled. "But who's going to do anything about it? I've already resigned my commission, effective upon my return to the United States. You'll be paid off and discharged as soon as we land, won't you?"

"Yeah, Nick, I will be." Then he would begin the trip back to the Natahala. At least that was his plan.

"But, you're right," Nick said, "it's getting pretty late. Maybe you'd better slip back on deck. I'd like it if you came back tomorrow night, if you'd like that, too."

"Deal," Third said. "Will you meet me on deck like you did tonight?"

"Sure," Nick said, cracking the door open and checking the companionway. Then he whispered. "All clear, Third. See you tomorrow night."

After he closed his cabin door, Nick reflected on what had just occurred. It wasn't like him to do something like that, he thought. It had been a very long time since he had done it the last time, back at the schloss his last summer there.

He had been one of the boys who had been allowed the honor of attending a special summer school that taught German history and culture. What made it even more exciting for Nick was that his family actually owned the schloss, and he would inherit it someday. His father had said not to mention that side of things, so he hadn't. But every time he saw the castle from a distance, he had the thrill of knowing that it would be his someday.

Upon arrival, each student had to make a pledge to keep the "secrets of the castle." The regime was a hard one: Cold showers very early in the morning were followed by long runs on trails through the forest. Exercise was followed by lessons that emphasized the purity of the German race and the necessity for world conquest. After two summers' time, the indoctrination course was completed, and each student understood that the world would be a much better place under German mastery.

Nick had always excelled in sports and enjoyed anything competitive, so he threw himself into such things with vigor. So had almost all of the others. The daily sports and exercise regimen had the objective of producing bodies that were as close to perfection as possible. They were a tough and good-looking group of young men. They were not only in their physical prime, but where also in their sexual prime as well, but without any normal outlet. Like all such young men, whether in an all-male school, a monastery, or a prison, they found other outlets for their lust.

One night, the sports master caught Nick in the act.

"You come with me." the tall muscular man said, "I'm going to give you a lesson you'll never forget."

It was not the lesson that Nick expected, and not one that he forgot easily. Since that time he had occasionally found release with his own sex. But his attractions were to women, not other men.

"Why am I doing this, then," Nick asked himself. "Why do you ever do it, his inner voice mocked in reply: because you want to. It doesn't mean anything. You're just looking for control and release." Nick knew that to be true.

The next night was a repeat of the first.

Afterwards, Nick said, "We'll be getting into San Francisco sometime tomorrow. I plan to stay there a few days, buy some clothes, things like that. Why don't you stay with me?"

Third thought about that. For the first time, he did not feel guilty. He was becoming comfortable with who he was. Maybe it was because Willan had so open and accepting. Maybe it was because God's answer really was that he should be himself.

"I thought I'd go right home," Third said, "but nobody knows exactly when to expect me, and I've never seen San Francisco. Sure, let's do that. How do we hook up?"

"Easy. Whichever one of us gets off the ship first will wait for the other one across the street from the end of the pier."

"OK," Third said, as he slipped out into the companionway.

Late the next afternoon, they were all up on deck. They sailed under the Golden Gate, docked, and listened to a Marine band playing martial airs to welcome them home.

Most of the mustering out had been handled on the ship. Third had only to see the paymaster and sign a couple of forms. Then he was handed his honorable discharge from the Army and was a civilian again.

He was a bit apprehensive as he reached the end of the pier. There were hundreds of people milling about. Then he saw Nick, grinning his boyish grin and standing on the base of a streetlight, so that he would be head and shoulders above the rest of the crowd.

They found a taxi just outside the gates of the Alameda Naval Station.

"Fairmont Hotel," Nick said to the driver as they got in.

"OK, Mac," the cabbie said, "but don't plan on staying there unless you got a reservation. Most of the hotels are really full up. Big convention in town. You might get in at the Y."

"Thanks for the advice," Nick said pleasantly, "but take us there anyway."

"Right," said the cabbie, shrugging.

The lobby of the Fairmont was crowded with people wearing gaudy convention badges. There was a party-like atmosphere. Nick maneuvered through the crowd, lugging his own two suitcases, with Third in tow.

"Wait here," he said, depositing Third and the luggage near a tall column. "Let me see what I can do."

He strode to the desk and waited there patiently for a clerk. There was a brief conversation. The clerk shook his head abruptly and tried to turn away, but Nick stopped him with what was obviously a command. Nick drew himself up and said a few more words, during which the clerk's haughtiness vanished, to be replaced with a welcoming smile. With a slight bow the clerk handed Nick a key and hit the bell, hard, summoning the immediate attention of a bellhop.

A cute little guy in a Fairmont uniform, complete with pillbox hat, appeared immediately and took charge of the luggage. Nick and Third followed him to an elevator that whisked them up to the top of the building. Double doors were opened for them, and they walked into a beautifully furnished suite of rooms. Third had never seen anything like it. He just stood there, dumbly, while Nick tipped the bellhop and took the keys.

"Wow," Third said. "I've never been no place like this."

"They told me they were full up, until I used my uncle's name. He's a 'somebody' in town, so the Fairmont couldn't exactly offend him. This is about all they had left and I can afford it for a few days, so I took it. It's got two bedrooms, though, and I don't want you to get the wrong idea. I plan for us to use just one.

"Yes, sir!" Third said with some enthusiasm. "What ever you say, sir." And they both laughed.

Chapter Twelve

Ft. Lauderdale, 1997

"Well," Mark thought to himself, "first things first." It was fairly late in the afternoon, so he wanted to find Jason. He carefully put away Paul Thomas's personal effects. Then, he stripped and put on a tight-fitting bathing suit that showed off his assets to their best advantage. He opened the door to the patio and stepped out onto the beach.

Jason spotted him almost immediately and came over to him. "Hi, handsome," he said, "I see you're back from your errand."

"Yup," Mark said playfully, "and ready for food and drink. What are you in the mood for?"

"Sex," Jason said, firmly. "Sex and then food and drink. But, definitely, sex first. I've been hanging out here for hours, looking at all these hunky men. I need attention, man."

"Poor baby," Mark answered, grinning. "I guess I will have to take care of you." And he did.

Later, they went out and had a relaxing evening, with both food and drink.

The next morning, Mark told Jason that it was back to business. So Jason went back to the beach, "to work on his tan," he said. But this time, he agreed to take a key card with him. Meanwhile, Mark put on his "Mormon missionary" outfit (black clericals with white shirt and striped tie) and set about switching cars around. He returned the rental car to the airport and caught a cab to the Ft. Lauderdale Police impound lot. There, he showed his identification and claimed the late Paul Thomas's car. It turned out to be a very nicely appointed and quite new Jaguar, which, he decided at once, he would not at all mind driving.

He drove back to the beach motel and carefully parked the shiny black Jag in front. The skinny kid at the desk (who actually had gotten a break) took it all in and said nothing. Mark just nodded as he crossed the lobby and headed for his room. When he got there, Jason was coming back inside through the sliding glass door that faced the beach.

"I thought you were going to work on your tan," Mark said.

"I did," came the response, "but, too much sun is bad for your skin."

Jason was just turning on the television when the telephone rang. Mark sat on the side of the bed to answer it. It was Lieutenant Collins.

"Mr. Taylor, I think you'll be pleased to know that the coroner has finished his work-up, and you can now claim the body of Mr. Thomas."

"I am very glad to hear that," Mark replied. "What was the outcome of the autopsy, if I may ask?"

"Accidental death by drowning," was the immediate response.

Mark was startled. He had seen the marks on the neck and they matched, almost exactly, other marks on other bodies that had resulted from death by manual strangulation.

Then the penny dropped: There weren't enough clues, and there was practically no evidence. He knew that medical examiners often worked very closely with the police. So, this case wasn't going to become a case at all. It was just another faggot dead in a swimming pool and nothing anybody wanted, or cared, to be bothered about.

"How awful," Mark said, relieved. "I will make the appropriate arrangements at once."

He hung up the phone. He took Talbot Smith's business card from his wallet, looked at it and dialed Smith's office number. When the receptionist answered, Mark asked for Mr. Smith and was given the option of his voice mail, a personally taken message, or calling back. Mark wanted to move, not to stand around waiting while the coroner had second thoughts. He wanted to get that body out of there.

"Kindly tell Mr. Smith that Father Taylor would like to speak with him urgently," was his equally smooth, firm, and professional response to the cool and indifferent voice of the receptionist. It got results.

"I'll slip him a note," she said. "Please hold."

In a matter of thirty seconds or so, Talbot Smith was on the line. "What can I do for you, Mark?" he asked in his best professional manner.

"I'm sorry to trouble you with this, Talbot, but I need some quick advice if you don't mind."

"Not a problem. Go on."

"I need your recommendation for a good undertaker who can handle a cremation fairly quickly."

"Easy. Smith and Bowden. Smith is a cousin. Use my name."

Mark knew perfectly well that the marks on Paul Thomas's neck weren't going to go away. He wanted to erase the evidence, and do that quickly. His request to Talbot Smith was short and to the point, "Please call them for me and tell them to expect me. It will be a matter of immediate cremation."

"Certainly, Mark," Talbot replied, "I'll take care of that within the next thirty minutes."

"Thanks, Talbot, I owe you a least a drink on the beach."

"Deal. Call back if you need anything else."

The two of them broke the connection simultaneously, and Mark crossed the room to get the telephone directory off the desk.

"Hey," Jason said, "What's with this "father" business?"

Oops. He'd let it slip. It was now or never. "The fact is, Jason, that I'm an Episcopal minister."

"And?"

"And—it's a bit complicated from there on. All I can say at this point is that my bishop asked me handle the details of Paul's death."

"Look," Jason said. "We've got to start being honest with each other. I know that you probably think I'm a cheap hustler, but I ain't. I already told you: I got standards. And you were right when you said that Paul was lonely and that I was kind to him. But I really did like him. I'm not for sale. Period. Now, it's time for you to open up, too."

"OK, Jason, I will. But you've got to trust me on parts of this because I promised that I wouldn't talk about some of it."

"That's OK, too," Jason said, "If you made a promise, you gotta keep it."

"Right. I'm a deacon, which means that I'm on my way to becoming a priest, if everything turns out the way it should. But before I went to seminary, I was a policeman. When Paul turned up dead, the Bishop asked me to take care of it."

"That's not all, though, is it?" Jason said, knowingly

"No, it's not. But, there's not much more that I can tell you."

"Then, let me tell you something: He was murdered."

Mark gasped. "How do you know that?"

"Because I saw it."

"But you said you didn't see anything."

"I was scared," Jason responded. "I didn't know who you were then, so I didn't know if I could trust you or not. You might have been one of them, even."

"I see," Mark said, understanding Jason's caution. "Can you tell me how was he killed?"

"I told Paul I'd follow him down to the pool. He put on trunks and left while I was in the bathroom. When I got to the pool gate, I saw two of them. There was this really big guy with kinda long hair who was choking him while the smaller guy held him. They pulled off his swim trunks and threw him into the pool. The big one said, "faggot," and spit in the pool. Then they walked off, and I heard this old car start up. It was awful. As soon as they disappeared, I tried to get him out of the pool, but he was too heavy for me."

Continuing Jason's story, Mark said, "So you ran for the office and reported it."

"Yeah, the clerk called for help and told me to hide out, so I did. I was scared shit-less. I snuck away and hid in the room with the door locked and the lights out. I didn't know what to do. I heard people prowling around, but I don't know if it was them or just people cruising real late. I felt awful that I couldn't help him."

"I'm not sure you could have helped him. He was probably already dead when he hit the water. I wouldn't worry about it too awfully much; you did what you could. If you'd tried to interfere with those thugs, you'd probably have ended up dead, too. Sometimes it's best to let the preservation instinct take over. Anyhow, I'm going to treat this like a confessional secret, so I can't tell anybody anything about it ever. Unless you tell me to."

"There's more," Jason continued, "I saw them again today. That's really why I came inside. I think they're still looking for me."

Mark was unnerved. "When was this?" he asked anxiously.

"Just about when you got here. I'm pretty sure they didn't see me, but they sure were looking around. They were in an old white Mustang with a bad muffler. It sure sounded like the car I heard start up right after Paul was killed."

"Rats!" Mark exclaimed. "Rats again! They were tailing the Jaguar. They must have staked out the impound lot to see who picked up Paul's car. Now they know where I am. And, as soon as they poke around a little more, they'll know you're here, too. This is really dangerous, you know. You're the only witness who can identify the killers, so you are in real danger."

"On the other hand," Mark continued, "the police just told me the coroner said was an accidental death by drowning, so the murderers are officially off the hook. That is, unless they're worried that you'll make some objection to that official find-ing."

"So what do we do now? Do I object?"

"I don't think so. But it's really up to you." Mark thought a moment, then added: "I think we should play this cool. We can just pretend everything's normal. We don't know about them at all. We've accepted the coroner's finding. So, first, I call the undertaker and get Paul's body cremated. Then I call my bishop. Then we go to Atlanta."

"And," Jason added, "We watch to see if we're being tailed."

"Right."

"Then," Jason said, "That's what we'll do. Nobody's going to listen to a little queer like me, anyhow. Paul's dead. I can't help him now." Tears appeared in Jason's eyes, but he brushed them away.

Mark gave him a hug and kissed him gently on the forehead. Then he called the undertaker and used Talbot's name, as directed. He got immediate attention and said he'd be right over. He didn't want to take Jason, in case he was being watched, and he didn't want to leave him. Finally, they decided the Mark should go alone and watch for the tail, if there was one. Jason would lock himself in and answer the door only if it was Mark. Just in case, Mark gave Jason both key cards.

Then, Mark drove in Paul's Jaguar to the funeral home and walked in. The receptionist greeted him professionally and produced a synthetic smile of sympathy. "How may we help you at this time?" was the question, asked with a honeyed voice.

"By telling Mr. Smith that Mark Taylor is here."

"Certainly, sir. Mr. Smith is expecting you." She dialed an extension, and Smith soon appeared. "How may we help you at this time?" was his question as well.

"I'd like to have you pick up a body at the city morgue."

"Certainly, sir. While we are doing that, you will want to pick out a suitable casket for the body's repose and have it fully prepared for viewing, won't you?"

"I want to have the body cremated at once and the ashes delivered to me." Mark knew perfectly well that Talbot had already conveyed this message. He wasn't pleased with Smith's attempt to increase his sales.

"Oh," Mr. Smith said, obviously disapproving and disappointed, "we will certainly provide that small service for you." The emphasis was on small and the intonation obviously telegraphed cheapskate.

"Thank you, Mr. Smith," Mark responded, "I'm sure that both your cousin, Talbot, and the Bishop of Atlanta will be pleased to know how helpful and cooperative you have been at this difficult time. Let me know when you have picked up the body. I want to see it as soon as you have it."

"You want to what?" Smith's professional poise evaporated with the shock of the idea.

"I want to see it as soon as you have gotten it here."

"That is most unusual. If it has been at the coroners, it may have been, uh, autopsied," Smith said, appearing to be uncomfortable.

Mark responded, "I have already seen it at the coroners'. I just want to make sure that no mistake has been made as to which body is which. Such things do happen. I am acting under instructions from the bishop, you will understand."

"But the immediate cremation? Isn't that a bit, uh, unusual?"

"Not at all. The gentleman wished to be buried in his parish churchyard, and they only inter ashes there."

"I see. Well, let me give some instructions, and I think you may plan on hearing from us later today."

It was about noon when Mark went back to the motel. He knocked three times, a pause and then two more. When Jason asked who it was, he said "Tom" as they had arranged. If he had said, "Mark," Jason would have known to call for help.

"All clear," Mark said, as Jason opened the door a crack. "No tail or anything out of the ordinary."

It was well past noon, and Mark suggested food. Jason was always hungry, it seemed, and he was ready. So, they walked down the beach in the sunshine and had a pleasant meal. Jason didn't see anything unusual, and neither did Mark. When they got back to the motel, there was a message waiting for them.

The skinny kid on the desk said, "You got a call from the Bowden and Smith funeral home. They said to tell you that they're ready for you. Gee, I hope everything's all right."

Mark reassured him. "Everything's just fine, thanks," he said.

Since the tail seemed to have disappeared, both he and Jason set out this time. Both of them went out to the Jaguar. Mark drove them across town to Bowden and Smith.

When they got there, Jason asked, "Do you want me to come with you? I'd kind of like to. You know, to sorta say goodbye."

"You can if you want to, Jason. I understand how you feel. But I don't think the body is something that you ought to see, or would want to see, for that matter. It's better to remember him as he was. All that's left now is just the part of him that remains after the soul has gone. It really isn't Paul any longer. And you can really say "goodbye" properly at his funeral."

"Then, I'm not ever going to see him again, am I?" Jason said, as the reality set in.

Mark smiled his most sympathetic smile. "Well, not for some time, I hope," he said.

After a pause, Jason got it. "OK, then. I suppose it's his body after all, so whatever he wants done with it is what's gotta be done."

"You're sure you're all right with this?" Mark asked.

"Yeah," Jason said. "Well, no. I'm not OK just now, but I will be. You go ahead and take care of things. I'll wait in the lobby."

"It'll only take a couple of minutes," Mark said, as they entered the building together.

Mr. Smith was waiting at the desk. "We have a couple of viewings going on," he explained. "Otherwise, we'd be closed at this hour. Please follow me." Obviously, Mark thought, they couldn't be bothered with a mere cremation. His dislike for Mr. Smith deepened.

Mark and Mr. Smith went into the basement of the building while Jason remained in the lobby. Smith showed Mark into one of the preparation rooms where Paul Thomas's body lay under a sheet. Before Smith could stop him, Mark walked up to the table and pulled the sheet free of the body. He looked intently at the face and neck area for closely and then in a more cursory manner at the rest of the corpse.

"This is Paul Thomas, alright," Mark said, "you can put it in the crematory container now. I'll wait upstairs in the lobby with Mr. Rogers. Let us know when you're ready.

After what seemed like an hour, but was only twenty minutes or so, Smith came out to them. "We're ready for you, gentlemen."

Mark and Jason followed him into a small room on the ground floor where the simple container rested on a church truck. Mark took out his pocket-sized copy of the burial service and began,

> *"With faith in Jesus Christ, we receive the body of our brother Paul ... Let us pray with confidence to God, the giver of life, that He will raise him to perfection ... that he may rest with all your saints in the eternal habitations."*

Then, turning to Smith, Mark said, "Let me know when to pick up the ashes, will you?"

"Certainly, sir." Smith replied, "It should be sometime tomorrow afternoon."

Mark and Jason walked slowly together back to the car. After they were out of the building, with its all-too-sweet smell of flowers and the equally sickening piped-in organ music, Mark hugged Jason to him and held him close for a moment. Then they got into the car and drove away.

In the rear-view mirror, Mark saw the old white Mustang swing into traffic behind them.

"Don't look, but, it's just as you thought," he said to Jason, "we're being tailed."

Neither of them turned around. Mark drove Paul's Jaguar straight to the motel and parked in front, as he had before. They went inside together, entered the room, and made sure that they used all of the locks. Then Mark took a loose shelf out of the wardrobe and wedged it into the sliding glass door, so that it couldn't be quietly opened, only smashed.

"I don't get it," Mark said. "Paul Thomas was only a church musician. Who would want to kill him, and why?

"Dunno," Jason said. "But they did. Maybe they just hate faggots."

"I think there's more to it than that," Mark said, "but I can't figure out what."

Their lovemaking that night was long and intense, as though love alone could overcome death.

Chapter Thirteen

Tulsa, Oklahoma, 1959

Neither Paul, Jack nor Martha ever spoke again of their contract negotiations in the trailer that fateful evening. Paul remained perfectly civil to the two of them, and they returned his civility, although Martha did so with considerable difficulty.

Paul attended the two remaining rehearsals and recording sessions. He taped his music, as promised, giving the best performance that he could. He delivered the tapes on time, as promised. Martha duly paid his rent and utilities. She even kicked in a hundred dollars a month until he started school in the fall, even though that hadn't been stipulated. She recognized the importance of good will in business deal.

After the last taping session, Martha tried to get Paul to quit his claim to any share in Jack Johns World Wide Ministry. He demurred, but kept the paper, saying that he would sign it on graduation day. Martha did not argue.

At the beginning of his freshman year, Paul figured out what his costs would be, and Martha herself brought him the check. "I'll never trust you alone with Jack again," she said, "so don't expect to see him without me around."

Paul said nothing, except to thank her for the check and to note that it did not include all of the one-hundred-dollars-a-week pocket money.

Martha retorted that she would pay that sum on a monthly basis, and Paul agreed, knowing that he still held the upper hand. True to her word, Martha mailed him a check for four hundred dollars and change every month. It was just another expense check, like the others that Martha wrote. If it bothered her to write it, she didn't let it show and Jack had sense enough to keep his mouth shut about it.

At the end of Paul's first term, just a couple of weeks after the Thanksgiving break, he was pleased and astonished to see that he had achieved an almost straight "A" average. He asked the registrar to send a copy of his transcript to "Rev. and Mrs. Jack

Johns," and the registrar did. Shortly thereafter, Paul calculated his expenses for the second term and Martha again wrote the check.

All that Paul's father knew about any of this was what Paul wrote to him. Paul said he had left Jack Johns Worldwide Ministry and was in college studying church music. He told his father that he had received an all-expenses-paid scholarship. Paul figured that Jack and Martha wouldn't contradict that. They didn't. Paul's father was pleased about his son's talent and worried about education at a Presbyterian college. However, he kept his concerns to himself and prayed earnestly for Paul's salvation.

When Paul's father wrote to Jack and Martha, they confirmed Paul's story. They said that they were in close contact with Paul. Martha promised that to keep a close eye on him.

But Jack was increasingly unhappy with the new family arrangements. He missed having somebody in bed with him. He missed the comfort of having Martha's warmth by his side, and he missed the excitement of having sex with Paul. Like most truly bisexual men, Jack enjoyed playing both male and female roles. Now, he could play neither.

All that was left to Jack was his strong sex drive, so his frustration grew and grew as the months went by. Outwardly, Jack made everything look fine. But Martha couldn't watch him all the time and take care of the children, the house, and the books. Sometimes, he made guest appearances, preaching at nearby churches. Martha couldn't go with him and mind the kids, too. Jack took advantage of those rare opportunities to find anonymous gay sex. As he became increasingly sure of himself, he became bolder in his adventures.

Then, one evening a couple of years later, Jack didn't return from the recording studio at his normal time. When he did, he appeared subdued and went quickly to his own bedroom.

When the suspicious Martha knocked at the door, and Jack said, "Come it," she found him under the covers. She smelled alcohol.

"All right," she said, closing the door. "What's been going on, Jack?"

"Nothing, Martha," was the reply.

She didn't buy it. "You've been drinking, haven't you?" she asserted.

Knowing it was no use, Jack admitted that he had been.

"Where?" she wanted to know.

"A quiet little bar I know of on Sixth Street," Jack said. "Nobody knows me there."

"I don't care if they do or not," Martha said. "You can't preach against alcohol and go out drinking in public places."

"It's safe enough," the slightly tipsy Jack retorted. "Nobody I preach to is likely to set foot in there, and even if they did, they sure as hell wouldn't tell anybody about it."

"Don't swear, Jack, it's not becoming to a minister of the Gospel," Martha instructed, not for the first time. "And what do you mean that nobody would tell about it? Of course they would, you ninny, it would be all over town in a couple of days."

"What I mean, my dear, is that the bar is a place where queers go to meet each other. Follow me on this: none of my radio flock knows what I look like. They aren't supposed to drink, so none of them are apt to go into a bar. Even if they did, they wouldn't go to a queer bar. And even if one of them was queer and did—and somehow recognized me—he'd hardly tell that on himself."

"Jack, I won't have it." Martha said, shaking her finger. "I see your point, but I still won't have it. You should not be doing such things. Have you been picking up men there?"

Seeing his opportunity to be completely candid with his wife for once, Jack said, "Yes. Sometimes I do. Even that's safe, though. We don't exchange anything but first names. I always say mine's Ed. Even if I see the same guy in the bar again, we don't speak. That's the way we handle it."

"What do you mean, "we," Martha asked, her eyes narrowing.

"I mean us queers," Jack said, loudly. "Us faggots. Us goddamned faggots, if you've got to know."

"Stop that," Martha demanded. "You stop that at once." She kept her voice low for the sake of the children, but she was apoplectic with fury. Her voice shook and she trembled all over.

"'Fraid of the truth, are you?" was Jack's slurred response. "Well, m'dear and loving wife, you made me what I am today." He rolled over, turning his back to her.

"Jack, this isn't over. You will not ever do this again, and that's final. If you do, I'll have your balls on toast for breakfast."

She walked out of his bedroom and silently closed his door behind her. She paused outside the door to compose herself.

After she had stopped shaking, she went into the dining room to tell the children that their father wasn't feeling well and not to disturb him. They knew better than to disobey. They finished their belated supper in silence. Then, Martha helped them finish the homework they had begun earlier. She supervised them while they said their "Down I lay mes" and tucked them into bed.

She quietly tidied the kitchen, turned out all the lights and went to her own room. She went to bed, but not to sleep. She had a lot to think about. And she wasn't thinking about Jack's fall from grace. Her thoughts were about Jack on television, and how important he was going to become when he could be seen as well as heard.

A lot of radio personalities, such as Jack Benny and Bob Hope had made the transition, and they had done so with great success. Radio had been good to Jack, too, Martha had reasoned, so television could be even better.

Jack's good looks, a growing following, a live audience to cheer him on, and suitable guest appearances by well-known personalities would, she felt sure, be a winning combination. She also knew it would take money to get into television. She thought about that part of it a lot.

But Jack's admission that he was to queer bars, and picking up men for anonymous sex in seedy apartments, and in cars in dark alleys created a new problem for her. Before Jack's face could ever become well known, any other attempt at blackmail similar to what she was already paying to Paul would need to be forestalled. She wondered how to do that.

Then an old saying came to her mind: "Better the devil you know than the devil you don't know." She forgot about making money for the moment and concentrated on that instead. Then she began to think of ways to mend her fences with Paul Thomas. She was thankful that she had decided to be civil to him. It was her instinct for self-preservation, she supposed, but it would stand her in good stead now.

Instead of mailing the next month's check to him, Martha called his dormitory and left a message asking him to call her.

Paul returned the call that evening. "Hello, Martha, this is Paul. Did you call me?"

"Yes, Paul, I did," Martha said. "I'd like to bring your next check to you, if you don't mind. I need to have a friendly, private chat with you."

Paul became immediately suspicious, but he just said, "Of course, Martha, I'll look forward to seeing you. Let's meet outside Tyrell Hall. My organ lesson is over at 3:00 tomorrow. Will that be OK?"

Martha only said, "Yes. See you then."

And she did. She was waiting on a nearby bench, smiling her preacher's wife smile, when Paul emerged from ivy covered stone building. The chimes in the nearby tower announced the end of class. They sat on the bench in the shade to talk. Students walked briskly by. No one paid them any attention.

Up to that time, Paul had been immersed in studying his music. Martha and Jack had paid his way, and, under Martha's management, they had done well financially, too. Now Martha wanted to change the rules of the game. She played her opening gambit.

"Paul," she said, as sweetly as she could, "I know I was pretty ugly to you about you and Jack. And, I suppose I was a bit unfair, too, in dealing with it. In spite of everything, you've held up your side of the bargain, and I think we have, too."

"Martha," Paul said, "I think you're right on all counts. I understand that what I said to you that night must have been a real shock."

Martha managed a little laugh, "Well, yes," she said. "It certainly was that. But I've come to understand that some men are just different. I suppose Jack's one of those and there's nothing to be done about it. The difficulty is that he's a preacher, and he has to be discreet. You do understand that, don't you?"

Paul, who had been having a few discreet affairs himself, in and around the music school and drama department, said he understood that all too well. "What's this about exactly?" is all he asked.

"Well," Martha said, "I want to know if you love him."

The question was nothing like what Paul expected. "Yes," he said, "I suppose that did fall in love with him. But that was before all of this." His expressive hand took in Martha, the music school building, and the rest of the campus.

"OK, then," Martha said, "let me rephrase my question: Do you still love him?"

"Honestly, Martha, I don't know. I think about Jack a lot; I think of him fondly. We had some good times together, but both of us were always worried about being found out. Now the situation is quite different."

"It needn't be, you know," was Martha's surprising answer. "The truth is that Jack and I have separate bedrooms now. I'm content with that arrangement, but Jack is terribly lonely and unhappy. I'm dreadfully sorry about that, but it's going to take a man, not a woman, to fix it."

"And you're asking me?" Paul asked her.

"Yes."

"How does Jack feel about this?" Paul asked.

"He doesn't know," Martha replied. "I didn't say anything to him because if you said no I think he'd become really depressed. Maybe even kill himself." Martha, of course, thought no such thing, but she knew where the *vox humana* organ stop was on Paul's emotions and she pulled it out.

"Please say yes and let me tell Jack the good news," Martha pleaded, her voice trembling slightly.

Paul was less enthusiastic. He agreed to meet Paul "to talk over old times, but nothing more."

Martha, her mission accomplished, went home to once again lay down the law to her errant husband.

After the children were in bed, she invited Jack into her bedroom and shut the door. She sat on her dressing table bench. He sat in the only chair. Neither of them even looked at the bed.

"Jack," Martha began, "I want to have a serious talk with you. Our ministry is doing very well. We're taking in a lot more money than we're spending, and we now have a couple of hundred-grand in the bank. It's all safe and secure. But our ministry's not; not if you're going to go out to drink and have sex with queers."

Jack started to say something, but Martha cut him off. "Jack, I'm not an unsympathetic person. I know that all men need sex regularly, and I know, now, that some men are just different. I understand that you one of those. I haven't been fair to you about that, and I want to be."

"And just how do you propose to do that?" Jack asked, "Have me neutered?"

"Don't be sarcastic, Jack," Martha said, controlling her ire. "I just want to find a way for you to have a safe outlet for your desires without compromising our ministry."

Jack was astonished. "What?"

"I mean it, dearest," Martha said, "I do love you in my own way. We have to work this problem out together."

"What on earth do you have in mind?" Jack asked, amazed.

Martha told him.

A few days later, the builders arrived to rehabilitate the old servants' quarters above the carriage house that now served Jack and Martha as a two-car garage. The upper floor was speedily turned into a very nice studio apartment, complete with king-sized bed. (King-sized beds were the newest things from Hollywood, now that the motion picture code no longer required twin beds for married couples in movies. Hints that adults actually had sex were starting to creep into movies.)

When the apartment was completed, Paul moved in. The old Hammond was resurrected for him to practice on if he wished. He didn't, much preferring the large pipe organ downtown at Trinity Episcopal Church. With no dorm rent to pay, Martha increased his weekly allowance to a princely sum of one hundred, fifty dollars.

The deal was simple: Paul didn't come to the main house. Jack visited him in the carriage house. Martha saved money on the dorm rent, even while adding to Paul's pocket money, and she had made a shrewd real-estate investment. She didn't ever think of herself as a whoremonger or of the extra fifty a week as payment to Paul for servicing her husband. For her it was just another business deal.

As soon as Paul was safely and regularly laying Jack, she went back to thinking about television. And, finally, she produced a business plan that was audacious, even for Martha.

She had, of course, been keeping track of their larger and more regular contributors. Jack's healing ministry worked miracles for some people simply because of the law of averages. Martha was quick to capitalize on that, as well as others who feared their impending journey into the unknown. She orchestrated a capital campaign to raise funds for their new television venture.

The motto was "Help us Help Jesus Help the World." Mailings announcing the need for financial support for Jack Johns World Wide Ministry went out in the mail. The slick mailer included a photo of Jack holding a large Bible. Men and women in hospital whites flanked him. They were holding packages with red crosses on them. A couple of them had stethoscopes around their necks. In the background a large silver plane sported a red cross, too, and the words "Jack Johns World Wide Ministry." Another photo showed Jack with a group of dark-skinned children, who were happily eating cereal from brightly colored plastic bowls.

The medical personnel were actually models hired from a New York modeling agency. The photograph of Johns and his "doctors and nurses" was superimposed over a photograph of a plane. The image of the plane had also been altered to add the cross and the lettering. The children were from a local orphanage. Jack's "JJWWM" had thrown a little party for them. It was his only visit to the place. Martha had arranged it of course, complete with photographer.

Jack had, at first, resisted the advertising scheme. But Martha held firm and prevailed. "We're not really promising them anything, Jack" was her response to his concerns. "People need to feel better about themselves. They like giving, just like they love feeling superior to others. When we get enough money, we'll do a lot of good with it, preaching the Word. The pictures just illustrate what could do, once the funding is in place."

So Jack agreed to include financial appeals, written by a speechwriter, in his weekly radio broadcast. The appeal for funds was well coordinated and effective, but it didn't net the kind of money JJWWM needed to expand. Even so, Martha toiled on. She still intent on becoming the executive producer of the JJWWM show.

The, an unexpected telephone call brought about big changes. Mr. Phillip Anderson, it turned out, was the principal backer of The Foundation for Religious Truth in America. He wanted to talk to Martha.

When he arrived for his appointment, he began by saying, "Mrs. Johns, The Foundation admires what you and Reverend Johns are doing to bring America back to its Christian foundation. We want to help you do that. I have brought a check to help with your current capital campaign."

With that said, Anderson handed her a check for ten million dollars.

Martha felt faint when she saw the amount on the slip of paper, but she managed to keep her composure. "Mr. Anderson," she said, "My husband and I are grateful for your offering. I promise that every penny will be used to further Reverend John's work to save this sinful world."

"And we are grateful for the fine work you are doing. If I may, I will be in touch from time to time to assist you in any way I can. In the meanwhile, should you discover you need additional backing, please let me know. The Foundation is always interested in reviewing grant requests."

Martha had her money. She lost no time turning dreams into reality. She bought a large warehouse to convert into a television production facility. An architect designed a façade that looked vaguely like a non-denominational church of some sort, complete with a very modern and very cheaply constructed tower. The architect had wanted to put a cross on it, but Martha rejected that idea. "Too Catholic," she said. Instead, they settled for a giant, gold-colored plastic bell. It housed a loudspeaker that played recorded chimes. The architect also designed the inside of the largest studio. It looked vaguely like a non-denominational church, too, with theater seating for about five hundred people.

The seats were arranged in a semi-circle with an imposing pulpit at the focal point. On the wall behind it, was the JJWWM logo: a globe surrounded by the name "Jack Johns World Wide Ministry." There were side stages on either side of the pulpit. Seats for a choir were located on one side, with phony organ pipes behind them. The other side stage was a living room set, with lavish gilt furniture, a fireplace, and a huge picture window looking out onto an idyllic country scene painted on a backdrop.

Absent from this pseudo-elegance was any sort of baptismal font or pool. There was no altar or communion table, no cross. "We just preach the Word," Martha had dictated. "We don't do that other stuff."

Having thus disposed of 2,000 years of Christian belief and sacraments as "stuff," Martha prepared to launch Jack's television career. But first she had to get him ready.

She hired a television acting coach for Jack. While the space was being fitted out with cameras, lights, and editing equipment, Jack toiled with learning how to act on television. Martha bought an electronic organ and hired professional musicians who usually played in dance bands to provide the different kinds of music that would be needed. A composer who normally wrote advertising jingles was hired to write opening and closing theme music for the show.

When Jack and Martha were ready to open, she used their dwindling funds to invite nearby fundamentalist congregations to attend their inaugural taping sessions on Saturday evenings. She even threw in a box lunch and souvenir key chains. The key chain fob sported a picture of a blond, blue-eyed Jesus on one side and a photo of Jack on the other.

It was all very tacky. But it appealed to Martha's taste, so it was surprisingly successful. It appealed to others of her class and education. She had never heard P. T. Barnum's dictum "never under estimate the taste of the American people," but she would have agreed with it.

Her efforts not only were making her and her husband rich; her efforts were also making Jack famous.

Now, almost four years after Martha's critical confrontation with Paul, Jack's fame came as a mixed blessing. In addition to the thousands of dollars that arrived by mail every day, there were other kinds of contact with the outside world that were less pleasant. People with unbalanced personalities wrote crazy and sometimes threatening mail. There were occasional writers, both male and female, who claimed to have had sexual affairs with Jack. Several women claimed to have had a child by him. JJWWM's team of lawyers handled these claims adroitly; some with binding agreements included a large financial settlement and a gag clause.

One day, just as Jack and Martha pulled up in front of the studio, a middle-aged woman, with a teenager in tow, confronted Jack. Screaming invective, she hurled a rotten egg at him. The woman had tipped off a local newspaper, and a cameraman was there to catch the picture. The photo showed an open-mouthed Jack and an astonished Martha looking in horror at the egg dripping off his face. The picture appeared in papers all over the country. The accompanying story included the woman's accusation that her teenage son had been fathered by Jack and that his lawyers had tried to shut her up. JJWWM had no comment on the story.

Martha decided that Jack needed a bodyguard. Preventing such occurrences was far easier than trying to spin the damage afterwards. So, she determined that both their home and the studio complex would have a complete, integrated security setup.

Just as he had agreed to Martha's arrangement with Paul, Jack readily agreed to this also. He was content to let Martha run things: she was making him a star.

Chapter Fourteen

Austria, 1956

Nick got off the train at the rustic station and looked once again at the magnificent green trees and blue sky of the Fatherland. He inhaled the clean, crisp spring air; slung his knapsack over his shoulder and began his walk to the von Hutton schloss about three kilometers away. He looked like any other American college boy on vacation in Europe.

He didn't mind the walk. In fact, he rather enjoyed it. His high school and college summers had been spent here, ostensibly studying "German history and culture." The Nazi indoctrination course had included plenty of hard physical exercise, including long-distance hikes. He was in prime condition. For Nick, three kilometers was just a short stroll in the woods.

And, there was a big difference this year. He was not returning to summer school. He was returning, instead, as heir-presumptive to the manor. This year, he would occupy the owner's suite at the castle instead of sleeping in bunks in the unheated and drafty part of the castle that had once housed its huge wine cellar. He would take warm baths instead of cold showers. He would go hunting, if he chose, or bathe in the nearby lake.

He would play host to a very important meeting. Himmler, now 56, would attend if that could be managed. It was very risky for him to reenter Germany or Austria. There was no statute of limitations on what the Americans called war crimes. If found, he could still be arrested and tried.

Nick knew the general purpose and outline of the three-day meeting. It had been decided to take the first steps in assuring the rise of the Fourth Reich. On the evening before the guests were scheduled to arrive, the schloss's students departed on a three-day field exercise that included long hikes by day and survival camping at night.

Nick and his guests would have the schloss to themselves, except for a few trusted members of ODESSA who worked there as servants.

The last of the guests arrived at about midnight. Among them was an elderly gentleman with a bald head, thick horn-rimmed glasses and a large, drooping black moustache. It was Himmler.

The men sipped fine old cognac around the fire in the great hall of the schloss. Business would be left until the next morning. Some of the junior members of the group, including Nick, had never met the great man himself. It was an opportunity to relax and get to know him personally. Nick felt greatly honored.

The meeting that convened immediately after the next day's early breakfast was not devoted to social chitchat.

Himmler opened the meeting with a formal address: "I want to first of all thank you for being here. For those of us who are older, there is still some danger. Those of you who are younger, although not wanted on the enemy's list of so-called war criminals, could still be in serious trouble if you were caught doing the dangerous work you do. I am grateful to all of you.

"It has been just over ten years since the collapse of the Third Reich. Those of us who have believed in the ultimate goals of that great effort have vowed to continue the struggle. All of us, young and old, who sit around this table have sworn to carry out this purpose.

"It is true that the winners write the history of what happened in any conflict. You have all been to school in this very building, and you have learned here the real truth of what our Fatherland was trying to achieve; for it is here that the real historic facts are preserved for generations to come.

"Before I continue, I must now ask all of you to reaffirm your loyalty to our cause. If any of you are unwilling, let him speak now and leave us forever."

They stood and Himmler led them in again in the oath the younger men had taken when entering the academy.

"I swear to you, our Leader, loyalty and bravery; to be always ready to stake life and limb in the struggle for the aims of the movement; to give absolute military obedience to my military superiors and leaders; I vow to you, and to those you have named to command me, obedience unto death, so help me God."

"Excellent!" Himmler said. "We now come to the point of this meeting. Please take your seats. As I have said, it has been just over ten years since the invaders occupied the Fatherland. During that time, the leadership of ODESSA has been studying the foe and making plans. It is now time for those plans to be put into action."

Everyone leaned forward eagerly to learn what would come next.

"We have decided that the Fourth Reich will rise in America."

There was a gasp of astonishment around the table.

"What? Did you think it would arise in the Fatherland? That has been tried already. It would be insane to attempt it again.

"No, my comrades, No! What is the most powerful nation in the world? It is now the United States. The British Empire has fallen. DeGaulle is an old woman, concerned only with being as offensively French as he can be. Italy? Phooh! The Soviet Union cannot sustain the communist ideal; it will go bankrupt. No, only America is emerging as the truly strong nation.

"Our task is to make use of that strength. We are few in number, but we have time on our side. A nation of mongrels, like America, will grow fat and lazy on its wealth. Like the Romans before them, the Americans will become content with bread and circuses. Then, we will act.

"But to use America, we must have the right people, in the right places, exerting the correct influence at the right time. That is the task of our young soldiers gathered here with us this morning. Each of you has either graduated from college or will graduate shortly. You will then fulfill your military obligation to the United States. You will do your best to be good officers and gentlemen, and you will win what awards and recognition that come your way. And, when you have done this, you will enter politics, or business, or education. And there you will become leaders in your field.

"Each of you has the native ability to do this, or you would not be here. By staying in contact with each other, you will learn much that will be of individual and mutual benefit. By supporting one another when support is needed, you will form a close-knit comradeship that will serve you well. And we who are now the leaders of the movement will provide you with guidance, with advice, and, when needed, with money.

"And one thing more. If you fall into any real danger of exposure, we will discretely handle that problem for you. You may be well assured of your personal safety, so long as you are not foolishly careless about your mission.

"Now, my young comrades, I name your leader: Nicholas Alexander von Hutton the Third. Stay in touch with him, and he will pass along the help and instructions that you may need."

There was a short pause while Nick gathered his thoughts to respond to this unexpected announcement. Then he stood and came to attention.

"Sir, gentlemen, and comrades: I accept this commission. In doing so, I acknowledge my undying duty to you and to the Fatherland. Seig Heil!"

The others rose and joined him in his salute, repeating after him, "to victory!"

After they had again seated themselves, Himmler went on, "I want now to read something to you, because it will guide you in the first part of your work." He pulled a single sheet of paper from his inside coat pocket, smoothed it out on the table, and read:

> *"The national government will maintain and defend the foundations on which the power of our nation rests. It will offer strong protection to Christianity as the very basis of our collective morality. Today, Christians stand at the head of our country. We want to fill our culture again with the Christian spirit. We want to burn out all the recent immoral developments in literature, in the theater, and in the press—in short, we want to burn out the poison of immorality which has entered into our whole life and culture as a result of liberal excess during the past years."*

"Those are the words of Adolph Hitler. The Fürher was a man of vision and great wisdom. He understood, more clearly than most people do, the influence of religion on the common man.

"The task before you can be divided into two parts. But, as you will shortly see, they must become one. The first part of your task is to infiltrate and influence America's Conservative Party. The second part is to infiltrate and influence fundamentalist Christianity. By combining these two goals into one movement, you can do in America what was accomplished first in Germany: the creation of a religion that supports the objectives of the state. That will make it easier to gain control of the populace.

"When you have become Conservative leaders, you should promise the electorate the same sort of things we promised in Germany: work for the unemployed, prosperity to businessmen, profits to industry, social harmony and the maintenance of peace and prosperity through a strong military."

"Sir," Nick interjected, "Am I to understand that this will be sufficient to control so vast and diverse a country as the United States?"

"No, Nick, not at all. There must also be a program to rid the United States of the unfit. But that is secondary. The creation of a "Christian nation" is the vital first step in this. From it comes control of the populace. Then you can begin to weed out the enemies of the "Christian nation." For us in Germany, the Jews were the first "enemy within." In America, I think it will be the homosexuals. Like the Jews were in Germany, they are America's despised minority.

"After that," Himmler continued, "we go after those of impure blood, the intellectuals and so on." Nick nodded his affirmation, as did the others.

"Yes. You see, gentlemen, Hitler wanted to purify and build a nation for all Aryans. Under the leadership and domination of our race, he was certain that a better world could be created. Our objective has not changed, but our strategy for achieving that goal has. We will wait until some natural disaster arises that will help us to rid the world of undesirables.

"People are always predicting the end of the world. Isaac Newton said it would come in 2060, for example. Near the end of the nineteenth century, the volcano Krakatoa blew up and caused worldwide concern. Sometimes there are huge earthquakes or hurricanes that do much damage. I simply do not know when the next catastrophe will occur or what it will be. But something of immense impact will arise. When it does, we must be ready to make use of it."

With that final comment, Himmler brought the plenary session to a close. The assembly broke up into three groups to organize themselves in the areas of business, politics, religion, and education. The rest of the meetings were held in these smaller groups. Under the leadership of older ODESSA members, plans were laid and details worked out for implementing them.

As their leader in the United States, Nick attended all of the sessions in rotation. He quickly concluded that he should coordinate the efforts in the political and religious spheres himself. He would use the education branch to bolster both of those through indoctrination of the young. He suggested establishing Christian religious schools for that purpose.

On the third and final day, the group had a formal luncheon to conclude their work together. At the close of the meal, Nick rose to propose a toast.

"Gentlemen, the toast is: "Success to our cause for the betterment of our world.""

The others rose, raised their glasses, and echoed his words. Then they all solemnly drank to the toast.

Then Himmler responded: "To Victory," he said.

"Seig Heil," They all responded.

Over the next twelve hours, the group discretely left the schloss by twos and threes. They departed by various routes in various ways to avoid calling attention to themselves. Nick stayed on for a couple of weeks more, digesting his new responsibilities. Then he too left to begin active duty as a reserve ensign in the United States Navy.

It was to lay the groundwork for his life in politics.

Chapter Fifteen

Ft. Lauderdale, 1997

Mark and Jason were still in bed when the phone rang the next morning. It was the mortuary, calling to say that Paul Thomas's ashes could be picked up at any time after 2:30 that afternoon. Mark said he would be there then.

With nothing else to keep them in Ft. Lauderdale any longer, Mark and Jason made plans to leave. Mark called the bishop to report, and called Talbot Smith and suggested meeting for lunch before he went to the mortuary. Talbot agreed and suggested one o'clock at the same beachfront restaurant where he had hosted Mark three nights earlier.

Mark and Jason packed their belongings, had a light breakfast nearby, and checked out before the noon deadline. Mark had dressed in jeans and a knit shirt and so had Jason. Mark's choice of clothing was deliberate. He assumed that the thugs would continue to follow. Mark didn't want them to know more about him or Jason than they already knew.

Traffic was heavy on A1A, so neither Mark nor Jason saw the Mustang. But they supposed it was there anyway. They drove directly to the restaurant where Talbot was waiting for them. He greeted Mark warmly and was charming when introduced to Jason. The three of them had a leisurely luncheon seated below the terrace awning. All of them enjoyed and commented on the view. Talbot asked if the arrangements made by his cousin's funeral home had been satisfactory. Mark said they had been, but didn't comment further. The check came just after 2:00, and Mark picked it up, figuring that it was his obligation to pay, as he'd brought Jason along. However, Talbot was quite insistent about paying the bill, so Mark gave in.

Jason said, "Thank you, Mr. Smith. I enjoyed your company even more than the good food." Jason gave Talbot a dazzling smile. Talbot was clearly charmed, and Mark felt a little pang of jealousy. "Oops," he thought. "I didn't expect to feel that!"

They parted company, and Jason and Mark walked back to the Jaguar. "Flirt," Mark said.

"Who, me?" Jason said with mock innocence. "Flirt? Never!" Then, after a pause, "He's a nice guy. I didn't think it would hurt anything to turn on the charm."

"It didn't," Mark replied, and he smiled.

The Jaguar purred to life. Mark slipped it easily into the traffic and headed it towards Bowden and Smith for the last time. "See anything?" Mark asked.

"Not so far," was the response.

"Don't look around, unless you're really casual about it," Mark instructed.

"OK" Jason said. Then after a minute, he suddenly pointed at nothing is particular and exclaimed, "Wow, look at that!" His gesture gave him a perfect opportunity to turn around and look behind them. "Gee," he said, with mock seriousness. "You missed it!" He turned back around. "They're there, all right," he reported, and settled down in his seat.

"Nicely done," Mark said. "Just don't do it too often."

A short drive and several streets later, they were back at the funeral home. "Stick close," Mark said to Jason.

"Don't worry," Jason retorted. "I'm sticking to you like Velcro, and self-preservation isn't the only reason." He grinned.

They both whet inside and claimed the cardboard box that contained Paul Thomas's cremains. Mark paid with the bishop's credit card, shook hands with Talbot's cousin, and they returned to the car. The Mustang was parked on the other side of the street, about a block away.

"They're not exactly hiding, are they," Mark remarked as they climbed in. "Maybe they're trying to intimidate us."

"Or maybe they think we're dumb," Jason said, "or maybe they're the dumb ones."

"Well," Mark said, "whichever it is, we're going to be very careful, and maybe a bit tricky, on our way back to Atlanta."

"Do you think they'll try to follow us there?" Jason asked, alarmed.

"I'd bet on it. And, if they do, I'd say you're in very real danger," Mark said gravely.

He pulled the Jaguar into the street and watched in the rearview mirror as the Mustang began to follow again. It was well after three, and they had a long drive ahead of them. Mark hoped he could make it to Orlando before nightfall. He wasn't about to be caught on a highway at night with a couple of murderous thugs following them.

As it turned out, they got to Orlando fairly early in the evening. They had all kinds of accommodations to choose from, but Mark was particular. He wanted an upscale hotel with several floors, one with all-night services and, therefore, a decent security setup. They settled for a Hilton.

"Good evening," Mark said to the desk clerk. "We would like a room, please. If possible, one on a higher floor away from the traffic noise. My cousin is afraid of hotel fires, so he's always more comfortable when he's near a fire stair. Can you do that?"

The clerk consulted the computer screen, hit a few keys, and said, "The only room we have left that meets those requirements is a no-smoking with a single king bed. Will that do?"

Mark turned to Jason and asked the question with a raised eyebrow.

Playing his part to perfection, Jason sighed, "I suppose so, if that's the best they can do."

The clerk gave Mark a sympathetic look.

Mark completed the transaction. They said, "No, thanks" to the waiting bellman and hustled their bags to the waiting elevator. When they got in and punched their floor, they looked back across the lobby. Two rough-looking men had just entered. As the elevator door hissed shut, Jason said quietly, "That's them."

"Not so good," Mark said. "If they check in, they'll pretty much have the run of the place. We'll stay in, order room service, and get the hell out of here very, very early in the morning."

"Sounds OK," Jason said. "But I'm sleeping on the side away from the door."

"If I let you get any sleep," Mark joked.

The elevator door dinged open. Their room was on the opposite side of the hall. The fire stairs were just a few steps away. Mark checked the locks, closed the door, and saw that the peephole in the door gave him a good view of the elevators. It was, all in all, a pretty secure location.

They showered together and tried to relax by watching television. They perused the room service menu and ordered. Mark included a bottle of wine.

They snuggled on the bed until there was a knock at the door. Mark said, "Who is it?"

"Room service," came the reply.

"Check," Mark said to Jason, who promptly looked through the peephole and then opened the door. He also quickly closed the door behind the waiter.

Mark signed for the meal, added a tip, and they both saw the waiter to the door. They closed it firmly behind him, and secured all of the locks. After dinner, they followed the same procedure when they pushed the rolling table back into the corridor. Then, they turned in for an early night after setting the radio alarm for 4:00 a.m.

When the radio shattered the peace with a bad country-and-western song, even more badly sung, at 4:00 in the morning, they did indeed get the hell out of there as they had planned.

However, they didn't take the elevator. Mark figured that one of the two men might be on watch in the lobby. They took the fire stairs instead. They trudged down the eight flights of stairs and crept carefully into the hotel parking lot. The Jag was nearby. The Mustang was only a few cars away, but there was nobody in it.

They dumped their bags in the trunk of the Jag and slipped away quietly. They hoped their remaining eight-hour drive to Atlanta would be uneventful.

Jason looked behind them several times, at first cautiously, but then more boldly. He saw nothing unusual. But Mark took an exit anyway, crossed the intersecting road, and parked near the ramp back to the expressway. That vantage point let them watch the traffic that had been behind them go by. They waited a while, but Mustang failed to appear. Presently, they resumed their journey north, secure in the knowledge that they'd given the old Mustang and its occupants the slip.

Jason was tired. He had slept hardly at all, and then badly, awaking at every noise from the corridor. Now, more confident in his own safety, he allowed himself to drift off into a welcome sleep.

While Jason slept, Mark took stock of the situation. Paul Thomas had certainly been murdered, and Jason had seen who had done it. Mark had now seen the thugs that had been tailing them just last night at the hotel. Those thugs had successfully tailed them until their departure early that morning. Were they still a threat? He wondered. He asked himself how he should act on what he knew.

On the one hand, he could make the whole thing public and insist on a proper investigation of the murder. But as a result, Paul Thomas's name would end up being dishonored, which was exactly what his trip to Ft. Lauderdale what supposed to preclude. Secondly, the thugs would reconnect with Jason and put him and Mark in danger once more.

The bishop had wanted Mark to avoid publicity. The coroner had already ruled the death an accident. Up until now, the Ft. Lauderdale police had made no connection between the dead man in the motel swimming pool and an Anglican composer, however famous in his own circles, and of whom they had probably never heard. The case was certainly closed, as far as the Ft. Lauderdale authorities were concerned. It was likely that the thugs were only chasing Jason because they knew that he had seen them. Once Jason had disappeared, they would probably figure that they had scared him off, and would give up on trying to find him. This all seemed reasonable to Mark.

Better, Mark finally decided, to let sleeping dogs lie. He would keep quiet about what he knew and caution Jason to do the same, unless it became absolutely necessary to reveal anything to anybody else. Better, by far, he thought, to preserve Paul Thomas's reputation than to try to avenge his murder, an act that would do Paul Thomas no good and very possibly do Jason harm.

By the time Mark and Jason got to Atlanta, Jason had awakened from his nap and they both were feeling safe. Mark suggested, and Jason agreed, that he should stay at Mark's Midtown apartment for the time being. They dropped off their bags and then walked to Burkhart's for a drink, then to a nearby restaurant, with a largely gay clientele, for dinner. They sat side by side at the table, laughed, and joked, happily out in the welcoming atmosphere of gay Midtown Atlanta.

Afterwards, they went home to bed, snuggled, made love, and slept deeply.

Mark's appointment with the bishop was set for 10:00 a.m. He slipped quietly out of bed at 9:00 and crept into the shower, leaving Jason asleep in the big bed. When he emerged a quarter of an hour later, Jason had coffee going, orange juice poured and bread ready to pop into the toaster.

"Over, sunny-side up, or scrambled?" Jason wanted to know.

Mark told him scrambled and sat down for the quick breakfast that he hadn't scheduled. As it was, he made it to the cathedral just in time. Mark turned over Paul Thomas's ashes and asked about the service. It was, the bishop told him, to be on the following Saturday. The bishop thanked Mark for handling the business, and then added, "There's a bit more to do, I'm afraid."

"Oh?" Mark said, a bit apprehensive. "What else?"

"As I have told you," the bishop said, "I'm the executor of the estate. But, I can't find his heir."

"Would you like me to help do that?"

"As you say," the bishop said, "a little more help is what I need."

"Who's the heir?" Mark wanted to know, supposing it would be a relative.

"I've checked the Atlanta address and phone number in Paul's will," the Bishop continued, "but they seem to be out-of-date. Nobody seems to have ever heard of a Jason Rogers. How do you go about running somebody like that down?"

"Oh," Mark said airily, "That I can do." He grinned inwardly. "When would you like to see him?"

"Do you know where he is?"

"I do."

"Then I want to see him as soon as I can. He certainly should have some say in the funeral arrangements, and there is the matter of the estate to settle, too."

There being nothing more to do in the bishop's office or at the cathedral, Mark took his leave, saying, "I'll call you as soon as I can speak to him."

He whistled his way across the parking lot and got into his own little car. It felt like a tin can after the Jaguar. That fine piece of machinery had been left, carefully parked, inside the gated parking garage where Mark lived. He and Jason had made certain that it was well out of sight from the street, just in case.

Mark drove home and let himself into his apartment. There he found a note with one word scrawled on it: "Pool," it said. Mark called the bishop and asked when it would be convenient for him to bring Mr. Rogers to the bishop's office.

To which the bishop replied, "right away, please."

Mark joined Jason poolside, where he was happily sunning himself and dozing in the warm autumn air.

"Sorry, fella," Mark said, shaking him awake, "but this pool's only for the poor slobs who live here. You rich guys gotta go somewhere else."

"Huh," Jason said, roused from sleep, "What cha talkin' about?"

"C'mon," Mark replied without further elaboration, "you've got a date with the bishop."

Jason stumbled along after Mark, full of questions, sleepily dragging his towel along behind him. A few minutes later, he was fully alert, dressed in chinos and an oxford shirt, nervously sitting in Mark's little car as they wound their way north in the heavy Peachtree Street traffic.

"What am I supposed to do?" Jason wanted to know.

"Just listen to what the bishop has to say, and answer his questions," Mark replied. "There's nothing to worry about. Just keep it simple, and don't volunteer anything about the murder. Anything the bishop asks, you'll have to tell him, of course."

Jason fretted anyway.

They entered the imposing cathedral by a side door, and Mark led the way to the bishop's paneled office. The secretary announced them, and they went straight in. Before Mark could say anything, the bishop crossed to the door and extended his hand to Jason, saying, "Good afternoon. You must be Jason Rogers."

"Yes," Jason replied. "I guess you must be Mark's boss, the Bishop."

"I am," that cleric replied, smiling. "I understand that you knew Paul Thomas."

"Yes, sir, I did."

"I take it you also know Mark," the Bishop continued. "Tell me about that."

There was a pause while Jason ordered his thoughts. "I was with Paul in Florida when he died," was his simple statement. "Mark met me there and brought me home."

"I hate to ask this of you," the bishop said, "but I suppose I ought to see some identification. Do you have a driver's license or something?"

To this request, Jason produced his license and handed it silently to the bishop, who glanced at the photo and the name, then handed it back. "Thank you," he said.

"I have a responsibility to the estate to make sure of who you are. I hope you understand that."

"Sure," Jason said.

"You see, young man, you are to inherit most of Paul's estate. A few smaller bequests, aside, you are to receive the bulk of it."

Jason's eyes got a bit bigger. "What?" he said. "Paul left it to me?"

"That's right," the Bishop said. "Almost everything he had. You are to receive his condominium, his car, the royalties from his music, and other belongings, as well as a small trust fund. It will take a few weeks to sort it all out. But you might as well take possession of the condominium and car. They belong to you anyway. I can advance some of the money from Paul's bank accounts as well. However, I have to keep most of it to handle his final financial commitments and finalize the trust. The Bishop of Atlanta is to be the trustee, you see."

Then, the bishop turned the conversation to the funeral. Jason and Mark learned the Paul Thomas had worked out most of his arrangements well in advance. Because he was so well known, there was going to be a very large crowd coming in from all over the country. Jason, as Paul's principal heir, was also to be the chief mourner. The bishop wanted to know whether Jason had any particular requests about the service.

Jason wisely said, "No," and that he would gladly leave all of the arrangements to the clergy.

"I think that's about it for now, then," the bishop said. "I'm sorry for the loss of your friend. He was my friend, too, so I know how you must feel. Please call me anytime if you need me."

Jason said his thanks and said that he would.

"I've no idea how you'll get into Paul's condominium," the Bishop said as an afterthought.

Mark responded to the question. "I do," he said simply. "The keys were among Paul's personal effects."

"Of course." The Bishop was glad to have that little problem solved, too, and said so. They finished saying their goodbyes and headed back to the Midtown apartment and picked up Mark's legal papers.

Going back up Peachtree Street, this time with Jason driving what was now his Jag, their route took them back past the cathedral on their way to the Buckhead condominium where Paul Thomas spent the last years of his life. The building itself was a tall tower with sumptuous grounds, secure parking, and a concierge at the desk.

The concierge recognized Jason right away, but registered surprise at Mark, in clerical collar and black suit. Jason explained their business only by saying that they were going up to Paul Thomas's apartment and that they had a key. The attendant buzzed them through into the locked elevator lobby. Jason, it seemed, was a regular visitor so Mark's official documents proved to be completely unnecessary.

The elevator whisked them smoothly to the seventeenth floor, where Jason led the way to Paul's unit. Jason unlocked the door and motioned Mark ahead of him.

Mark looked around and was impressed. The condo had a spectacular view, luxurious furnishings in its spacious living room, and a large balcony overlooking the busy streets far below.

Jason stood silently, staring straight ahead. Then he fell to his knees and began to sob, his head in his hands. Mark dropped to his knees beside Jason and held him.

"It smells like him," Jason said by way of explanation, as he snuffled away the last of the tears. "It just came over me, all of a sudden. I'm going to miss him." He wiped his eyes with the back of his hand. "Sorry," he said to Mark.

"There's nothing to be sorry about," Mark replied. "Grief's perfectly natural when somebody you love dies. It's best to let it all out."

"I hope I never lose you."

"Me, too."

The stayed there, kneeling on the white carpet, holding each other for a long, long time.

Chapter Sixteen

Korea, 1960

By the time that Nick got to Korea in the fall of 1957, with two years of active duty remaining, the war itself was long over. Things had settled down to a stalemate along the thirty-eighth parallel. Tensions rose and fell regularly. When they were high, shots were exchanged. However, Nick's period of service was marked chiefly by boredom. He was consigned to shuffling papers at desk in Seoul.

Two years later, he was delighted to board ship and head home. His wedding was to be in June. He had become engaged during college to a pretty young creature whose family was already well connected to his own. They had opportunities to meet when Nick had leave, and they had taken full advantage of those. Other than that, his fiancée has spent the better part of three years planning her wedding. It was to be one of Tulsa's main social events of the year.

Third was not eager to go home. He enjoyed his time with Nick in San Francisco. He'd never been in a really big city before, so at first he was intimidated by it. Nobody had paid any attention to them as they walked along, nor when Nick had showed him the discreet unmarked door that led a gay bar.

Nick walked right up to the door and knocked, whereupon a small shutter slid back and a pair of eyes peered out.

"Friends of Dorothy's" Nick said.

The door opened, and they quickly moved inside. The door closed behind them, and the shutter quickly slid shut. They were in a small, narrow space, divided from the bar itself by a heavy black curtain. The doorman pushed the curtain aside for them, and they entered the dimly lit and smoke-filled room.

Nick moved to the bar and ordered drinks. Then he led Third to an open spot along the wall, where they sipped bourbon with a splash. They had one more drink together and then left the place. They had only gotten about a block away and on the other side of the street, when several police cars swooped down, and the door was broken in.

Nick just said, "Move on. Don't look back. Walk on up the street and around first the corner. We need to disappear as quickly as possible. But don't do anything to attract attention."

"What's going on?" Third asked as they rounded the corner.

"A raid. Queer bars are always getting raided. We got out just in time. I think there's probably a way out the back that the police don't know about, but it's nasty if you get caught."

"What do they do?"

"Beat everybody up and then arrest them for resisting arrest."

"You're kidding."

"Nope, not a bit. It's what cops do when it's a slow night."

The next day, Nick and Third had parted company. They exchanged addresses and Nick added his Tulsa telephone number, "just in case you're ever down my way."

Since enlisting in the Army, Third had been home twice. Both times had been for funerals. The first was for his father, Jabez, who had fallen from his perch in a tree while deer hunting. His gun had fallen with him and had discharged when it hit the ground, killing him instantly. The second was for Shrimp, after his body had been recovered in Korea. Both of their bodies now lay beneath the green sod of the little valley in the quiet cemetery next to the Baptist church.

During his service in Korea, Shrimp had sent the bulk of his Army pay home. So had Third.

Junior had used the cash to pay off what was left owing for the tractor and to buy a Bendix washing machine and a refrigerator. He was also able to put an electric pump in the barnyard well and a pump and pressure tank for water from the spring. Junior drove himself, determined to do well for his extended family. He had married, too. He and his wife planned to have two or three children to keep the farm going when the women, who were aging rapidly, could no longer carry so much of the burden.

It was into this changed valley that Third was going home.

Third caught a train to Chicago, then one to New York, then to Asheville and finally a milk-train to Greenville. After that, he took the bus to Wests Mill. From there, he decided, he could walk the eight miles home. He'd done a lot of marching and walking in the Army, so eight miles was nothing. He slung his duffel bag over his shoulder and set out. He'd only gone a good half-mile, though, when a truck pulled up beside him and stopped.

"Ain't you Third?" the dark-skinned driver asked.

"Sure am," Third replied.

"Well, git in then. I go right past your place. Glad to give a fellow veteran a lift."

So Third threw his duffel bag in the back and climbed into the passenger seat.

"Thomas Moore's my name," the driver said.

"Third White," said Third, "but I guess you already know that."

"Yeah, sure do."

They chatted on about their various experiences during the war and where they had served. When they pulled up in front of Third's place, they shook hands quite naturally and Third said thanked his driver for the lift.

When he reached the porch, Junior was standing there frowning.

"What'd you go and do that fer?" was his greeting to Third.

"Whatcha mean?"

"Why'd you ride with that nigger?

"Look, Junior," Third said with tired exasperation, "all I did was hitch a ride. I was glad to have it, and if you don't like it, you can lump it."

Third stomped into the house and went up to his old room. He dumped the duffel bag on his bed and went back downstairs to wash up. Nothing more was said about Third crossing the racial divide until after dinner. By then, he'd had a chance to catch up with his kin and meet Junior's new wife, who had inherited the adjacent farm from her first husband.

After supper, Junior took him aside. "Look, Third, things have really changed around here."

"So I see," Third replied. "Running water, electric appliances; even a new tractor. Pretty soon you'll have a telephone, too."

"And, another thing," Junior continued, "and I don't rightly know how to say this to you, but I'm not sure we can afford to take on another hand around here."

Third was silent for a while, considering his options.

After a while, he spoke his piece: "You know, Junior, you're only Grandpa Jeb's great-nephew and I'm his grandson. By rights, this place'll come to me when Grandpa goes. So, I suppose I've still got some say about it. Now, I'm not gonna make no fuss. I'm glad you've done what you've done, and I know you've worked hard to make everything better. I'm not gonna deprive you of what you've earned. But, I'm not gonna give up what oughta rightly be mine, neither. I guess I'll go away for a spell, and let you run things. I'd like to try my hand at something besides farming. After Grandpa goes, then we'll see how things stand."

They talked this over with old Jeb the next day, and he agreed. It was to be Third's farm if he wanted it, and he'd put that down in writing. They shook hands, all around, and the deal was sealed.

At his first opportunity, Third went into Wests Mill and called Nick in Tulsa. He told him to expect him in about a week. He couldn't wait to shake the dust of that narrow little valley off his feet. He promised himself he'd never return, if he could help it.

However, Third's arrival in Tulsa was not exactly what he had expected.

Nick met him at the train station, as promised, and asked, "Where are you planning to stay?"

When Third said he had hoped to stay with Nick, Nick replied, "I'm married now, Third, and my wife knows nothing about my gay side. I'm afraid you'll have to stay at a hotel."

Third wasn't happy about that, but he agreed, and Nick found an inexpensive motel room for him. As soon as they got inside, they got into bed together. And, as soon as it was over, Nick left, saying, "I have to get home to dinner. I'll call you tomorrow."

Third spent most of the day in the stuffy little room waiting for the phone to ring. When it finally did, it was Nick, calling to arrange to meet for dinner.

Bishop's Restaurant in downtown Tulsa was a rambling old place, with lots of little dining rooms and private booths. It was to one of these that Nick and Third retired. After they had ordered, Nick told Third how things stood, as gently as he could.

"I hope you'll stay in Tulsa," Nick went on, "I can help you get a job."

"Look, Nick," he said. "I know that I'm just a hick from the South, and you're an educated rich fella with a lot going for you. But, I'm not going to be some secret that you have to keep from your wife."

"I'm truly sorry, Third," was Nick's response. "I didn't mean for you to fall in love. I only intended for it to be a little fling for both of us."

"Let's leave it a clean break, so neither of us owes the other for anything," Third said.

Nick picked up the check, but Third insisted on paying half. His pocketbook couldn't afford it, but his pride said he must. They shook hands with each other in front of the restaurant and each went his separate way.

Third felt alone in the world, unloved and unwanted. It wasn't only Nick's rejection, but also his self-imposed exile from the Natahala farm and his kin. He had to make his own way, but how?

He had only his separation pay to keep him going, so he took any job that came along. He was, at various times, a dishwasher, a janitor and a night watchman. His income from these jobs was meager and the work he did was dull. But Third was tough. His upbringing had taught him that and his Army experiences had reinforced the lesson. He doggedly kept at it, living frugally in a rooming house in a seedy neighborhood, and constantly looking for the opportunity to better his situation.

Third was surprised when, several months later, his slovenly landlady called up from the lower hall to say he had a telephone call. He was even more surprised to hear Nick's voice on the other end.

"Hi," Nick said. "I had a devil of a time tracking you down."

"Hello, Nick," Third said, his heart thumping, "it's good to hear your voice."

"I'm glad to hear yours", too," Nick replied. "First off, this is sort of a business call. You made your feelings pretty clear, so I'm not calling to ask you to revisit that. I hope that's all right."

"It's fine, Nick. You said 'business.' What's on your mind?"

"It'll take a bit of time to explain," was Nick's response. "Can you get away this weekend?"

"Yes."

"I'll stop by and pick you up Friday at 6:00. You'll need clothes for a weekend at my cabin on Grand Lake. Nothing fancy. No funny stuff, either; you'll have your own bedroom. And my other guest is straight. It's important, OK? So don't stand me up."

Intrigued, Third just said, "I'll be here. See you then," and he hung up.

On Friday, Nick arrived right on time in his black Continental sedan. Third threw his small bag into the back seat.

"So, what's up?" Third wanted to know.

"Lets wait till we get there," Nick responded. "I want you to meet a guy who's looking for some help from somebody just like you."

"So long as it's legal," Third replied, laughing, "I'll take it."

Nick laughed, too. "Oh, it's legal alright. It's about as legal as it can get."

They drove along, mostly in silence after that. The trip to Grand Lake took just over an hour. Nick's cabin turned out to have eight guest suites, a library, and huge living room with floor-to-ceiling windows, and a spectacular view of the lake. It also had a caretaker, a quiet and strong-looking blond man who got Third comfortably settled in one of the guest suites.

"Cocktails at eight, sir," he said as he withdrew, closing the door behind him. Third consulted his watch and found he had just twenty minutes. He took a quick shower, put on a pair of neat jeans, a plaid shirt he had ironed carefully, a pair of neatly polished, worn shoes, and a navy-blue sweater.

He walked into the living room just before eight, to find Nick and an older man sitting in front of a small fire in the gigantic fireplace. Both of them rose.

"Third, I'd like you to meet Tom Kemper. Tom, this is Third or more properly, Jabez White the Third."

Kemper was dressed very much like Third, in jeans, shirt and sweater. But there the similarity to Third's casual attire ended. Everything about Nick and Tom's clothes said "money," while Third's attire screamed "poverty."

But before Third could become too self-conscious of the difference, the servant appeared and asked for drink orders. Tom had a martini, and Nick asked for Scotch. Third followed Nick's lead and said he'd have the same. When it came, it was a smooth as silk and hit him like a sledgehammer. He decided he'd better take it easy and not let his head get to muzzy. After all, this was business.

The others had seconds, but Third just nursed his first.

Dinner consisted of a Château Briand, roast potatoes and an assortment of vegetables. It was delicious. It was followed by an after-dinner drink that the men took into the library, where another small fire burned in the grate. Nick closed the doors.

"Third," Nick said. "Thanks for coming. I'm grateful that you trust me enough not to ask a lot of questions. The fact is that I was in Navy Intelligence during the war. That's how I met Tom. Tom still does that sort of thing, and he's looking for some help. That's all I know, or should know, about it, so I'll make my exit now." With that, Nick left the library and closed the doors behind him.

Tom looked at Third for a minute. Then: "Third, what sort of clearance did you have during the Korean action?"

"Sorry," Third said, "I can't tell you that. It's classified."

"Quite right. I happen to have already gotten that information from another source. If you had told me, I would have politely ended our private conversation at this point. Of course, we would have had a nice weekend here on the Lake, but nothing more would have come of it."

"In other words, I passed," Third said.

"Yes. At least for now," Tom said, smiling. "I suppose I need to begin by describing the work I do in a general sort of way. I work for the government in an obscure little agency practically nobody has heard of. We investigate various kinds of things that might be criminal in one way or another. Sometimes our investigations take several years."

"Years? Why so long?"

"Because some criminals are very clever. Essentially, we spy on them to find out what they're doing. It's all quite legal, of course: we get warrants and all that. To do our work effectively, we sometimes plant an agent in the operation to feed us inside information."

"Is that what you're asking me do to?"

"I'm asking you if you think you'd be interested in doing it."

"I don't know. I'm not interested in being shot at or killed. I had enough of that in Korea."

"We wouldn't put you in that kind of danger. For example, we have a man working for us as a janitor in a bank. He empties the wastepaper baskets. The contents of a couple of them don't go into the trash. He flattens the papers out and puts them in a large brown envelope. He puts that under his clothes and drops it in the mail the next day."

"That's it?"

"That's it for him. Your assignment, if you take it on, will be a bit more complex. But nothing that you can't handle with your Army background."

"OK, so it's easy and safe, you say. If that's the case, why not use a regular agent?"

"Because they are agents. We have to invent backgrounds for them. They have to pretend to be somebody else all the time. You can be yourself ninety-nine percent of the time. You'll be much harder to spot."

"And, second question: How much does it pay."

"It will pay a G. S. level 3 salary. Not princely, of course, but then you'll be drawing another salary from your employer as well. Combined, it will be quite handsome. But you mustn't appear to live above your means."

"Sounds like I'll need a savings account," Third said, grinning.

"Sounds like," was Tom's smiling reply.

Chapter Seventeen

Tulsa, 1962

After his initial conversation with Tom, Third excused himself and went off to bed, a bit tipsy from the unaccustomed drinking that he had been doing with Tom and Nick. There, he slept deeply, in spite of the strange turn his life had just taken.

Tom and Nick stayed up later to toast their success before the living room fire. Nick had done a good job of recruiting, Tom told him; Third was perfect for the assignment. He was exactly the kind of person that they needed to get inside the JJWWM operation.

The next day there were official documents to sign, and a sizable check to bind the agreement. After these formalities had been completed, the three men shared a pleasant brunch before Nick drove Third back to town and dropped him a block away from his rooming house.

Tom had said that it would be two or three weeks before Third heard from him again. "We'll need a little time for a background check," Tom had said, "although with Nick's endorsement, its really a matter of form."

Nevertheless, the time passed slowly for Third. He was eager to start his new job, eager to find out more about what he would be doing.

After almost four weeks, Tom called early one morning. "Hi, Third," he said casually, "Its Tom. How about coming over for a cup of coffee and a doughnut around the corner from your place?"

"When?"

"Now, please."

"Sure. Be there in a couple of ticks."

"Order your doughnuts, and read the paper," Tom instructed. A click broke the connection.

Third walked over, trying to contain his excitement. Tom was there in a booth, looking innocuous, absently paging through the morning paper. As Third approached, Tom stood up, looking right past him. He tossed some change on the table and walked out.

Third sat in the empty booth. He ordered a couple of doughnuts, a cup of coffee, and an orange juice. When his order came, he ate absentmindedly and paged through the paper. The envelope was between the fourth and fifth pages of the sports section. Third finished his breakfast, folded the paper under his arm, paid the check, and left a generous tip. Then he, too, walked out. Tom was long gone. Third walked back to his rooming house.

He was more than a little astonished when he read his assignment. He was instructed to move to new lodgings and continue with his current employment. He was to look for a certain person, photo attached. The picture looked vaguely familiar to him, but he dismissed it. His new room would provide a good view of a "fag bar" that had an entrance on the alley. When he saw this person enter the bar, he was to make contact and strike up a friendship.

It all sounded a bit chancy to Third. He wondered if Nick had told Tom to use him because he was queer. He wondered who the vaguely familiar face was. With nothing to lose and everything to gain, he followed his odd instructions to the letter.

Tulsa was experiencing a summer heat wave. His new room was on the second floor at the back of the rooming house. It overlooked the alley. When he returned to it from work that first evening, he opened his room's single window to let in the sultry summer night air. The room remained unbearably hot. He lay down, naked and sweating, on the narrow bed. A single small electric fan served only to stir the humid air, but brought no real relief. He got up, put the only chair near the window and sat naked on the hard wood, trying to catch any stray breath of cooler air that might come his way.

The bright green door across the alley was constructed from heavy grooved planks arranged in the shape of a chevron. It was freshly painted and had a small opening in it. A green enameled reflector surrounded a single light bulb that hung over the door and cast a circle of light on the asphalt paving below.

The bar was tiny. It was located in the back half of an old brick building. Its dimly lit and unmarked green door was the only entrance. Inside, it was like most gay bars of its time: dark, filled with cigarette smoke and very quiet. More than anything else, the owners and habitués alike wanted the security of anonymity. For some obscure reason, the bar was called The Third Thursday, although it was open anytime it was legal for any bar to operate. Mostly, the cops left it alone.

Occasionally, a furtive male figure would appear out of the gloom of the alley, step up to the door and knock. Something was said, the door opened, the figure slid inside, and the door closed quickly. This performance was repeated over and over, but Third did not see his man that night, or the next, or the next.

Faithfully, each evening, Third repeated his routine: a quick, cheap meal out after work. Then, he went back to the rooming house, took a shower to cool off, and then began the vigil by the window. After eight hours of hard work, it was hard for Third to stay awake until the bar closed at midnight. But he persevered.

Then it happened. On his fifth night of keeping vigil, he saw the man. He looked different than he had in the photograph. He was wearing a dark glasses. Even so, the shape of his nose, his height and, the long flowing hair all matched. Third quickly dressed with care in a formfitting knit shirt and a pair of Army uniform pants. It was already a bit after 11:00, when he went out, and the rest of the rooming house was quiet. His route took him around the corner from the rooming house and to the mouth of the alley. He saw no one as he left the sidewalk and turned into the alley's darker shadows. The only light burning at the back of the rooming house was in his room.

It was only a few feet, but it seemed like a hundred yards to Third. Finally, the door was before him. He swallowed hard and knocked.

It seemed to him that the sound reverberated up and down the alley. Surely, people would turn on bedroom lights and look out of windows to see what was happening. Of course, nothing of the kind happened. The little window in the green door just slid quietly open, and a pair of eyes peered out.

"Uh, uh," Third muttered, trying to say something to the peering eyes. He felt his face grow hot, and he broke into a sweat. But the door swung open for him and he stepped inside, escaping the exposure of the alley.

"First time?" a friendly voice said.

"Uh, yes," Third answered. "Except once in San Francisco."

The voice parted the entrance curtains for him and resolved itself into a muscular young bouncer with a crew cut, blue eyes, and a smile that matched the friendly voice. "Welcome to The Third Thursday," he said.

His target stood in one dark corner, apart from the others, surveying the scene. He wore a pair of dark blue work pants, and a chambray shirt with the sleeves rolled up. Even though the bar was dark, his sunglasses still obscured his eyes.

All heads swiveled and all eyes focused on the curtained entrance as Third came into the room.

"Thanks," Third said to the doorman. He smiled back and, now feeling more confident, headed towards the bar. "A Bud, please," he said to the bartender as he laid a Franklin half-dollar on the bar. The beer was produced, and the half-dollar taken. Change appeared and Third left a dime tip. He took a swallow of beer and sighed. He was amazed at how relaxed he felt. He sipped his beer out of the long-necked bottle and pondered how to make his approach.

That decision was taken out of his hands. A friendly voice said, "Hello. Have you been here before?"

"I've been in town a while," Third answered, "but this is my the first time in here." He turned, and his gaze took his target at close range. The man smiled at him and Third smiled back.

"Ed," Jack said, holding out his hand.

Third took the hand and said, "Third."

"What?"

"Third. It's a kind of nickname."

"Oh. All right then, Third, glad to meet you."

Their hands remained clasped, and they stayed that way as the man moved closer. "Let's move away from the bar," Jack suggested, so Third followed him back to the corner from which Jack had come.

"You must be from the South," Jack said, to keep the conversation going, "whereabouts?"

"South Carolina," Third said, "a farm near a little town called Wests Mill."

"So, what brings you to Tulsa?" Jack asked.

"I came to see a friend," Third answered, "but things didn't work out. I decided to stay on and try to find a job."

"Sounds like a tough break," Jack said comfortingly as he moved behind Third and put his arms around him. Holding him, Jack said, "If you're looking for a friend, I'm available."

"Thanks," Third said, leaning against Jack's chest. "I guess I need to be held right now."

Jack's arms hugged him tighter. "We all need to be held sometimes," Jack said. "We all get lonely." They stood quietly for several minutes while Third sipped his beer. Then Third made his decision. He reached out, put the bottle down on a nearby table, turned and kissed Jack shyly on the mouth. Jack returned the kiss with practiced ease.

They backed away slightly from each other and looked into each other's eyes. Then they moved together again and shared a longer and more passionate kiss. "Come home with me," Jack said. "We need each other."

Third simply nodded, and they walked out of the bar together.

Jack's car was parked a couple of blocks away. They walked along the quiet streets, reached the car, got inside, and Jack pulled away from the curb. As soon as Jack had the car moving, he put his right hand on Third's thigh.

The carriage house was only a few blocks from the bar. Jack parked the car in the garage and took the stairs up to the studio apartment two at a time. Third followed suit. They undid buttons and zippers as quickly as they could. Clothes dropped to the floor. Jack flipped back the bedclothes. Naked, they embraced once more and fell together upon the cool, crisp sheets. Afterwards, Third fell asleep in Jack's arms.

Jack remained awake for a while. He reflected that his prayers had been answered. He had been alone ever since Paul left for Washington, and he was getting desperate for sex, for a man to hold, for the kind of companionship that Martha had never been able to offer him.

Then, Martha's father had died unexpectedly, and she had packed herself and the children off to the funeral in Illinois. She planned to stay with her mother for a couple of weeks at least. Jack had a couple of guest appearances to make, as well as recording his regular Sunday preaching. None of that could be cancelled, Martha had decided, so she and the children had gone without him.

Jack was elated. He had never cared for Martha's parents and certainly didn't want to see his mother-in-law again. She still despised him. She still thought that he had gotten Martha pregnant and then left her.

Now, he was alone for at least two blessed weeks, and he had planned to take full advantage of that. Of course, Martha had insisted that he behave himself, and Jack had solemnly promised that he would. He had no intention of keeping the promise when he made it, but it satisfied Martha.

This was only the second night of her absence, but Jack had scored. And, he reflected, he had scored big. Third was strapping, handsome, passionate, eager, and well endowed. He was everything Jack wanted in a man, and, if he played his cards right, he would have everything he wanted for at least a couple of weeks. While Third slept next to him, Jack laid out a plan that he hoped would keep Third around for keeps. Then he, too, fell asleep.

When they awoke the next morning, they made love again. When release finally came it was the most intense that either of them had felt for a very long time. Their bond grew deeper. Jack put his plan to keep Third around into play then and there.

"Look," Jack said. "If you're looking for work, I think I can help you out."

"Doing what?" Third wanted to know.

"First," Jack replied, "I've got to level with you. I'm married."

"And I'm leaving," Third said, as he got out of bed he picked up his boxers.

"Please, Third," Jack pleaded. "Please wait and hear me out. My wife knows everything."

That stopped Third in his tracks. "What do you mean?" he asked, his boxers at half-mast.

"My marriage to Martha is one of convenience," Jack said. "Nothing more. I tried to be straight. I did all the right things. I got married. We have two children. I'm still gay. I always will be. Martha knows that and we've worked it out."

"So," Third said, "It's OK for you to play around with guys." The boxers were up around his waist, now.

"Play around? No, actually it's not!" Jack went on, "I'm a minister on television. Jack Johns World Wide Ministry is its name. I have to appear straight and happily married. Don't misunderstand, though. Martha is a very good, very strong woman and I love my children. But, Martha and I have had separate bedrooms for years, now. And I have to be very discreet."

"So, how to you manage that?" Third wanted to know.

"Until recently, I had a live-in boyfriend. He's gone off to Washington, now, and I'm alone again. He lived here, in the carriage house."

"And your wife, uh, Martha, knew about it?"

"She arranged it."

"Really!" Third was surprised. "She actually set it up for you to have your boyfriend here at your house?"

"Yes," Jack said simply. "She did exactly that."

"No shit!"

"What I'd like is for you to live here now," Jack said. "I can offer you employment with my ministry in some capacity and you can live here in the carriage house. How would you feel about doing that?"

Third thought it through. It seemed a bit odd that the government would want him to spy on a television preacher. On the other hand, his assignment was really going very well. He was in as instructed. At the very least, he would have a clean, comfortable apartment, one with air conditioning. And, his second, secret government salary was going into his savings account. If they wanted him in, in more than one way, that was OK, too.

Third's answer was direct. "Deal," he said.

Of course, Jack was delighted. They sealed the bargain with a kiss and went to the main house where Jack cooked breakfast. Afterwards, he called in to JJWWM headquarters and said that he'd be in a bit late; he had an important errand to take care of first.

They drove to the rooming house, where Third paid off his landlady and removed his scant belongings. Jack helped install him in the carriage house, told him to relax for the rest of the day, and happily went off to work. When Martha got home, he reasoned, she would be faced with a fait d' accompli. He hoped. And, anyway, he'd have Third to bed nightly for a while at least.

Third waited until Jack had been gone about fifteen minutes. He found a pen, paper and an envelope in the main house.

On the paper he wrote the date and the single word *In*. He addressed it to the Post Office box that was scrawled on a scrap of paper stashed away in his wallet. The Johns' desk also supplied a stamp. He walked to the corner, deposited the envelope in a mailbox, and walked back.

The first step of his mission had been accomplished

Chapter Eighteen

Tulsa, 1962

Martha came home just three days after Third moved into the carriage house. She returned, disappointed, from tending to the aftermath of her father's funeral. Things had not gone smoothly; she had quarreled with her mother about the funeral arrangements. She had also expected something from the estate, but found that all of it had gone to her mother. She and the children arrived back at the house just after Jack left for JJWWM headquarters.

Unknown to Martha, Third was in the carriage-house apartment, getting ready to take a shower. All Martha saw was that the windows were open and that somebody was moving around inside. She had already decided that their operation needed a security setup. If there was a prowler in the carriage house, that would be even more evidence of that need.

For interim protection, Martha had armed herself with a .38 revolver. She kept it loaded, and stashed in a locked drawer of her dresser. She took it out, cautioned the children to stay in the house, and headed for the studio apartment. Cautiously, she crossed to the apartment stairs and climbed them. At the top, she threw the door open, and pointed the revolver toward the interior.

A startled Third stood facing the door, wearing nothing but a startled expression. He put his hands in the air.

"Just who the hell are you?" was what Martha wanted to know.

"Look, lady," Third responded, "I don't know who you are either. So let me get my pants on before we start introductions."

"Fine!" said the fuming Martha, but she held the gun on him while he dressed.

Third was not particularly embarrassed. He didn't turn his back on the gun. Not bothering with underwear, he pulled on a pair of jeans, tucked his manhood inside, and buttoned them up. Then he added a T-shirt.

"OK, lady," he said, leaving his hands at his side. "My friends call me Third. I've been staying here with Jack the last three days. Now why don't you put that silly little popgun down before I take it away from you."

Cowed, for once, Martha was speechless. She stood there, mute, looking at Third and considering the situation. Finally, she put the gun down on the bedside table and crossed the room to a chair and motioned to another.

Third sat down, too. "I suppose you must be Jack's wife, Martha. He told me all about you."

"I'll bet he did," Martha said.

"Yes, he did," he retorted. "In fact, he told me just about everything. Such as separate bedrooms and you finding male companionship for him."

"What did you say your name is?"

"Third," he responded. "It's a kind of nickname. I'm named after my grandfather."

"And what do you do, besides fuck my husband?"

"Right now, I'm between jobs."

"Oh, I see," Martha said with disgust in her voice. "A cheap hustler."

Third was more than a little irritated by Martha's manner and he let it show. "Now, you look here lady," he said, "I'm no hustler. I've just finished my hitch in the army and I'm looking for work. I'm about out of money, and Jack took me in. He told me, first thing, about your marriage of convenience. Otherwise I wouldn't have stayed. And he said he might have a job for me."

"Oh, he did, did he? I wonder what he thinks you'll be good at besides screwing him."

"He said "security," but he wanted to talk to you first."

Martha was again silent while she took a second, hard look at Third. Having come upon him buck naked, she had already seen that he was lean and muscular.

"What kind of training did you have in the Army?" She wanted to know.

"Basic training, hand-to-hand combat, a little judo, using a rifle; the usual. My specialty was signals; field radio and that sort of thing."

"You look like you're in pretty good shape," was Martha's response to that. "And, if you were operating a field radio you can't be exactly stupid."

"No, ma'am," said Third, politely, realizing that the confrontation had turned into a job interview. "I'm anything but dumb. It may not have acted like it, but I can be polite, too, as well and throw my weight around."

"And why would that be important, do you think?"

"Well, if it's a security job for a church, brute force wouldn't look very good, now, would it?"

It didn't take Martha long to decide. Here was somebody who could bed Jack regularly, keep him from scrounging for sex in back alleys, and could be employed legitimately as well. He could probably intimidate almost anybody just by looking fierce. He was well spoken, and knew how to be polite. He was, she reckoned, the answer to her need for setting up some kind of security. And, while she tried him out, she would be getting two services for the price of one. She decided to be generous.

"O.K., Third," Martha said, "you're on the payroll. I'll give you a trial period of one month and see how you work out. We'll discuss the details tomorrow in my office at 9:00. Be on time and don't even mention that you've ever met Reverend Jack Johns. Got it?"

"Yes, ma'am."

Martha stood and walked towards the door. Third opened it for her and then closed it quietly. As soon as Martha got back to the house, she rounded up the children and headed for JJWWM headquarters.

When she got there, she turned the kids over to Jack's secretary and strode into his office, shutting the door behind her.

"Martha!" Jack said, smiling and looking pleased, "I didn't expect you home this soon."

"I'll bet you didn't," she retorted. "Otherwise I wouldn't have found Third parading round naked in the carriage house."

"Martha, I can explain," Jack started. But she cut him off.

"Don't bother, Jack; Third already has. I've agreed to try him out for security. You'd better hope he's a good fuck, because he's going to be doing that, too."

"Martha, my dear, you're a jewel. You wouldn't know a good fuck if it bit you on the ass. And, yes, he's quite good in that department. So, you'd better hope he works out in security because he stays."

They glared at each other, each wanting the upper hand. It was Martha who spoke first. "OK, Jack, we'll work together on this. Just keep you bedroom activities in the bedroom and make sure your relationship's professional here at the job."

"Fine," Jack responded. "Just make sure you treat him professionally, too. We're not going to need any of your snide remarks."

"Agreed," Martha said. "He works under my supervision here, in a completely professional way. What he does on his own time is his business. We'll say that he lives in the apartment to provide off-hours security at home as well."

Thus it was settled between them. Third stayed to do his job and also watch the JJWWM empire grow. He reported for work each day. First, he found out what the routine was around the studio complex and who everybody was. Then he looked into what happened when Jack traveled somewhere and what the risks were in doing that. With that background information, he began to evaluate what kind of security setup was needed.

Jack was becoming very well known. He appeared on his own regular television show, of course. True to her promise to Peter Anderson and The Foundation for Religious Truth in America, Martha also steered him to other public duties, too. He was often the token clergyman at political meetings, said grace at conservative fund-raisers, and was photographed with ambitious politicos who wanted their faces to become as famous as Jack's already was.

As a result, Jack was becoming a major mover and shaker in the "Take Back America for God" movement, an initiative funded by The Foundation for Religious Truth in America.

What America had to be taken back from was never completely clear to the millions who supported the idea. Nonetheless they rallied to the cry. Some wanted to take American back from so-called activist judges, with whose rulings they disagreed. Others wanted to take it back from the niggers to whom it had been given by those ultimate activists, the justices of the Supreme Court. A large group was sure it was the abortionists, while others were certain it was the queers. Isolationists wanted to get the country out of the United Nations. All of them wanted action before their supposed enemy took over America.

Martha understood that the conservatives were using the vague threat of "them" to gain support from a vast mass of people who equated God with country. All of these people agreed that they all wanted a so-called "Christian nation". Which meant one that excluded those with whom they disagreed.

Martha also coveted the political power that could be harnessed if Jack became a leader in the conservative movement. It was a perfect fit for the apocalyptic message her husband preached: The world would soon end. The Rapture would take God's chosen up bodily into Heaven. America's enemies, within and without the country, would be left to endure the destruction of the Earth as the four horsemen of the Apocalypse were turned loose in the final battle with Satan. Then would follow the thousand years of peace, ruled by those who were saved.

Martha made sure Jack stayed on message. She worked closely with Peter Anderson's Foundation for Religious Truth for fund Jack's message on an ever-larger network of televisions stations.

Six short years after Jack went on television, Jack and Martha's corporate savings were huge. It was what Martha's accountants called "serious money." So serious, in fact, that they needed to start spending it before the Internal Revenue Service started asking questions.

Martha told Jack, it was time to reinvest the money to grow their operation again. Pleased with their success under Martha's management, Jack readily agreed.

It was shortly after Third joined JJWWM, that Martha began to execute their expansion plans. There were two new construction projects. One was to be an office building in downtown Tulsa. The other was an expansive mansion on the outskirts of the city. Both of these edifices had the purpose of projecting Jack's success and, thereby God's stamp of approval on his ministry.

Both projects boasted the best of every new architectural idea. The projects were spurred ahead by Martha. She spent their cash wisely, but was willing to pay for speedy, high quality work, so projects took only a couple of years from inception to completion.

Jack applied his fundamentalist theology to their sudden success and decided that it was a blessing from God, delivered to them because they were doing His will. He concentrated on making sure he did not stray from the fold of the blessed. Martha told Jack that he should revisit the sermon themes that had proved fruitful, and then concentrate his efforts on those same messages. He followed her advice.

Martha took no religious view of their newfound wealth. She was certain to was the result of her own hard, shrewd work to guide Jack in fruitful directions. From her point of view, their success would continue to increase only so long as she could retain and exercise control.

Their views of the source of their success were diametrically opposed to each other. And Martha's was most certainly the one that lay much closer to the truth. Recognizing this, Martha encouraged Jack to continue to think as he did. It made manipulating him easier.

So Jack warmed his ego in the belief that God had set His seal of approval on Jack's work. But Martha's road was harder. She wasn't used to fame and wealth, so she worked tirelessly to ensure their success did not evaporate.

Third had achieved his first objective. He occupied a position of trust. He had done his homework and applied logic to what he found out about the JJWWM operations. He plugged holes in security, made sure the part-time guards did their work properly. When Jack went to public functions, it was Third who occupied the position of chauffeur.

Martha's plans for expanded facilities gave Third and his handler, Tom, a new opportunity. What neither Martha nor Third knew that funds from Operation Aurum were being funneled to JJWWM through Peter Anderson and The Foundation for Religious Truth in America. The new buildings were being planned to provide the security that Martha wanted. Video reports from security cameras would give ODESSA an opportunity to get first-hand reports. Martha asked Third to work out the security details with their architect. Third agreed to, and the first thing he did was ask Tom for help.

Unknown to any of them, Tom also worked for ODESSA.

Chapter Nineteen

Tulsa, 1962

When Paul Thomas finished his studies in sacred music, it was time for him to move on. He and Jack Johns had parted company in the carriage house. They had, by that time, been together, off and on, for nine years. Despite their problems, they had grown very close.

Jack stood in the driveway and watched Paul back his little car into the street. Then, sighing deeply, he went back into the house to have breakfast with Martha and the children.

Paul had completed his bachelor's and master's degrees in sacred music and was now moving to Washington, DC.

His considerable talent and the earnest recommendation of his teachers had won him an audition at the Washington National Cathedral. The quick airplane trip to DC was followed by his audition the next day. A week later he was invited to be a Fellow in Church Music. The Cathedral fellowship paid a reasonable stipend, and he would be able to study with some of the most outstanding Anglican musicians in the world. It would be a yet another challenge, but he had come to enjoy challenges.

Paul had loaded his meager possessions into his little car the night before, and set out that morning on the drive to the District of Columbia. He had planned to drive straight through. He followed U.S. Route 67 a few miles north and then switched to Route 60 to cross the Mississippi at Cairo. He pressed on through Kentucky, but finally gave up in Lexington and caught a few hours' sleep there. When he awoke, he drove the rest of way.

He arrived a day early for his second visit to Mount St. Albans in Georgetown. Again, he took in the impressive Cathedral that was still rising from its foundations. Only the sanctuary, great choir, crossing, north transept and part of the nave had been completed above ground. Even so, the building was already massive. He poked around the huge cathedral close until he managed to stumble over the dean's office. There, he asked for directions.

The receptionist was pleasant and welcoming. "Why Mr. Thomas, we didn't expect you until tomorrow!" she exclaimed. "How nice that you're a day early! Just let me make a call."

She spoke briefly to somebody on phone. Then to Paul: "It's all arranged. Just go down the hill, take a left and you'll see The College of Preachers. Go right in, and they'll take care of you. I'll let the choirmaster know you're here."

Paul did as instructed and soon found himself standing in the two-story lobby of the Tudor-style building that housed the College.

"Mr. Thomas? We were expecting you tomorrow, but it's not a problem. Just get your things and bring them in. Then, park your car outside in one of the places, and I'll show you up." The handsome guy who managed the College was cheerily helpful. "Tom Watson, at your service," he added, offering his hand.

"Paul Thomas," Paul said, automatically, as they shook hands. "I'm sorry, but I don't quite understand the arrangements."

"Oh," Tom said, "didn't the choirmaster or the dean tell you? We're putting you up here until you find permanent quarters."

Paul could only say, "How nice," which it was, and "thanks," which he felt was insufficient gratitude.

Paul followed Tom, as instructed, and found himself trudging up the stairs and down the winding passageways to a monastic room at the rear of the building.

"We thought we'd put you here," Tom said, "because that door at the end of the hall connects with a path that goes straight to the music suite. It'll be handy for you. Dinner's at 6:00 in the refectory. Just come back downstairs."

"If I can find it," Paul thought.

Paul had never seen anything quite like this place. The furnishings were sparse, but well made in the Craftsman style. He unpacked his clothes and put them away neatly. Then he went on a voyage of discovery. What he discovered was a beautiful building with a rooms like his, most of which were empty, communal bathrooms, an imposing library with a high ceiling, and a refectory, or dining room, which was even grander. Nearby was a little chapel, laid out (he was to discover later) like one in a monastery. Adjacent to the chapel was an alcove with a small, but very fine, organ. And there was also a cloistered garden.

With time to spare before dinner, Paul went back to the chapel. The organ was unlocked and soon the chapel was filled with music as Paul played a meditation of his own spontaneous improvising. A bit before 6:00, he reluctantly shut the instrument off, closed the cover, and went back to the refectory.

There were about a dozen men present. Each of them was wearing a priest's collar, except for him and Tom Watson. Paul felt out of place, but the rest of them made him welcome. One said grace, and they sat down to a simple, but well-prepared dinner. With wine, Paul noticed, somewhat surprised.

Dinner conversation flowed freely. Paul mostly just listened, only explaining his presence when one of the priests asked out of politeness. The priest replied, "Then, that must have been you playing the chapel organ. Quite lovely."

Paul could only respond by saying, "Thank you."

The conversation moved on, and tended towards the biblical and scholarly. Paul had trouble following it. Nevertheless he paid attention and was comfortable enough to join the others for a glass of port and after dinner coffee in the library.

Each of the visiting priests was there to do individual research. The College was between sessions, and that was why the building was mostly empty and there was a spare room for Paul.

When the after-dinner coffee party broke up, Paul went back to his room and then out the back door. The towering apse of the cathedral loomed above him in the twilight. He followed a path to his right and presently came upon another cloister that separated the cathedral Garth from the rest of the grounds. He went in, looked around, and then climbed the side steps up to the Women's Porch. The doors to the north transept were bolted shut, but he could see in through the glass to the dimly lit interior. From within came the sound of the organ. Someone was practicing. Knowing that he would have to wait to play, he continued his walk. Soon, he came upon the stone yard, where the dressed, unset stones awaited their turn to be hoisted and mortared into place.

It was getting dark, so he returned to the College, went into his room, and prepared for bed. It was only about 10:00, but he was tired, and the narrow bed beckoned. He put on a bathrobe and wandered down the hall to bathe. He showered in one of the curtained-off cubicles, toweled himself dry, and returned to his room. He had noticed, with a strange sort of comfort, that there were no locks on the bedroom doors. It gave him an odd feeling of safety to be in a place where no locks were needed.

The next morning, he arose early and had breakfast with the other temporary inhabitants of the College.

After breakfast, he tracked down his new boss, the well-known organist and choirmaster Paul Callaway. Callaway explained that Paul's duties included playing for some of the smaller services in the tiny Bethlehem Chapel, rehearsing either the men or the boys of the choir when they broke into sectional rehearsals, and accompanying them during the major services when the Choirmaster wanted concentrate exclusively on conducting.

Then, Callaway introduced Paul to the precentor of the cathedral (the priest in charge of arranging the complex services) and finally, the famous Dean of the place, Francis Sayer, the senior priest in charge. A few weeks later, when the next session of the College was about to begin, Tom invited Paul to move into Tom's apartment in the DuPont Circle area of the District. Tom had made no secret that he was attracted to Paul. For Paul the attraction was mutual, so he didn't need a lot of persuading. However, Paul was worried about what people at the cathedral might think.

Tom's response to that was simple: "As long as we don't make any grand announcement, nobody's going to care. A lot of the men in the choir are gay, you know, and so are some of the cathedral staff. 'We don't make windows into men's souls,' to paraphrase Elizabeth Tudor."

They settled the details; Paul packed all of his earthly possessions back in his little car and moved again.

Paul was kept very busy with his part in the cathedral's worship. Even so, he also began to compose. At first the work was simple arranging for use during services. However, before long, he had sent off a full-length composition. To his delight, it was published.

In his off time, Paul and Tom explored Washington cultural and hidden gay life together. Both of them recognized that their relationship was destined to be brief and they made the most of it.

Shortly before Paul's fellowship was to end, he began to think about future employment. He wanted a full-time job as an organist/choirmaster, although they were scarce. He wanted it in a fairly large church with a good instrument. And, most of all, he wanted it to be an Episcopal church. He had fallen in love with the beauty of the prayer book services and could not imagine ever being completely happy with anything else. He also knew that his chances for getting everything he wanted were slim.

During his time at the cathedral, Paul had kept in touch with his major professor. It was through him that Paul learned that the post at Trinity Church in Tulsa was open. He had played that organ often and had substituted there a few times when the regular organist was away.

Paul knew that there would be many other, more senior and more experienced applicants for the post, but he applied anyway. He was thrilled when the letter came saying he was invited to audition. The rector remembered him and said he was glad Paul had applied. The field had been narrowed to three, and the audition was to be blind.

Each of the three finalists would play Trinity's fine Moller from behind a screen, so that only their music could speak for them. Each finalist was to be allowed an hour of rehearsal on the previous day. That would allow them time to become familiar with the instrument, the acoustics of the church, and record their registrations. That was, for Paul, a home-field advantage.

Nevertheless, Paul selected the music for the audition with great care and practiced it every spare minute he had. To test his skills in improvisation, he asked various people to name a hymn tune and immediately began to improvise upon it. He did his best to hone his skills and worked until the very last minute before he was time to catch his plane.

The audition was to last twenty minutes. He had been asked to prepare twelve minutes of music that showed a mastery of a wide range of styles of composers. Following that, a verger would present him with music to sight-read. During the last five minutes, he was to improvise on a theme that would be given to him at the beginning of the audition.

When the time came, a confident Paul played well. The sight-reading turned out to be simple enough, and when asked to improvise on the hymn-tune *Sine Nomine*, he was elated. It was a favorite. At the end of the audition, a disembodied voice said simply, "Thank you, we will let you know." And Paul walked away, went to the Tulsa airport, flew back to Washington and waited.

It didn't take long. The call came the next morning. He had the job.

Paul's return to Tulsa was the reverse of his trip to Washington two years earlier. He found a small house near campus and set about furnishing it. The first royalty check from his first published work came through just in time. He didn't have to actually scrimp when it came to furnishing his new home, so he didn't.

After Paul's return to Tulsa he reconnected with his former teachers and with old friends from Trinity. He was uncertain about how, or whether, he should approach Jack and Martha. Ultimately, the decision was made him.

Martha always read the church page in the Saturday edition of the *Tulsa Tribune*. It was one of her ways of keeping up with what was going on in the local churches. A short article announcing the new organist/choirmaster at Trinity caught her eye. Her hand went immediately to the telephone, dialed, and got Paul's new number from information.

When her call came, Paul did not particularly welcome it. Nevertheless he was polite. When Martha invited him to see the improvements at JJWWM headquarters, he reluctantly agreed.

Paul had only been to the converted warehouse once before, while he was living in the carriage house apartment. He really didn't want to go back there, yet he was curious and wondered what Martha really wanted.

Paul arrived at the appointed time and was greeted at the front desk like an honored guest. His escort proved to be a somewhat older, but very good-looking man, in a dark suit. He had a military bearing, and Paul assumed him to be a security guard.

"Hello, Mr. Thomas," the man said, "just call me Third; everybody does."

"OK," Paul responded, "if you'll just call me Paul."

"Let me show you around, Paul," Third said. "Mrs. Johns is tied up at the moment, but she will see you soon."

Third showed Paul through the building and commented on some of the latest improvements. Paul noted that the offices and other work areas had become crowded with many more workers crammed into them, than had been the case only two years before.

Eventually, Third and Paul arrived at Martha's office, where Third dropped Paul off and then disappeared.

Martha rose from her desk and came around it, hand extended, to greet her former employee and nemesis, and her husbands former lover. "Hello, Paul," she said, smiling, "It's good to see you again. Congratulations on your new appointment."

"Thanks, Martha. It's good to see you, too," Paul responded, even if he didn't feel it.

"Please sit down. Can I have someone get you a cup of coffee?"

"Oh, no thanks, Martha. I'm fine."

"Well, what do you think of the place?" Martha wanted to know.

"It looks like you're doing very well," Paul said. "You certainly have a lot more people here that when I left."

"Yes, the ministry's doing very well," Martha said with a smile. "We are planning to move to larger quarters. Jack's got his own little network now, and I'm sure it'll continue to grow."

Paul, who had seen a couple of JJWWM's productions on television, agreed. "I'm certain it will, too, Martha. The productions are very appealing."

"Thank you," Martha said, genuinely pleased. "We work very hard at it." She continued, "Of course, there is always a downside to the kind of fame Jack has now."

"Really?"

"Oh, yes," she continued. "We get all kinds of cranks claiming all sorts of things. We've even had men claim to have had sex with Jack. Disgusting, really. I have had to sic the lawyers on several of them."

Paul already knew of the iron fist inside Martha's velvet glove. He gave her as good as she sent. "I can't imagine such a thing, Martha. Even if it was true, I'm sure you wouldn't let it get in the way."

"Certainly not," she said firmly. "I can't allow that at all. I hope you'll come back and visit again. Perhaps Jack would have time to say hello on your next visit."

Paul took his cue and stood up. Martha pushed a button on her desk, and Third appeared promptly at the door.

"Thanks for coming, Paul. I'm glad could talk."

"Good luck with your work," was Paul's only reply. The encounter had not been pleasant. On the other hand, he had not expected it to be.

Third walked Paul back through the building towards the reception area. Third said, "I take it you've known the Johns for some time."

"Yes," Paul responded. "Jack and I used to go on the road with a tent revival. But that was years ago. I was in high school then."

"And afterwards?" Third wanted to know.

"I lived in their carriage house while I was in college."

"I see," Third said. He thought it through as they walked along. Then: "I live there now, Paul."

"Do you?" Paul exclaimed. "Perhaps we should talk one of these days."

"I'd like that," Third said. "If you're in the phone book, I'll give you a call."

"It's a new number, but information has it. Paul Thomas."

They shared a manly handshake at the reception desk, but the looks they exchanged conveyed the humor of the situation.

Chapter Twenty

Tulsa, 1963

Third had heard nothing from his handler, Tom, for several months. In fact, he half-way suspected that the entire matter had been forgotten. But, every month when he checked his secret savings account, the amount of his promised salary had been deposited. Then, early one Saturday morning, the phone rang.

"Hi," said a cheerful voice. "How about a doughnut and a cup of coffee?"

"Uh, OK," Third replied sleepily.

"See you at 10:00," the voice said before the connection was broken.

Third roused himself with a hot shower, shaved, and dressed casually. He made his way to the doughnut shop and arrived just before 10:00. He was about to enter, when he noticed the car parked at the curb. It was black and had dark tinted windows. Just as he approached the car, its right rear door opened.

A hand appeared, and Tom's voice said, "Hop in." Third did. As he closed the door, the car slid away from the curb.

"Hi, Tom," Third said. "Long time no see."

Tom laughed, "Nor hear, either."

"Yeah. I thought you'd disappeared."

"Nope. Just waiting for the right time."

"And this is it?"

"Sure is," Tom said. "I hear the operation is expanding."

"Yes."

"New office building and a new house at the same time."

"You're well informed."

Tom laughed again. "To quote our diseased neighbor, Will Rogers, 'all I know is what I read in the papers.' There's been plenty of coverage."

"Yeah, Martha thinks it's good publicity."

"I suppose it is, from a business point of view. I also hear that you're her fair-haired security chief. Good job."

"Thanks. Yeah, she pretty much leaves all the details of that to me. In fact, I'm in a little over my head, trying to sort out how to set up a good surveillance system for the new building."

"I'd make that buildings, plural, if I were you. You'll need security at the mansion, too. Why not just tie it all together?"

"Good idea," Third said. "Except I have no idea how to do that."

"I've got the perfect security consultant for you," Tom said. "Here's the information. His firm will help you sort everything out and make sure the system goes in just right."

"Martha will probably want to bid it out. It'll be a lot of money."

"Oh, don't worry about that. He'll be the low bidder. Just let me know who the other bidders are, OK?"

"Not the amount of the bids?"

"No, I won't need that. No need to open and reseal envelopes or any of that spy-novel stuff."

"OK, you're the pro; I'm the amateur. How do I get the information to you?"

"We'll need to set up a dead drop."

"A what?"

"A dead drop. It's a place where you can leave a message for me to pick up later. That way, no meeting takes place. The pace of things is going to speed up now, and you're going to be busier. They trust you now, so it's time to go to work. Have you ever been on the University of Tulsa campus?"

Third shook his head, "No, no reason to."

"Drop by the library and look around. There are carrels in the library stacks where the grad students can do research. Each little cubicle has some storage space and can be locked up to secure the student's materials. We happen to have access to a carrel. Here's the spare key. The student's name is Carol Harmony. It's an apt moniker; she's a music student."

"So she's one of us?" Third asked.

"No need for you to know that or for you to meet her. In fact, it would be better if you didn't run into her by accident. Do you know somebody who would be a courier for you?"

It was Third's turn to laugh. "Yes," he said, "And he's a musician and he teaches there part time."

"O.K., Third. Here's how it works: You put your information in this." Tom said.

He handed Third a big, bulky brown envelope. Inside was a thick book titled The Oxford History of English Music: Volume 1: From the Beginnings to c.1715. Third opened it to find that the pages had all been glued together and the center of the book hollowed out. The space inside was pretty big.

"Clever," Third said. "My courier just unlocks the carrel and puts the book on the desk, locks up, and walks away."

"Yes. Then you signal my courier to pick it up."

"How do I do that?"

"Easy. You wear a business suit to work every day, don't you? Wear a plain red tie."

"That's it?"

"That's it. You won't see him, but he'll see you. If I want to send you a message, it will be in the carrel waiting for your courier. He looks for a second book, just like the one I gave you."

"O.K.," Third said, "I've got it. Use Carol Harmony's carrel in the T.U. library stacks. Leave the information inside this book. Pick up the second copy of the book to get instructions. Wear a red tie next day."

"That's it."

The car dropped Third about two blocks from the carriage house where he still lived. He took with him the key to the carrel, the information about a security system contractor, and the book. It really was all quite simple. Except, of course, that he had to talk his target into being the courier. He hoped that would go well, too.

Jack and Martha were out of town for a few days, doing a round of book signings at high-profile churches. The children were both away at boarding school. Third was alone in the carriage house.

He took a deep breath, picked up the phone and dialed Paul's number.

Paul was busier than usual. It was the middle of Lent, so he and his choir were hard at work preparing for the musical glories of Easter. His special Easter compositions and musical arrangements had been finished long since. But, like all new music, it was being tested in rehearsal and minor adjustments were being made.

For that reason, Paul was well past his normal hour when he returned from choir rehearsal on Wednesday evening. It had been almost three weeks since his first meeting with Third at JJWWM. Third was the person furthest from his mind when the phone rang.

"Paul Tomas," he said into the receiver.

"Sorry for the late call. I phoned earlier, but you were out."

"Oh?" Paul said. It took him several seconds to realize who the caller was. Finally, it was the guarded tone and the decided Southern accent that gave Paul the clues he needed. "How are you?" he asked.

"Fine. Just thought I'd drop by for that cup of coffee you offered me."

"I'll put the pot on," Paul replied, knowing perfectly well that he would do no such thing. No coffee had been offered when they had met months earlier. Drinks would probably be in order, though.

"Great. I'll see you in fifteen minutes or so."

They broke the connection simultaneously.

"Hmmm," Paul thought. "He's certainly being cautious. I wonder about what."

It didn't take long for Paul to find out. The doorbell chimed twelve minutes later. When Paul opened the door, he saw that Third was in a tight-fitting T-shirt and a pair of very tight-fitting jeans. Paul liked what he saw.

"C'mon in," Paul said, smiling. "It's 'Third,' isn't it?"

"That's right," Third replied, laughing. "You remembered."

"I wasn't sure it was you on the phone."

"Oh," Third replied, "And you are accustomed to letting strange men into your home at all hours of the night, anytime they call up?

"Your accent gave you away," Paul said, grinning. "And it also depends upon how strange they are,"

"I can be pretty strange."

"Then you'll always be welcome. How about a drink?"

"I could use one. What are you offering?"

"Well, there's bourbon, Scotch, gin, vodka, rum, beer and white or red wine."

"Sound's like you're running 'Paul's Friendly Neighborhood Bar.'"

"Well, I am a Whiskeypalian, you know. And wherever three or four Episcopalians are gathered together, there's bound to be a fifth."

"Scotch, then," Third said, laughing at the old joke. "Just rocks, please."

Paul poured the drinks into two of his good cut-crystal glasses. He handed Third his with a cocktail napkin and said, "Cheers."

"Right," Third said raising his glass, "and here's to Martha, too."

"Martha? How'd she come into the conversation?"

"Just wait," Third said, "till I tell you all about it."

"About what? If it's dirt about Martha, I can't wait to hear it."

"Whoa. Half a second, guy. First, I've got to know a couple of things, if you don't mind."

"Like What?" Paul wanted to know.

"We've both lived in the carriage house, right?"

"Yes."

"Does that mean you slept with Jack Johns there?"

"Before I answer that, this conversation is getting pretty personal for a couple of guys who don't know each other. I want to keep things very confidential."

"Oh, so do I, believe me! I'll swear to confidentiality on a stack of Bibles, if you want me to."

"I think I can take your word for it," Paul said, seriously, "and you can take mine."

They solemnly shook hands on it.

"Let's start over," Third said. "I sleep with Jack in the carriage house. Did you?"

"Yes. It's a long story."

"You tell me yours and I'll tell you mine."

"Jack seduced me when I was sixteen," Paul said, simply. "I wanted him to, of course, or I would have stopped him. But he did. Then I went on the road with him when he was doing tent revivals. Later on, Martha, Jack, and I came to a parting of the ways. Martha wanted me out of the picture, and I used what happened with Jack to make them send me to college."

"Blackmail." Third said, putting a name to the crime.

"If you like, yes. After a year or so, Martha asked me to move into the carriage house to 'take care' of Jack. I did. After all, they were paying all my college expenses. That would have come to an end if there had been any public scandal about Jack. It was as much self-preservation on my part as anything else. I guess, in retrospect, Martha kind of blackmailed me back. Now it's your turn."

"Mine's a bit more complicated, so, I'll start with the very secret part." Third took a deep breath before he said, "I'm a paid informant for the government."

Paul stared at him open-mouthed, but said nothing.

"You heard me, Paul. I'm in the pay of the government. They think that there's something fishy going on at JJWWM and they want me to find out stuff. They tell me what to look for and I get it for them."

"And …?"

"And, they set me up to target Jack. I got lucky. He picked me up in a bar the first time I saw him. Took me back to the carriage house and we fucked. When Martha found out, she had one big fit, but ended up hiring me as head of security and kept me on to sleep with Jack, too."

"Yeah," Paul said. "Martha, the pimp. I like the image."

"Well, we've both whored for her, haven't we?"

"Yes. We have. After all," Paul said with a light laugh, "it was for money, after all. Different motives, of course, but still it was for money."

"And, in my case, it still is."

"But you are queer, aren't you? Or are you just being gay for pay?"

"Oh, I'm queer, all right. I started having sex when I was fifteen. It was with my cousin. I guess I just never outgrew it. That worries me, sometimes. They always said in church that queers go to hell. I've tried to change, but I can't. I've prayed about it a lot, but nothing's happened. So, I guess I do the best I can and either go to Hell or find out the Bible's wrong."

"What kind of church?" Paul wanted to know.

"Baptist."

"Oh," Paul said. "Fundamentalist and evangelical. 'fungicals,' I call them. No knowledge of church or biblical history. I know, I was once a Baptist, too."

"Well, I don't know about that, but the Bible says, 'Thou shalt not lie with mankind as with a womankind: it is an abomination.' You can't deny that."

"I wouldn't dream of denying it. It says exactly that. Now let me put it in context for you. The Council of Jerusalem, which was presided over by James, the brother of Jesus, decided that people didn't have to become Jews or obey Jewish law in order to be Christians."

"How do you know that?"

"It's a matter of historical fact. And I'll quote some scripture back to you, just to prove the point. St. Paul says, "Because the Law worketh wrath: for where no law is, there is no transgression." Got it?"

Third thought for a moment or two. "Yeah, I think so. If there aren't any rules then there's nothing to condemn people."

"You got it."

"But if there aren't rules, that's lawlessness."

"The idea is that if you love God and those around you, no other rules are needed."

Third didn't say anything and Paul figured he'd said a bit too much. Their glasses were practically empty, so Paul offered a freshener.

"Oh, OK, thanks. I will." Third responded, absently.

When Paul came back from the kitchen, Third said, "Thanks for the Bible lesson. That church of yours seems to make more sense than what I've been told all my life."

"I think it does, too. Remember, I grew up 'fungical,' too."

"Well," Third said, "Back to business, I guess. I didn't just come here to discuss Jack and Martha. I want to recruit you to help me."

Paul became instantly wary. "Doing what?"

"Dropping off a package for me from time to time. You don't need to know a lot more than that. Actually, it's pretty easy."

"OK, tell me and we'll see."

Third told him about the dead drop at the library, which was all Paul needed to know. Somewhat reluctantly, Paul agreed to "give it a try—once" but nothing more. And that was good enough for Third. They sat, nursing their drinks, until Third said, "I guess I really ought to be going."

"Or staying," Paul said, having made his decision.

"Well," Third said, "Jack and Martha are out of town for a few days. I won't be missed 'at home,' so, yes. I'd like that. You need to understand, it can't become a regular thing, you know."

"I know. That's probably better for me, too. Less chance for gossip."

They finished their drinks and headed off to Paul's bedroom, where Third spent the night. Although they got little sleep, the night was nonetheless a satisfactory one.

Chapter Twenty-One

Tulsa, 1963

Once Martha had decided that a new, high-profile office building and an appropriately grand mansion were next on the agenda, she had let nothing get in her way.

The JJWWM operation had grown so much that it was housed all over Tulsa. Their lawyers were in one building. Their accountants were across town from there. Other parts of the operation were in other buildings, scattered here and there. It made good business sense to consolidate their operations for greater efficiency, better control and increased profit.

Martha was getting accustomed to having money and power, but she also feared losing it. Any number of things could cause that. Jack's homosexuality might be discovered. Their separate private lives might be disclosed and publicly disgrace their supposedly perfect Christian marriage. Their secret proprietary methods used to extract offerings from Jack's faithful followers might be disclosed or stolen. Someone might set up a rival operation and siphon off some of their income. The possibility of internal theft was a nagging problem. Nobody had been caught yet, which probably meant that cash was going out the back door without anybody catching it.

For all these reasons, Martha wanted a top-notch security system. She wanted to be able to monitor all parts of the vast JJWWM operation. She had already charged Third with this responsibility in a general sort of way. Now she was eager to get more specific about security and operations monitoring. But, she didn't know how to go about that.

She called Third to her office.

"You wanted to see me, Miss Martha?" Third asked as he arrived.

"Yes, Third, I do. I'm still concerned about security in our new building. I want things buttoned up tight. I want to know everything that's going on. And if something happens, I want to know how it happened, who did it, where and when. Does this make sense to you?"

Martha sounded uncertain about her vague description of what she wanted.

Third recognized that his boss was well out of her element. She rarely sounded uncertain, but she sounded uncertain now. Third was delighted that Tom had already positioned him to take advantage of Martha's temporary weakness.

"Miss Martha," Third said, turning on his considerable Southern charm, "don't you worry about that. I've been working quietly along those lines myself. I think I've identified exactly the right person to tell us how to set everything up."

"Can we trust him? Will he be discreet?"

"Why don't I get him to come around and meet you? You can judge for yourself, if you like."

"Do it as soon as you can. No time like the present."

That sounded a lot more like the old Martha. Third knew he had scored. This was going to be a turkey shoot. As soon as he got back to his own office, he called the man Tom had recommended. An appointment was made for the very next day.

Mr. Byrd was a mousy little man with thick glasses, a bald head, and a quiet, efficient manner. He took Martha's outstretched hand in his dry little one and shook it firmly, looking here straight in the eye. Martha liked him instantly.

"Mr. Byrd," Martha began, "Reverend Johns has become a very well-known religious leader, as you may know. He wanted to meet you himself. But, you will understand that his very busy schedule prevents that on such short notice. He has asked me and Third to have this initial meeting with you and then set up an additional meeting with him if that becomes necessary."

"Oh, Mrs. Johns, I certainly understand. While I would be honored to meet the Reverend personally, I had not expected to do so. No, no. I am just here to assist you and the Reverend Johns ministry in any way that I can."

"That is very kind of you, Mr. Byrd. You are most understanding. You will appreciate that Reverend Johns employs quite a large staff. However, they are scattered around Tulsa in a number of different locations. It is the Reverend's desire to bring his little church family all together under one roof."

"Of course, Mrs. Johns."

"You will also understand, I am sure, that they are all very human. So, sometime one of them might fall from grace."

"And," Mr. Byrd continued for her, "if such a thing were to happen, the Reverend would want to know about it so that he could provide the appropriate pastoral counseling and moral support."

"Exactly!" Martha said, smiling her best preacher's wife's smile. "You understand perfectly! And," she went on, "we are always here for those who wish to visit us personally. Some of them, I am sad to say, are really dreadful sinners."

"I'm sure," Mr. Byrd responded, "but then you run a hospital for sinners, do you not?"

"Oh, indeed, we do!" Martha said. "So, you see, we need to know what our visitors may be doing, too."

"Well, then," Mr. Byrd said, "suppose I spend a little time with Mr. White here, going over your architect's plans. Then, I can propose a comprehensive security system, custom built to meet your exact requirements."

Martha managed to maintain a her smile as she said, "You will understand, of course, that the plans themselves have security features that we would not want to share with any outsider."

"Naturally," Byrd said smoothly, "I would expect to sign a confidentiality agreement before seeing them. And, with your permission, perhaps we would find a little corner here in your present offices, where our systems designer could work. That way, neither your plans or our work would ever leave your control."

"Fine, then," Martha said, bringing the interview to an end, "Please do as you have proposed and work the details out with Mr. White—or Third, as we know him here."

"I shall, Mrs. Johns. This has been an honor and a pleasure."

The self-effacing Mr. Byrd and Third withdrew from Martha's office and set about their work. Martha was satisfied, and Third was ecstatic. Apparently, for the businesslike Mr. Byrd, this was a job for which he was well prepared. Certainly, his part of the work, done primarily by an on-site designer, went quietly and smoothly.

By the time the office building and mansion were substantially completed, the security systems were completed as well, tested, and in perfect operating order. The bill was huge, but Martha signed the final check without a qualm.

The new offices were opened with much fanfare. Political bigwigs, business leaders and socially prominent families received engraved invitations to an opening gala fund-raiser for JJWWM's ministry. In keeping with its conservative image, no liquor or wine was served, but the food was excellent. The keynote speaker extolled Jack Johns' work and the money flowed in. It was a highly successful evening. Martha had secured a place in society for herself and her husband. Now, all she had to do was maintain it.

The gala, held in the vast, three-story vaulted atrium of the new building, also provided Third with an opportunity to test his new surveillance equipment. His newly hired staff operated remote cameras, hidden microphones, and recorders. They worked initially under the supervision of engineers sent by Mr. Byrd, so everything went without a hitch. Better yet, Third understood it all. He had planned every detail with Byrd's company. So he knew where every piece of equipment was, what it did, and how to operate it.

There were several different parts to the JJWWM operation, and Third had security supervision of it all.

The public side of the downtown operation was staffed entirely by good-looking, younger specimens of humanity that represented protestant America. They were mostly fair-skinned, but a few token darker people were to be seen. It was, after all, representative of the world Jack supposedly served. But none of them suffered from any blemish. Since they served a great healer and preacher, why would any of them have an illness of any kind? Martha wouldn't stand for it.

These perfect specimens were the people at the reception desk, the ones who pulled security duty in the public parts of the building, who ran the large and expensive gift shop and who appeared on television in support of their star.

If someone from the public side fell ill, he or she was told to stay away until they were better. JJWWM paid for sick leave. If the illness could not be cured the employee was given the option of moving to the private side or termination.

On the other hand, the people who worked on the private side could be just anybody who was willing to work hard to contribute to the operation's bottom line. Martha didn't care, as long as they were willing to sign a contract that bound them to secrecy for the rest of their lives.

Employees who worked on the private side came and went by the staff door. They did not venture into the public parts of the building when it was open. Instead, they reported to the mailroom and the counting house.

The mailroom prepared mailings to viewers and solicited money in a variety of ways. Workers in the counting house, which operated twenty-four hours a day, took care of the incoming mail and money.

Hidden television cameras were everywhere. Where they might prove useful, hidden microphones were employed as well. Camera images were fed into banks of television monitors. Third's cadre of security personnel watched these around the clock. If something unusual appeared on any of the screens, a nearby microphone was turned on and a recording was made of the incident.

In addition to the cameras, there was a warren of secret passages and catwalks above ceilings, where Third's staff of watchers could see almost anything they wanted to observe more closely. Of these, several were quite naturally in the mailroom and counting house.

Incoming mail often almost included a Prayer Card. These were mailed regularly to contributors. They asked the recipient to provide the name of someone who needed prayer. Prayer Cards had pre-printed number codes on them. Prayer Card information was transferred to punch cards for mechanical sorting and information storage. The cards themselves went into the trash. Every day, at the noon service in the tiny chapel, one of the JJWWM junior ministers prayed for the "concerns of all who had sent Prayer Cards." Which was the cynical extent to which JJWWM kept its promise.

Meanwhile, state-of-the-art automated printers were grinding out letters that said that the prayer had been uttered. The vaguely worded letters, with personalized salutations, went through an expensive machine that operated a real pen to apparently sign Jack Johns' signature in heavenly blue ink. A new Prayer Card and the personalized letter were mechanically inserted into their own personalized envelope. Then they were stamped with a real postage stamp, and dumped into mailbags to go to the post office. Although mass-produced, the mailings looked like personal messages from the famous Jack Johns himself. In reality, Jack never saw any of them.

Jack also received unsolicited letters. A mid-level supervisor reviewed each of them for anything useful. If prayers were asked for, they were added to the Prayer List, which meant that the sender was drawn into the Prayer Card operation. Sometimes a miracle of healing was reported. The odds were in favor of that. A certain percentage of really sick people simply get better, as most physicians know, for no apparent reason. When such miracles were reported, a different letter went out. The supervisor inserted appropriate wording into a form letter. The letter went into a flat envelope, along with a photo of Jack. The letter was mechanically signed, of course, and the photo was not only signed but also personalized with the recipient's name. A glossy brochure was added to the materials, along with an appeal for funds. It went out in a large manila envelope with real stamps on it, too.

Some of the letters were abusive or threatening. Those went to the legal team. Although that was a separate corporate entity with its own letterhead, the lawyers worked exclusively for Martha and Jack Johns in the JJWWM headquarters building.

Each threat was carefully evaluated. Those that fell into the "fruits and nuts" category, as Martha called it, were simply ignored, but the names were kept on file. If the threat was repeated, it was then taken more seriously. Each letter that alleged some kind of misconduct on the part of JJWWM, or Jack himself, was handled separately. The lawyers demanded evidence of dates, names, and places. Usually, these were easy to debunk.

The very rare threats of actual violence were reported to the authorities and Martha's lawyers followed up to make certain that all these threats were investigated thoroughly.

Still, Martha continued to worry about any threat that might spoil her financial success. She gave little thought to the faithful. Those humble folks were simply milked for income. It generally worked quite well. But not well enough to suit Martha. Never having had much prior to the recent successes, Martha always wanted more.

After consulting her lawyers and accountants, she set up several shell corporations. They had names in which the words 'ministry,' 'crusade,' or 'church' were featured. Each was a tax-exempt religious organization. And like the JJWWM operation itself, each was careful not to transgress the commandments of the Internal Revenue Service.

Those JJWWM Prayer Card mailings that didn't pay off, or that stopped paying, were transferred to one of these other secondary operations. The scams, clever and varied, appealed to the human desires for wealth, health, happiness, and love.

A lucky believer might receive a "coin" from the Holy Land, stamped out of heavy gold cardboard. Recipients were instructed to wrap their largest bill (or a generous check) around it and send it back. This 'faith seed offering' would be returned to them tenfold, or a hundredfold, or even a thousandfold, in the fullness of time as a sign of God's love. Only faith and prayer were required.

The JJWWM gospel was simple: Wealth, health, happiness, and love were the rewards to be reaped from faith, prayer and offerings. Poverty, sickness, unhappiness, and loneliness were the fruits of unbelief.

Printed-paper 'healing scarves,' were sent out by the thousands. Each had the imprint of Jesus' wounded hands on it. One was to pray the enclosed prayer in secret, telling no one, and then place his or her hands in Jesus' own to be healed. Healing would be gradual, of course. Recipients were told the blessed scarves were scarce. They needed to be shared with others, and should only be kept one day. Delay was selfish. Of course, an offering to send the scarves to others was also needed. Jesus "prayer rugs" were a similar scam.

The offering of blessed candles, accompanied by earnest prayer, could work all sorts of wonders. The cheaply scented wax, in a glass container, would burn for seven days as a "continuous prayer." A paper label depicted Jesus at prayer. Just return the enclosed card and the free candle would be sent. A minimum offering of twenty dollars was suggested. Choose: green for money, red for love, or white for a visitation from the Holy Spirit. These were only a few of the ingenious ideas that Martha's team of marketers came up with.

Each scam had one common thread: money had to be sent prior to the time the miracle was expected to occur. If people were somehow disappointed it was obviously their fault: perhaps they hadn't prayed earnestly enough, or sent in a large enough offering.

Then, there was the even more interesting, very private side of the building, that only a very few trusted employees knew anything about.

In Jack's office, there was an observation room behind a beautifully framed one-way mirror. For this office, there was a complete, self-contained television camera setup as well. It had it's own control room with recording capacity. Martha screened tapes of meetings between Jack and important people. Some yielded useful information. Some tapes even went into a fireproof vault. One large and two smaller conference rooms were similarly equipped. The tapes from meetings in those rooms were reviewed, too.

Ostensibly, Jack and Martha lived an idyllic Christian life in their beautiful gated home on the Tulsa outskirts. In fact, they were rarely there. Their "home" had simply been built as a showplace. They used it for entertaining important guests, for fund-raisers for JJWWM's favored causes, and for the "photo-ops" that got them national coverage in the media.

The Johns' mansion was surrounded by a high fence and had electrically controlled gates. It set back from the road at some distance and shrouded in trees and shrubbery to make even professional observation difficult. The public parts of the house, such as the main salon and the huge dining room were equipped with surveillance equipment, too.

However, the most secret part of Third's responsibilities had to do with the private apartments in the JJWWM headquarters.

In reality, Jack and Martha lived very separate lives in two private apartments in their headquarters building. Jack had one large one; Martha had another. There were other, smaller ones as well, but few knew anything about any of them. One of these was used by Third. Two others were used by a couple of senior members of the security service.

There were also hotel-type suites that were used by guests, or by Jack and Martha's personal physician when he needed to be there over night.

Third had recruited all of the members of the security service, and he had done his recruiting very carefully. He hired manly men, like himself, who looked straight, enjoyed being gay, and were willing to stay in the closet for a secure and well-paying position in life. They worked out in their private gym, ate at their own table in the executive dining room, kept to themselves and lived discreet lives when off duty.

Third kept his ever-watchful eye on everything. Not only for Martha, but secretly for Tom, too.

Chapter Twenty-Two

Tulsa, 1963

Jack Johns still had a wondering eye and had become interested in a handsome young man who had just joined the security force. The young man, recruited by Third with that hope, was pleased by the attention he got from the famous man. He also made Jack feel young again, so love, or at least something that passed for it, bloomed once more in the private apartment Jack occupied in the JJWWM ministry building.

Third passed this new intelligence along, just as he passed along all kinds of information to his handler, Tom. Third took his documents and recordings to Paul's house and put them in the hollowed out Oxford music history book. Paul would take it next day to the dead drop and Carol Harmony, whoever she was, would pass it along.

Paul had only promised to try the thing once. Later, he admitted to Third he had been so nervous that the feeling everybody was watching him had been impossible to shake.

"I know the feeling," Third said. "The first time I met my handler, I was certain that people would start yelling and pointing at us. I felt the same way again when I started copying recordings of private meetings."

The books used for the dead-drop were constructed very cleverly. First of all, they were large, worn and heavy. Any unevenness in the pages could be put down to age. There were twenty or so loose pages in the front of the Oxford books that made them look legitimate if they were opened casually. The spine appeared to be broken just at the first page of the lid. And a magnetic catch held the lid of the cavity shut. After checking with Third, Paul had added his bookplate to each of the books in turn. If necessity required it, Paul could even been seen appearing to read the front part of the book.

"I still get nervous, you know," Paul said.

"I know. I do, too. But when I first started this work, they told me to be wary of becoming too confident. They said that if I ever got comfortable with this line of work, I should get out."

"So complacency is a warning signal?"

"I guess so. It probably pays to stay a little nervous."

"Then I'm in good shape," Paul said. His laugh was just a bit forced.

Paul had become an adjunct professor at the University, so it was nothing unusual for him to be seen around the campus or in the music section of the library. However, a residual felling of reluctance about playing courier for Third haunted him. But, he reasoned, if it was something the government had asked Third to do, there couldn't really be anything wrong with helping his friend out.

On this particular morning, he had a private lesson to give on campus. He met his student and did the usual things in the usual way. The Oxford book was in his briefcase. After the lesson was over, he walked the short distance to McFarlin Library. There he appeared to consult the catalogue before going up into the stacks. He got off the tiny elevator at the appropriate floor and went in search of the book he had looked up. He slipped it into his briefcase and nonchalantly stopped momentarily at Carol Harmony's carrel. There was nobody else around, so he quickly unlocked the door and switched the Oxford books.

Afterwards, he went back down to the main level of the building to check out the book he had taken from the stacks. It was routine. Librarians never asked to check his briefcase. After all, he was an adjunct professor. But the graduate student on duty at the checkout desk that morning decided to be officious.

"Do you have any other books in your briefcase, professor?" he asked in a superior tone.

"Yes," Paul said. "One. It's mine, though." Paul pulled out the book, casually flipped open the cover and showed the disappointed kid his bookplate. "Thanks for doing your job, though," Paul added. "After all, some of these books are hard to replace." He smiled agreeably to the assistant as he turned and walked out the door.

Despite his apparent nonchalance, his hands were shaking slightly, and his palms were wet with sweat. But he knew that his demeanor had remained calm. He began to feel elated. The sudden release of adrenaline, accompanied by his success gave him an instant thrilling high. He came to realize that this was what hooked criminals and spies. That feeling of success was a better reward than any cash payment could be. He wondered if Third felt the same way. He decided to ask him.

Paul brought the subject up the next time Third came to visit. His answer was unequivocal.

"Yeah, Paul, I know what you mean. Sometimes, I think I'd just do it for the thrill. That and putting it to Martha."

"Is she getting under your skin?" Paul asked.

"She's more like a burr under my saddle," Third said, laughing. "The woman is a real bitch. I don't know how Jack stands her."

"Well, my guess it's not love and hasn't been for a long time," Paul said. "I'd say it was fame, money and she's got the goods on him."

"On the other hand, she can't very well spill the beans without ruining everything for herself, can she?"

"Right," Paul said. "I guess they're both hoist on their own petard."

"Alright, college boy, what's that mean?"

"When knights used to storm castles, they'd sometimes use a dagger to fasten a sack with explosives to the castle gate. The sack was called a petard. They had to light the fuse first and then run for the gate through a hail of arrows. In the rush, they might catch their clothes in the dagger, and boom. Up they'd go with their own bomb."

"You think this thing's going to blow up?"

"Well, no. At least not right away," Paul said. "But if it did, they'd both go up with it."

"Yeah, I've been thinking about that. We might go up with it, too. Look, Paul, I know you're the only guy in the world I can trust. Will you let me do a couple of things?"

"Like what?"

"Well, first off, I've been making copies of the copies, if you know what I mean. I want my own record of what I've given you to send on. But, if Martha starts nosing around, I may have to stash them someplace away from the office. I really don't have anyplace to put anything truly private. If I give anything to you, will you keep it for me?

"Sure, why not? I can keep them locked up with my own personal papers and manuscripts. Just let me know."

"Great. Second, I want to add your name to my secret savings account. If I get run over by a streetcar or something, I want you to have the money."

"Tulsa doesn't have any streetcars," Paul replied.

"But you get my drift. I might have an accident anyway."

"Something could happen to me, too. I'd better give you the combination to the filing cabinet."

"And you'd better sign my bank account signature card, too, the next time I come. I don't want anybody knowing about that money. It would compromise what

I've been doing for the government. If you're on the account, you can just take the money and nobody would be the wiser. You've earned half of it anyhow."

"OK, partner-in-stealth, it's a deal." They kissed to seal the bargain.

After that their spying, and personal liaison, became routine. Third was glad that Jack's new lover was occupying Jack's bed nightly. He was falling in love with Paul, so his feelings for Nick were rapidly fading away.

Nick was occupied with business and family. He rarely thought of Third. And, as instructed by ODESSA, he needed to start his political career.

To begin, he decided on a seat in the U. S. House of Representatives. The liberal incumbent was known in some circles as a womanizer. Nick used one of his connections to set the man up. The representative was successfully photographed during a raid on a brothel. Only a few of the more salacious tabloids dared carry the photo, which showed him in a round bed with a bare-breasted woman on each side. The story broke just two weeks before the electorate made their choice.

In 1961, at the age of twenty-five, Nick won the election hands down and successfully served two terms. He made a name for himself by exposing some illegal connections that led to highly placed persons in the opposition party.

Mindful of his responsibility to influence conservative Christians, Nick also began to pay serious attention to who was who in that sphere. Some of them were obviously too old, or too liberal, or just plain nuts, as he told himself. Through his contact Tom, Nick had discretely placed inside men in several groups that he wanted to know more about. That included the JJWWM operation. Fortunately for Nick, Third had taken the bait.

Next up for Nick was a seat in the Senate. In 1965, at just age thirty, Nick was very young to run for such a post and few of the political pundits gave him much of a chance.

Nevertheless, campaign contributions poured in from all over. Some were legitimate; some were from ODESSA fronts. Nick traveled tirelessly all over the state. If a dozen or so people could be assembled, he would go and talk to them. His name recognition shot far up in the polls.

His opponent was loyal member of Nick's own Conservative Party. Unseating him was made more difficult by his reputation as a good family man. But, research showed that his opponent had serious financial troubles and his marriage was strained. A carefully doctored photograph was sent to the Senator's wife. It showed her husband in bed with a handsome young man. In Washington, two days later, his opponent jumped from the Q Street overpass to Rock Creek Parkway below. A speeding cab hit him as he fell.

When interviewed by the press, Nick said, "Although we disagreed on where our party is headed, I had great personal respect for him. My wife, Nancy, and I have already expressed our condolences to his family, and our prayers continue to be with them and all who loved and respected him."

Nick's first term in the Senate was quiet, as befits a freshman Senator. One does not join "the most exclusive club in the world" and immediately begin to make waves. Nick was successful in being unobtrusive, too.

Meanwhile, the information that Nick got, via a courier and dead-drop system, was encouraging. It was clear that Johns believed what he preached, or at least he appeared to do so. Of the lot, he seemed to be the up-and-coming choice. It also became clear that his wife, Martha, was the real power in the JJWWM operation. Nick decided to pay her a visit.

At the appointed time, it was Third who met him at the door, as he did all-important visitors.

"Good afternoon, Senator Hutton," Third said. "Mrs. Johns is expecting you. Please follow me." There was not even a glimmer of recognition on Third's face. Nick was more than a little pleased by that.

Third announced the visitor to Martha's plain-looking secretary, who repeated that the Senator was expected. She opened the door for him herself and announced, "Senator Hutton."

"Thank you, Anne," Martha said smoothly, "that's all for now." Then, to her visitor she said, "Please sit down. We are honored by your visit, Senator. Unfortunately, my husband is engaged in a pastoral emergency. However, I will be glad to assist you in any way I can."

"Actually, Mrs. Johns, I should probably talk to you first anyway. You may know that I am deeply committed to the high moral standards that under gird our nation's greatness. Unfortunately, our country seems to be slipping away from those. I have watched the Reverend Johns on television for some time now. I believe he shares my view. As a private citizen, certainly not in any official capacity, I would like to encourage your husband's ministry by making a substantial contribution to it."

Nick took an envelope from his pocket and handed it across the desk to Martha. She slit it smoothly open with one of her long, highly polished nails and removed the check.

"Thank you, sir," she said. "My husband and I are very grateful. This will be of great assistance to our ministry."

Nick saw her eyes glitter with greed as she said it. His test had worked. He had the right target.

"There is just one favor I'd like to ask in return," Nick said.

"What would that be?"

"My wife and I are planning a fund-raising party for my next campaign. It will be one of those one-hundred-dollar-a-plate dinners for about three hundred guests. If your husband would consent, we would like you to be our guests and for your husband to say grace."

"I'll make every effort to arrange that for you," Martha said, rising from her chair. "Just have your people call my secretary with the details."

"It was a pleasure meeting you, Mrs. Johns."

"And mine as well," Martha said as she escorted him out of her office.

Nick's political career continued to flourish. As it did so, he also nurtured his relationship with JJWWM and worked closely with Martha help make Jack Johns even more famous.

Contributions from many sources helped Martha to grow her operation. Some of the largest contributors were blinds for ODESSA. As a result of Jack's talents, Martha's efforts and the influx of money through Nick's contacts, JJWWM gained worldwide fame, and built huge fortunes for all of them in the process.

Chapter Twenty-Three

Tulsa, 1985

Martha sat in her office high atop the Jack Johns World Wide Ministry building in downtown Tulsa. The windows of the corner room gave a grand view of the river and the distant Osage hills. A life-size portrait of the Reverend Jack Johns hung in a heavy gilt frame behind Martha's desk.

By now, both Jack and Martha were aging. Jack remained tall, slender and athletic appearing. His striking features and full head of silver hair made him instantly recognizable. A large retinue of specialists accomplished his carefully maintained appearance: a personal trainer, dietician, personal physician, masseur, make-up artist, hair stylist, and manicurist. Speechwriters now wrote Jack's sermons. He was waited on hand and foot and cared for like the highly profitable property that he had become. The real operation of JJWWM was in the hands of various departments, all of which reported to Martha. Jack was a star, and that only.

Time had not been as kind to Martha. In her drive for success, she paid much less attention to her health and appearance than she had to Jack's. She had always had a kind of sturdy peasant build, with wide hips and large thighs. More weight meant sagging breasts and a triple chin. Worst of all, she now had arthritis, and she suffered badly from it. Most of the time, she used a cane, and on particularly bad days a walker. Naturally, she could no longer appear regularly in public, not as the crippled wife of a world-renowned healer.

It was from Martha's executive suite that JJWWM was really run, not from the Reverend's showplace office. The top floor had long since been dubbed "Heaven" by the lesser mortals who worked for the Johns' ministry. For those who were summoned there to be confronted by an angry Martha, "Heaven" was more like Hell.

Martha looked down at the desk clock, put down the financial report she was reading, and pressed a button. Almost immediately, Third entered her office from a side door.

"2:00 a.m. meeting tonight, Third. At the house. High security. No record of this one," she said, "Nothing at all, clear?"

Third said, "Yes, ma'am. Understood." He bowed slightly and left the room as quickly and quietly as he had come.

Back at his desk, Third summoned the leader of the off-duty security team. Sarge, as intimates knew him, appeared almost immediately, having sprinted up one flight of stairs from the floor below.

"What's up?" Sarge asked.

Third looked at the physically fit ex-Army sergeant standing before him. He complimented himself again on his choice of subordinate. Sarge knew how to carry out any assignment Third gave him. On duty, he was all business. Tonight would be no different.

"Extra duty, Sarge," Third said.

"When and where?"

Third gave his orders: "At the mansion. Check the grounds, and then set up an outside perimeter. I don't expect any trouble, but if we have an intruder, I want him removed quickly and quietly. Scare the shit out of him, too, but no rough stuff unless I give the order. Have your men in place by midnight. I want them well armed. It's going to be cold and could take some time, so make sure they have water and energy bars. I'll recall you myself, when it's all clear."

Sarge went to collect his team, feed them, and get them ready for the nights' work. It didn't take long; they all lived in the building.

Late that same night, as Third had ordered, a black van with darkened glass and running without lights, entered the mansion grounds via the back gate. It slid to a stop in deep shadows near the six-car garage. Seven men emerged cautiously out of the vehicle, closing the doors very quietly behind them.

Six of them formed a semicircle in front of the seventh. They were all dressed alike: each wore black boots with crepe soles, black fatigue pants, a black sweatshirt, a black outer jacket and a black ski mask. Sarge, who was the seventh man, spoke to them in a low voice, knowing that the sibilants of a whisper would carry farther than his softly spoken final orders. Each man confirmed that he had his hunting knife and a loaded .38 police special. At a nod from Sarge, they dispersed.

The grounds were subtly lit. The low level of illumination made the grounds look dark. But in reality the guards could see anything they were looking for.

Two of the men walked in opposite directions around the mansion, looking into the shrubbery and checking the darker corners. Two more did the same with the garage. The last two stood sentry at the front and back gates. Nobody was found. Sarge gave a hand signal, and the men melted into the shrubbery and the shadows along the edge of the property. Sarge disappeared, too, nearest the house. The black van glided silently away.

Sarge did his radio check. One by one, each man confirmed that he was receiving, and then all fell silent. It was cold. A barn owl called from the distance, but got no answer. In a scant five minutes, it was as though nothing had happened and as if nobody was there. Third's invisible security team took up its silent waiting vigil.

At almost exactly 2:00 a.m., a three-vehicle convoy pulled up at the gate. A black van preceded a black Lincoln with tinted windows. Another black van followed. Their timing was perfect, even though they had driven in darkness from the small secondary airport near Broken Arrow over unfamiliar terrain. They were expected. Sarge's security team did not stir.

Third was there too, but he was inside the mansion. Neither the watchers on the grounds, nor those in the vehicles could see him. Immured in the basement, Third sat at an extensive security console, watching the array of television screens. When the three vehicles appeared at the front gate, he pressed a button and the massive wrought iron gates swung open silently.

Thus far, everything had gone according to plan. But Third's next action was not supposed to be on the night's agenda. He slid his hand under the security console and pressed a concealed button. Far away in a locked room next to his downtown office, automated equipment began to do what Martha had forbidden. He was recording the meeting just for his own personal archive.

Third has long since decided that his double agent role was not what Tom had pretended it was. Third had long ago figured out that 'Tom' was an assumed name. For another thing, Third had reported some outright scams and the government had done nothing about them. Furthermore, his work had been going on far too long, almost twenty years. During that time, he had amassed almost a million dollars in his secret account. Paying that much for the information he provided didn't make sense to him. Then, there were the ties to important political figures, including Senator Nick Hutton, which had begun to look pretty shady. Something was clearly up, and Third wanted to know what. So he had been recording everything that he thought was important for his own self-protection.

As soon as the gates opened, the convoy turned their lights odd and drove slowly up the drive. Following instructions, they turned onto the service drive that led to the rear of the huge house. As they were making their way to this secluded entry, Third left the console and hurried through the palatial home to meet the visitors. They all arrived at their destinations simultaneously. Vehicle doors opened. Disguised in his butler's outfit, Third opened the back door. Eight men emerged from the vans. One took up a post outside the rear door. Seven others, dressed entirely in black, disappeared into the shrubbery next to the house. At the same time, three men emerged from the car and entered the house.

Security was now complete. The visitors had supplied men for the inner perimeter, while the Johns' men kept watch over the outer one. And Third was inside the house; the last line of defense if one was needed. Martha and Jack viewed Third as quiet and efficient, the man to be trusted in an emergency.

Without speaking, Third bowed the three men through the kitchen door and escorted them into the wide hallway just beyond. From there, it was a short walk to the huge dining room, where their host and hostess waited.

Just outside the dining room, the remaining guard took up his post. Third ushered the other two men inside and then stood near the sideboard where glasses and decanters sparkled. The silver ice bucket was frosted from the cold within.

"Refreshments, anyone?" Martha asked, playing hostess. She gesturing carelessly towards the sideboard where Third stood, ready to play bartender. Getting no response, she nodded to Third, "We'll wait on ourselves if we want anything later."

Third took his cue, bowed his best butler's bow, and left the room, closing the door tightly behind him. He nodded to the stoic guard at the door and began his own routine, patrolling the interior of the vast house.

The meeting ended just before 4:00 a.m. The guests departed, taking their security people with them. Third recalled Sarge and his men. Their black van returned almost immediately, and they departed as silently as they had come.

Next day, Third reviewed the recording he should not have made. He listened and watched in increasing horror as he pondered what to do. Presently, he went out into the security group's reception area and told the secretary that he had decided on some fresh air and a bite of lunch away from the office. He'd be back about 1:30, he said.

Third followed his announced schedule to a 'T,' except that he added a private phone call while he was in the restaurant.

Paul got Third's urgent message when he got home that evening. Third sounded worried and serious. When he showed up at Paul's just before midnight, he told Paul everything about the meeting. Paul agreed that it was very, very serious.

"I'd better tell you my news, too. It's good and bad, both." Paul said, sadly.

"Shoot. It can't get much worse than it is already."

"I've decided to move to Atlanta."

"What?" Third exclaimed, dismayed.

"I know. I just happened today. My Rector was among the nominees to be the new dean of the Atlanta cathedral. His appointment was confirmed yesterday. He wants me to go with him as organist and master of the choirs. It's a big promotion. It's full-time, not part-time, so I won't have to take private students any longer. And

I'll have time for composing, too. The only fly in the ointment is that I will be leaving you. Unless you want to come, too. Can you?"

"I wish I could. I'd like to quit, but I can't. It may not be safe to. I don't want to drag you in any further, either. Your move to Atlanta may actually be a very good thing from that point of view. Let me sort this out, first."

"I wish I could help in some way, but I don't know what to do."

"I got you in, so it's my job to get you out. No arguments, Paul. It's my responsibility, not yours."

Together, they composed a message to go to the dead-drop the next day. It said,

> *"Urgently recommend setting up new drop. Courier leaving Tulsa for new job. Please advise."*

Two days later, Martha saw the announcement in the Tulsa Tribune that Paul Thomas had accepted an appointment at St. Philip's Cathedral in Atlanta where Trinity Church's former rector was now dean.

She filed that piece of information away in the back of her mind for future reference.

Chapter Twenty-four

Atlanta, 1986

Paul's move to Atlanta went as smoothly as any long-distance move ever does. He took up his new position at the cathedral and settled in easily. It cannot be said that either his teaching stipend or his part-time job at Trinity paid munificently. However, he also had an income from the various musical works that he continued to compose. Third had dipped into his secret savings account and given Paul a generous parting gift as well. It was enough to buy a large unit in one of Atlanta's first high-rise condominiums.

Third had rented a post office box, and Paul wrote to him there. He expressed his thanks for the financial assistance and sent some photos of the condo, too. He said he hoped that Third would visit when he could. When he could, Third did.

In the 1980s Atlanta's Midtown neighborhood was the center of gay life and Paul was drawn to the festive atmosphere, the parties in private homes, and the rest of the increasingly open way of life in the bustling city.

At one particular soirée, Paul paid particular attention to the young bartender on duty. They exchanged a few polite words when Paul went back to the bar. And, Paul noticed, the young man kept looking at him. The party broke up fairly early and Paul decided to stop at one of Midtown's many bars for an after-dinner drink before heading home. Just as he was finishing his rusty nail, he spotted bartender from the party heading his way.

"Hi," the young guy said, "my name's Jason."

"Hello, Jason, I'm Paul. Will you join me?"

Jason did. It became an arrangement that is common in the gay world: a young man who offers companionship and an older man who provides stability and assistance. They saw each other regularly after that.

Paul learned that Jason's life had not be at all easy up to that point. At age fifteen, Jason's orientation had become obvious to his parents. Their fundamentalist preacher recommended regular beatings and Jason's father followed his advice for almost a year. Finally, Jason could take no more and struck back, hitting his sadistic father so hard that he knocked him to the ground. Next morning he was given twenty dollars and a one-way bus ticket to Atlanta, "where all the rest of the God-damned queers are," and told never to come back.

When Jason got to Atlanta, he found out he was not alone. There were a lot of kids about his age who were throw-aways. Most of them engaged in prostitution, acted as 'mules' for drug dealers, or committed petty thefts.

Jason tried to do better. He managed to find a sympathetic restaurant manager who took Jason on as a dishwasher, even though he was underage. A connection was able to provide Jason with a fake Georgia driver's license that showed he was eighteen. After that, he started dancing as a go-go dancer in a gay nightclub.

After a couple of years, he was able to work his way into freelancing as a waiter or bartender for a catering company. He got a tiny apartment for himself and was finally, if barely, self-sufficient. He was determined to hang onto that. And that's how he met Paul.

Their friendship was casual at first. And, at first, there was nothing sexual about it. Paul still felt a strong attachment for Third, who he missed very much. Like most long-distance romances, it was hard to keep alive. It gradually drifted into a simple friendship while the mutual attraction between Paul and Jason deepened.

Then, in 1996, Third called out of the blue to say he was coming for a visit. Paul said he'd be glad to see him and introduce him to Jason.

"Better not," Third said. "What we have to discuss is what you might call old business, if you get my drift."

Paul said he did. Then he went about trying to explain the sudden appearance of an old boyfriend to Jason.

Jason gave Paul a hard time about it, just for the hell of it, but ended up saying, "If I can't trust you now, I'll never be able to. It's fine. Really it is." And he disappeared for the weekend.

When Paul picked Third up at the airport, Third was all business.

Soon as they had settled down in Paul's living room, Third said, "I want to take out an insurance policy, Paul. I hope you'll agree to be it."

"What did you have in mind?"

"What you agreed to before you left Tulsa. I just want to know if you're still up for it. I want you to stash away a file folder for me."

Paul remembered his promise well enough. "Sure. Do I know what's in it?"

"Yeah. That last unauthorized recording we discussed. That, and some other papers and things. Taken together, they're the goods on Martha, Jack, and the great Senator Hutton."

"Why now?"

"Because I'm pulling out and I don't want any trouble. I'm 55 now and I want to quit this business before I grow ulcers."

"So you're going to tell them that you have a record, its stashed somewhere, and that if anything happens to you, the whistle blows."

"Exactly."

"Fine, I'll hold the stuff for you, if you want, but I'm sure nothing bad's going to happen. You'll be fine. You'll see."

"I sure hope so," was Third's worried reply.

Third handed over a slim brown accordion file, its flap closed and tied shut. Paul took the file and Third followed him into Paul's study. There, Paul dialed the combination lock on the bottom drawer of his filing cabinet and placed the folder inside.

"Done," he said.

They went out to dinner, and Third went back to Tulsa the next morning.

Jason's arrangement with Paul continued. It was an arrangement whereby he earned his own way and was also able to enjoy a nice place to live, an occasional night out, or a short vacation somewhere inviting. It worked quite well for both of them.

In was on the last of those short vacations that Paul had been murdered.

Now, just days before Paul's funeral, Jason and Mark were making their first visit to what had been Paul Thomas' condominium. While Mark admired the view and the appointments, Jason kept recalling times spent there with Paul.

Finally, Jason said, "Let's go. I don't want to stay here any longer. It's still Paul's place; I feel like I shouldn't be here."

Mark understood. "OK. We can lock up and leave if you want. But look, Jason, we've got to come back sometime. You need to clear out Paul's clothes and things. I'll help, if you want, but it really does have to be done."

"Right." Jason said. "But let's wait until after the funeral. It seems like I'm rushing him into his grave."

So the two of them drove back to Mark's little Midtown apartment. They were silent as they drove down Peachtree, Mark lost in his own thoughts.

As they got out of Mark's little car, he said quietly, "Jason, you'd better stay here with me until after the funeral. And you don't have to go back to Paul's condo, you know. You could just clean it out and sell it if you wanted to. No more memories, that way."

"I think I'll keep it," Jason said. "I can change things around, you know, and fix it up the way I'd like to have it. Then it'll be mine. Right now it's still Paul's."

"Sounds good," Mark said, relieved. "You'll stay here with me until you get that done, won't you?"

"You're making it sound kinda temporary," Jason said. "Not going to dump me, are you?"

"No way. I'm being awkward, I guess. I just want you to be free to do what you want to do."

"I'm the awkward one," Jason said. "What I really meant is 'we.' We'll do the condo over, the way we want it and we'll live there, together. That's what I want."

"Be careful what you ask for," Mark said, "because that's what you'll get."

As they reached the apartment door, Jason said, "Swim?"

"Sure."

In the bedroom, Mark changed into a pair of swim trunks while Jason put on a Speedo.

"No thong?" Mark wanted to know.

"If you want," Jason said, "but my husband wouldn't like it. He's a clergyman. I have his reputation to think about."

They spent the rest of the afternoon at the pool, splashing each other in the water and sunbathing. That evening, they were very domestic, cooking at home and going to bed early.

The funeral on the following Saturday was at the cathedral. The Bishop had asked Mark if he wanted to be the deacon for the service, but Mark had demurred. He felt his place was beside Jason.

The cathedral was packed. Paul Thomas' many friends and admirers had come from near and far for this final tribute to him. Most of the music was selected from among his many compositions. As a result, the dignified service was transformed into a soaring tribute, not only to Paul, but also to his belief in a life everlasting.

Mark sat with Paul in the mourner's pew, and guided him through the unfamiliar liturgy. Dressed in a new dark suit and black shoes, Jason carried out his role of chief mourner with quiet dignity.

Afterwards, the funeral procession wound its way down Peachtree. Although the service had been at the cathedral, Paul's ashes were to be buried in the churchyard at All Saints in Midtown. The crowd filled the small courtyard to overflowing for the brief and simple burial service. Near the bronze statue of Jesus in the Garden, a small opening had been dug in the sod. There, with quiet dignity, the bishop deposited Paul's earthly remains.

"Ashes to ashes, dust to dust, in the sure and certain hope...."

Then the bishop put the first scoop of earth into the ground. Then Jason and Mark stepped forward to take their part in filling the grave. When they stood up, Mark could see the tears that streamed silently down Jason's face.

They were silent on their way back to the Midtown apartment. Finally, Mark said, "Did you love him, Jason?"

"Yes, but not like I love you."

"I'm not sure what you mean."

"Well, he was a really good friend and all. We had good times together, and he did things for me that I couldn't have done by myself. I liked being close to him, but there was something missing that I have with you."

"What's that?"

"I liked being with Paul. But I feel like I'm a part of you and you're a part of me. I never felt that with Paul."

Mark choked up a little, but managed to say, "I feel the same way."

After the funeral, it was easier for the two of them to settle into a domestic routine. Paul took up his new duties at All Saints, where he was now the junior member of the clergy staff. Jason was now unemployed.

"I can't very well go back to my old life," Jason told Mark. "and I really don't want to. I did what I did because I could make a living, not because I liked doing it. And it wouldn't be good for your reputation, either."

"Well, you're the guy with money. You can do as you please, can't you?"

"Yeah, I can. I've been thinking about that. I need to be able to do something that will let me move pretty easy."

"Meaning?"

"You know. You won't be at All Saints forever. You'll want to move on. When you do, I'll need to be able to pull up stakes and move with you."

"Any thoughts about what?"

"I like to draw. I thought maybe some kind of design work. But before we start into that, we have the condominium to do."

Mark was relieved hear Jason say that. Jason was ready to move on, to leave his attachment to Paul Thomas behind and begin a new life.

"OK," Mark said, "I can help you this Saturday, if you like."

"I'll start tomorrow," Jason replied. "I need to deal with Paul's old clothes and stuff myself. Then the two of us can work on making the condo ours."

For the next two days, Jason drove up to the Buckhead condo in his Jag to collect, box and bag all of Paul's personal effects. Each afternoon he drove back to the Midtown apartment that they shared.

Jason was puzzled by Paul's filing cabinet. The top three drawers were ordinary ones, but the bottom drawer was fitted with a combination lock. He asked Mark about it.

"Valuable papers, I suppose. I guess we ought to open it."

"But we don't have the combination," Jason objected.

"People usually write that kind of thing down somewhere," Mark said, "It's a stupid thing to do, but people can be pretty stupid. Let's go up and check."

They returned that evening and searched. Mark looked around on Paul's desk, and even checked the undersides of the drawers to see if it was taped to the bottom of any of them. He had no luck with that. Finally he turned to Paul's address book and went through it page by page.

Finally, he said, "Got it."

"Where?"

"Under E: "Efas, R. L., phone number (012) 031-0046.""

"Huh?"

"'Efas' is backwards for safe and I've never seen a phone number like that one. And look at the initials. The combination is Right 12, Left 3, Right 46."

Mark was right. The bottom drawer opened on the first try. Inside were the usual papers: the deed to the condo, insurance documents, the title to the Jaguar, etc. There was also a note about a joint savings account number in Tulsa and an accordion file folder with its flap tied shut. It was labeled "JJWWM."

"I'm tired," Jason complained. "It's getting really late."

"You're right," Mark said. "Let's take this stuff back to the apartment. We can go over it later."

The next Saturday, the two of them went to the condo together, armed with a measuring tape, ruler, pencil and paper. They intended to start figuring out how to redo the place and wanted to sketch out room plans and to make lists. There was a surprise waiting for them when they unlocked the door and stepped inside.

The whole place had been tossed. Pictures were off the walls, furniture overturned and ripped open, drawers had been thrown open and the contents scattered.

Jason was aghast. "We've been robbed!" He said.

"Burgled." Mark corrected him. "Robbery happens when you're there."

"Do you think they're still here?"

"No. They're long gone. And they were pros, too. The door was locked, remember? We had to use your key. And they had to get past the concierge at the desk, too. That, or get up here through a locked fire stair. They knew what they were doing. The question is, what were they after?"

"Should I call the police?"

"Not just yet. Don't touch or disturb anything, but try to see if anything's missing."

Jason walked carefully through the condo, stepping gingerly over the contents that were strewn everywhere.

"I don't see anything missing," Jason said after a while. "The computer's here, the television and music system, too. I think all of the silver's here. What were they looking for?"

"Dunno. Go ahead, call the cops and report it. They're not going to find anything, but it'll put building security on alert."

Jason and Mark waited for the police to arrive. The they waited some more, while the Atlanta police carried out their efficient, but time-consuming investigative routine. They had questions for Jason. They had questions for Mark. They had questions for the concierge. Finally, they officially concluded what Mark had unofficially decided in two minutes: whoever broke in was a professional who didn't find what he was looking for. There were no real leads to follow, but the police would beef up patrols in the area for a while.

Neither Mark nor Jason said anything about an old white Mustang. It and its occupants had long disappeared, so that danger had been the farthest thing from their minds. Now that worry was back.

They hadn't seen the Mustang because it was parked, at that very moment, outside Senator Nick Hutton's lake house on Grand Lake of the Cherokees.

Chapter Twenty-five

Tulsa, 1997

Nick's houseman, who opened the lake house door, had the deferential and polished manners of any good butler. He did not immediately recognize the man who was standing there.

"Did you have an appointment?" he asked, knowing perfectly well that no appointments with the Senator had been scheduled; and certainly not at the lake house.

"No, I don't," was Third's reply. "Please tell the Senator that Third White needs to see him urgently."

"Please come in, sir," was the deferential response. "Kindly wait here while I enquire."

The houseman disappeared into the recesses of the lake house, but was gone barely a minute before he returned.

"Please follow me, sir," he said as he headed in the direction of the library.

The door was already open. He ushered Third through it and announced him. Then the houseman closed the door softly behind him as he went away.

Nick retained an outward composure. Inwardly, he was fuming. "This is an unexpected surprise," he said pleasantly.

"I didn't want to call," Third said, "I didn't think you'd want me to show up at your office or anything like that. I'm trying to be discreet."

"Discretion is always appreciated, Third."

"Thanks. I hoped you would understand. I know you're busy, so I'll get right to the point. I want to quit. I haven't told Martha or anybody yet. I wanted to talk to you first."

"Third, I appreciate your loyalty. Certainly, you can transition out if you really want to."

"I want to. Of course, I'll work with you to get somebody else in place, first, if you like."

"I appreciate that offer, too. Of course, you have a legally binding, lifetime, non-disclosure agreement with the Johns' Ministry, do you not?"

"Yes, I do."

"That's good. You know a great deal about the close connection between the Conservative Party and the Johns. That should never become a matter for official scrutiny or public comment."

"Of course not."

"Third, I need to be blunt about this. I am not calling your loyalty into question, but I need to tell you that whistle-blowers do not always fare well. Some of them even end up dead."

"I thought that you might say something like that, Nick. I have no intention of ending up dead. So let me be blunt, too. I have what you might call a life insurance policy. Stashed far away from here are some documents and video recordings that will reach official hands if anything unfortunate should happen to me. The recordings include your secret meeting at the mansion with Martha, Jack and Tom."

"You surprise me, Third. You really do. I supposed you trusted me."

"I did until I found out about the Nazi connection. Nevertheless, I'll keep still for my own good. Now, Nick, you just be a good boy, and let me slip off into retirement and all will be well for all of us."

"You seem to have planned this out quite well," Nick said with an appreciative smile on his face. "Ok, Third, you've got a deal. Go ahead and hand in your resignation. Let me know which of your subordinate to approach and I will call on him."

Nick stood to indicate that the meeting was over. The two men shook hands and Nick ushered Third out the front door. Then, he returned to the library where he sat lost in thought for some time. Finally, he picked up the phone and made an appointment to see Martha.

The next day, smiles wreathed Martha's face as she greeted the senator at her office door.

"Nick, what a pleasant surprise," she exclaimed as she closed the door behind them.

"Not so pleasant, I'm afraid, Martha," was Nick's gloomy response. "I have discovered something that could do your Ministry a great deal of damage."

"Oh?"

"As you know, I sit on a number of Senate committees and have quite a few friends on the Hill. Naturally, private information sometimes comes my way."

"Go on."

"I hate to tell you this, but it appears that your head of security—what's his name?"

"Third."

"Yes, Third, has been spying on you for some time."

"What? Spying?"

"I'm afraid so. I think that it's been for one of the ultra-liberal groups. I just don't know which one yet. I'm trying to find out."

"Well," Martha said, pursing her narrow lips, "I've got some news for you, too. And it fits right in. He's just resigned. He must have found out that somebody's cottoned onto what he's been doing."

"That would make sense, wouldn't it?"

"Yes, it would. How much has gotten out, do you suppose?"

"It's hard to say," Nick said with apparent sadness. "I'll try to find out and scotch it, of course. I just wonder if he's confided in anybody you'd know of."

The penny dropped for Martha. "That little son-of-a-bitch Paul Thomas."

"Who?"

"A friend of his, a very close friend, if you know what I mean. He used to work for Jack and me when we were first starting out. He's about as two-faced as they come. I'll bet Third shared a lot of pillow talk with him before that weasel Paul left town."

"When did that happen?"

"Oh, I don't know. '94 or '95; thereabouts. He got a cushy organists church job in Atlanta. Some Episcopal cathedral or something. I forget exactly what."

"I don't know how I could check up on him," Nick said. "I guess we'll just have to trust to luck about that." He rose. "Sorry to be the bearer of bad news."

"Well, I'm sorry that we've been nursing a cuckoo in our nest," Martha said. "We're well rid of him. I'll have to do a real house-cleaning now. No telling who else is involved."

They shook hands at the office door and parted company. Martha was deeply disturbed, which was fine with Nick who was secretly elated. "Paul Thomas," he thought. "Shut him up for good. That'll scare the shit out of Third and whatever this Paul may know will die with him."

Nick returned to the lake house and turned plan into action.

Half an hour later, Nick's houseman politely ushered two men into Nick's library. They were both rough looking, crude and clearly out of place. Nevertheless, Nick knew them well and valued the important services they provided.

They were an odd pair. Butch was small and wiry. His companion, called Tiny was a head taller and a hundred pounds heaver than Butch. Butch was the brains while Tiny supplied the brawn. They lived in a small and very comfortable, isolated cabin on Nick's large lake property. Officially, they were caretakers for place. Nick also used them for certain kinds of chores that needed doing, and when necessary, what was euphemistically called wet work.

When they were out and about, Tiny usually drove Butch's old white Mustang. It was disreputable looking and noisy. Both were intentional. Under its unglamorous exterior was a powerful engine and finely tuned suspension system. Hidden switches could be used to disable the tag lights or the rear lights altogether. Concealed compartments held a variety of weapons. It was a very useful machine.

"Orders, sir?" Butch asked.

"Yes. Get that car of yours on our cargo plane and fly to Atlanta. Find a Paul Thomas who works at an Episcopal cathedral. I think he's the organist. Follow him and take him out in as disgraceful a way as you can. Snuff him, and do your best to destroy any reputation he's got."

"Then report back here?"

"No. Search his house. There are going to be some files and probably at least one computer disc. Look through his stuff and find anything that's related to the Johns or our operation. Toss the place and make it look like robbery. Get the stuff, get out and bring what you find to me here."

"Got it," Butch said, and repeated the orders back.

"That's it," Nick said, "do it."

They departed on their errand.

In Atlanta the found out there was only one Episcopal cathedral. St. Philip's Web site had the names of the staff on it, along with their photographs. Paul Thomas was listed as "Organist and Master of the Choirs." There were two possible Thomases in the phone book, but the other one was a carpenter living in Marietta.

They found the right Thomas living in a high-rise condo and staked it out. He followed the same routine, leaving for the cathedral around 8:45 in the morning and returning sometime in the afternoon or evening. Then, early one morning Paul emerged, accompanied by a young man. The two of them put some luggage in the back of his Jaguar and drove away. Butch and Tiny followed as a discreet distance as their target drove to the Interstate and turned south.

"When do we take 'em," Tiny asked, impatient for action.

"Don't know yet. Let's give it time. We'll get our chance."

Their target drove on and on, stopping only for food and gas. They finally arrived in Ft. Lauderdale a bit after dark. Butch watched them check into a motel that had a new looking rainbow sign out front.

"Get out of the car and follow them to see which room they get," he said. "Don't do anything, got me?"

"Yeah."

"Then meet me across the street at that gas station."

Tiny did as he was told, while Butch parked the Mustang on a nearby side street. Tiny reported back to say the room number was one at the back of the motel.

"It's a queer joint, Butch. Naked guys hanging out by the pool and everything."

"Perfect."

The two of them skirted the property and staked the room out from heavy shrubbery at the edge of a lake. After several hours, their target emerged. He was wearing swimming trunks. He went towards the pool. They followed. It was cool for Florida and the pool was deserted.

Just as Paul Thomas was sticking a toe in the water to check the temperature, Tiny sprang from behind him and throttled him. When he fell, dead, to the pool deck, Butch pulled off his trunks and threw them into the shrubbery. They rolled the body into the pool.

"Faggot," Tiny said, and spat into the water.

Then, they saw Jason looking on in horror. Before they could react, the young man fled like the hounds of hell were at his very heels. They watched the room for a while, but Jason didn't return. Then they heard sirens and hid.

The police came and went. After a while, they saw Jason again, but he had another guy with him.

"This is getting messy," Butch said. "I'd better call in."

Nick's orders were simple. "I agree it's getting complicated. Follow them and see what they do and where they go. You can be obvious about it. That should frighten the guy that was with Paul Thomas. If they start to make trouble with the police, take them both out. Otherwise, leave them alone. Two more deaths might look exceedingly odd."

"Right," Butch said, "got it," and hung up.

Tailing the Jaguar was easy. Butch and Tiny were able to follow it all the way to Orlando and then the trail went cold.

"They musta slipped outta the hotel in the night," was Tiny's helpful suggestion.

"No shit, Sherlock," said a disgusted Butch. "Well, it's Thomas's Jag, we'll just pick it up again in Atlanta. No point in trying to chase it down now."

They didn't call in again until after they had tossed Paul's condo. When they did call in, Nick called off the hunt. "Fly back and report in. I want to give this some more thought."

When they got back to the lake house, Butch got right to the point, "We think we know where it is."

"The files, you mean?" Nick asked.

"Yeah. There's a filing cabinet with a combination lock. It's in the library at that Paul guy's condo."

"How do you know?"

"We went there and tossed the place, just like you said. But those two queers showed up and we had to scoot out the back."

"Can you open it?"

"Not easy. Security's pretty tight and we'd probably have to make some noise. Getting it out in one piece would be even harder."

"Look," Nick said, obviously displeased. "I pay you for results, not for reporting problems."

"We got an idea, boss," Tiny said, speaking for the first time.

"Yeah," Butch added, "Tiny thinks we oughta grab the little queer. He'd be easy to handle."

"And this is going to help us how?" Nick said.

"Easy. We trade him for the papers and stuff. His boyfriend's gonna want his little boy-toy back; he's some kinda pussy clergyman. He's not gonna give us any trouble."

Nick thought about it for a minute or so while the two men continued to stand nervously before him. Finally, he spoke. "Alright. But, I want this quick and clean. And I'm going to send another man with you. I'm going to tell him to help you, so treat him nicely and make him a part of the snatch team. His name's Third. When you've got the files, kill all three of them. Make it look like a shoot-out between the three of them. And grab Third's I.D. I don't want anybody to know who he is. Clear?"

"Sure, boss," Butch said and Tiny nodded in agreement.

"Here's what I want done. Grab the little queer—what's his name?"

"Jason."

"Take him to someplace in town that's secluded, so nobody will see what's going on. Make it during the night."

"We can use the courtyard at the church where the other queer works," Butch suggested. It's in the middle of town, but you can't see into it very well and it's pretty dark."

"Yeah," Tiny said, "and the other queer knows where it is alright." He sniggered.

"That sounds fine," Nick said, "I'll leave that up to you. Pretend to work out the details with Third. But I want this clean. That means I want them dead. All three. And bring those files to me! I don't want any more screw-ups, clear?"

Both men nodded they understood.

"That's all. Wait for my final orders," Nick said, dismissing them.

Cool and efficient as ever, the blond houseman showed them courteously to the front door and locked it behind them.

The two of them went back to the cabin to wait.

Nick called JJWWM's main number and asked for Mr. White. When he was told that Mr. White no longer worked there, he asked if there was another number. The cheerful operator said there was and gave it to him. Nick dialed it right away.

"Third," he said when the phone was answered, "there's a problem that could blow up our deal. I need your help one more time to make sure that doesn't happen."

Third agreed to return to the lake house. There, Nick told him what had to be done.

Chapter Twenty-Six

Atlanta, 1997

On Sunday, after the last morning service, Mark and Jason headed up to the condo. They wanted to finish straightening up the mess the burglars had made. Jason pulled the Jaguar into its assigned parking place and they both stepped out, joking merrily to each other.

Mark never knew what hit him. The next thing he was aware of, a matronly lady was kneeling by him, slapping him gently on the face.

"Did you faint, Father?" she asked as his eyes fluttered open. "Shall I call an ambulance?"

Mark's head hurt like hell. "No." he said, "No ambulance. I think I must have tripped and hit my head. I'll be all right now, thank you."

"Are you sure?"

Mark was feeling more alert. "Yes. I promise I'll get checked out. Thank you so much for your help."

The kind lady left him a bit reluctantly, but when he walked steadily off in the direction of the building entrance, she drove away, only glancing back a couple of times to check on him. As soon as her car disappeared, Mark went back to the Jag. Jason would not have left him there willingly. And if he had gone for help, he would return shortly. Mark gave him fifteen minutes. Then he knew something was seriously wrong.

He decided to drive back to Midtown first, just in case Jason might be there. When he got in the car, he found a neatly printed note, folded and taped to the steering wheel.

"We've got Jason. Go to your apartment. Wait there for instructions."

He did as ordered. However, Mark was not idle while he waited. The condo had been burgled, but nothing had been taken. That pretty much narrowed it for him. Whatever they were looking for had to have been in the bottom drawer of the filing cabinet. He spread those items out on the dining table and went over them. They were all innocuous, except for the accordion file marked "JJWWM." He opened that.

Inside, he found an old contract between Paul Thomas and Jack and Martha Johns. It seemed that the now world famous evangelist and television personality had sent Paul to school. He read on.

The other papers were reports from a later date; most of them were computer generated. They pointed to an unsavory and potentially explosive connection between the Reverend Johns' television ministry and the Conservative party. How Paul Thomas had come into possession of these papers Mark could not imagine.

He found a photocopy of a handwritten note that said,

> *"Urgently recommend setting up new drop. Courier leaving Tulsa for new job. Please advise."*

Even more odd, he decided. Clearly, Paul Thomas had been tied to something that wasn't quite right.

The last things in the file were five identical computer discs. Identical, that is, so far as Mark could see. None of them had any sort of label at all.

He put everything back in the file folder and waited. The hours passed slowly. He told himself to contain his anxiety, that they were making him wait to worry him. And he worried, anyway, even as he made tentative plans.

It was past 4:00 a.m. when the call came, Mark was waiting for it. Even so, he let the phone ring a couple of times before he answered. Mark tried to keep my voice calm. "Hello," he said, trying to sound sleepy.

"We have your precious Jason," the gruff voice said. "Either we get the papers or he'll end up at the bottom of the river." The voice was deep, solid, uneducated and with a hint of the mountains in it. A thug.

"What papers?" He said, apparently surprised.

"We have Jason. Bring those papers from the filing cabinet and you can have him. If you don't show, he dies."

"I'll do whatever you tell me to," Mark assured him. "Please let me talk to him," he pleaded.

"Mark, don't!" came Jason's voice before it was cut off.

"Meet in the All Saints churchyard," the man said, "in fifteen minutes. Bring the papers." Then the connection was broken.

The church was several blocks away, so Mark had very little time. Just what they wanted, he supposed. But he was already dressed in black sweats and mostly black jogging shoes. He quickly added a black knit cap, black gloves, and a black scarf against the autumn chill.

Next, he tore the flap off the file folder, stuffed the folder into his waistband and pulled the sweatshirt down over it. He ran out the door. But he didn't drive. He ran. Fast. By cutting through a couple of empty parking lots and up a couple of alleys, he made it there in less than ten minutes. And that gave him a scant five minutes to spare, to scout out the situation and plan a rescue. Not much time.

He stopped, first, in the shadows near the MARTA station to catch his breath. Low clouds swept the tops of the tall buildings around him. Traffic was almost non-existent on West Peachtree Street. In the distance, a siren wailed. Nearby there was no sound, no movement.

He caught his breath, wrapped the black scarf around the bottom of his face and pulled his cap down. He jogged out of the shadows, hoping that any watchers in the churchyard would see only a city dweller out for an early morning run.

His route took him down Ponce de Leon Place, behind the Parish House and out of sight of the churchyard. There, he jumped the low stone wall. A few steps brought him to little-used side door. Fumbling in the dark, he slipped his master key in the lock, turned it, and opened the door. He stepped silently inside and quickly turned off the alarm system.

The stairwell between the old and new parish houses was made almost entirely of glass. Light filtered dimly into it. In that dappled darkness, Mark climbed quietly up the stairs. He paused at the first landing, again catching his breath, and peered out. Dressed from head to foot in black, and with his face and hands muffled in black, he hoped to be invisible to any watcher.

Mark could see nothing unusual. Except, perhaps, that the churchyard was darker than normal. A quick look confirmed that some of the exterior floodlights were out. "Probably shot out with a pellet gun," He concluded, a common enough trick used by burglars, he knew from previous experience.

There was enough light to see the general shape and layout of the churchyard. And still he saw nothing. So he moved on, a shadow among the shadows, down a long corridor to another window at another vantage point.

There were two of them. One large, one small, both rough-looking men. He recognized them almost at once from the lobby of the Hilton in Orlando. They were standing under a post light in the middle of the churchyard. The larger one had his arm around Jason's throat. It appeared to rest lightly there, but could instantly become a chokehold. The other looked around watchfully, checking the locked gates with his sweeping gaze. His hands hung at his sides. As he turned, Mark could see the .45 semi-automatic pistol in one of them.

Jason just stood there, quiet, alert, and scared.

Still, Mark continued to stand at the edge of the window, barely breathing, frozen in place as his police training had taught him. He knew if he didn't move at all, any movement in the shadows would become obvious. So he waited a bit longer, but not the slightest movement betrayed anyone else. There were just the two thugs and Jason standing there in the misty rain.

Time was ticking away. Now it was on Mark's side. As much as he wanted to rush in to the rescue, he gave it ten minutes more. They wanted something, so they would not immediately carry out their threat, but they would begin to become nervous, he hoped.

Mark oozed back into the darker shadows and felt his way down another staircase to the ground floor, crossed a small lobby, and entered the parish kitchen. Here again, light from the outside filtered in. The service door for the kitchen led directly into the churchyard. It was almost exactly opposite the streetlight where the men stood. Mark silently slid back the bolts so that the door would open when he turned the knob. Then he turned on the alarm and sprang into action.

Mark yanked the door open and slammed it shut behind him. That closed off the ominous warning beeps for the alarm that was sure to follow. He had one minute before the alarm sounded and alerted the remote monitoring station.

"Here!" he yelled rushing towards them, "Here are your Goddamn papers!" He pulled the folder out from under his clothes and threw it towards them. Papers and computer discs flew everywhere. His completely unexpected, sudden, dramatic entrance startled them, as he had hoped that it would.

Tiny tightened his hold on Jason, but Butch fell for Mark's ploy. He started to reach for some of the papers. It was his first and last mistake. Mark gave him a vicious kick on the side of the head, and he slumped to the ground. His gun clattered onto the concrete.

Mark lunged for the gun, and Tiny moved to grab the gun, too. His grip on Jason loosened momentarily. When Jason felt Tiny's grip go slack, he slipped down under his arm and turned toward Mark.

"Run!" Mark yelled.

Jason needed no encouragement. He swiveled away and sprinted towards the little cemetery at the top of the churchyard.

In those few moments, Tiny had grabbed the gun. He turned to fire at the fleeing Jason. Mark moved to interfere, and grabbed Tiny's wrist, just as the gun went off. Jason dove for the grass and disappeared from view behind some shrubbery.

The two men struggled for control of the gun. As they did so, the one-minute timer on the alarm expired. The shrill siren of the alarm began to sound, echoing off the tall buildings that surround the church.

Suddenly, the gun went off again. First Mark saw white, then red, then black, and then nothing.

When he came to, a paramedic was leaning over him, working on his shoulder. I hurt like hell. Nevertheless, he tried to sit up, but the paramedic restrained him.

"Just take it easy, buddy," he said. "I don't think you're hurt that bad, and we'll have you on your way to the hospital in no time."

A second face appeared beside his, this one topped by an Atlanta Police Department hat. "Is he awake?" the face asked.

"Yeah," the medic said. "But take it easy."

"Tell me what happened," the cop said to Mark.

But Mark wasn't going there, not yet. "I am a member of the clergy of this parish," he told him, "and I came down here in response to a call for help. There was a young man here. What happened to him?"

"You mean that little hustler?" the cop asked.

"We are all God's children," Mark rebuked him. "What happened to him?"

"Oh," the cop said, with more respect, "He's OK. He's talking to my partner."

At that moment, Jason's welcome face appeared beside those of the two strangers.

"Thank God you're OK, Father," Jason said, telegraphing what he had told the cops about their relationship. "He is OK, isn't he?" he asked the medic.

"He will be," the medic replied, "as soon as we get him into the ambulance, which is right now." Another medic and a cop appeared with a stretcher. They got Mark on it, raised the wheeled frame, and rolled him towards the street. Apparently, they had been climbing over the churchyard wall, because the gate was still locked.

"The key to the gate's in my left pocket," Mark told them, thereby saving himself a potentially painful lift over the wall and establishing his bone fides at the same time. He could see the cop's attitude adjust again.

"I really do need to find out what happened, Father," was his next remark. "What can you tell me?"

"There were two of them," Mark said.

"No," the cop said, "there were three."

"Three?"

"Yeah. We're still trying to figure out who the two others were. But we know who the dead guy is."

"Dead guy?" Mark said, groaning as they lifted him into the ambulance.

The cop climbed in beside him. "Yeah," he replied.

Jason climbed in on the other side. "I'm coming, too," he said.

"No, you're not," retorted the cop. "Out!"

"He comes," Mark said.

"Oh, all right," said the cop, in deference to him. Then to Jason, "Just keep still."

"Right," said Jason. And he wisely did so.

At that point the medic's face reappeared. "We're giving you something for pain," he said, "and starting an IV. Nothing to worry about." Then, turning to the cop, "No more questions now. He's in no condition to talk, and he's under the influence of narcotics."

"Right," said the cop. "It can wait. He's not going anywhere."

The cop stepped out and the ambulance pulled away from the curb, lights flashing and siren wailing.

"Where are you taking me?" Mark asked.

"Grady," came the response. "They do lots of gunshots there."

It didn't take long for the morphine to begin to take effect. Mark kept looking at the ambulance ceiling, but the tiny perforations in it kept going in and out of focus. By the time they reached Grady Hospital, Mark felt like I was floating about 4 inches off the stretcher. When he tried to talk, he had trouble getting the words out.

"I must sound pretty drunk," he said to Jason.

"Yeah," Jason said with a grin.

"You need to make a phone call for me," Mark said. "Call the rector. The number's in my wallet."

"Right," Jason said.

While everybody was doing paperwork, Jason got the number and went off to make the call. Mark was wheeled into a curtained off area in the emergency room. Jason stuck his head through the curtains. "Mission accomplished," he managed to say, before the nurses shooed him away. They gave Mark another hefty dose of something, told him they were taking him to surgery, and not to worry; everything would be fine.

Mark didn't remember much after that until he woke up in recovery, swathed in bandages. His wakefulness lasted maybe two minutes before he fell asleep again.

He was vaguely aware of being wheeled down endless corridors and into elevators. When was fully awake again, he was in a private room and it was daylight. Jason was sitting by the bed, watching television with the sound turned down low. The morning news was covering the shooting in the All Saints churchyard.

"A security guard employed by the internationally famous television evangelist Jack Johns was found shot to death in the churchyard at the historic All Saints Episcopal Church," is what the pretty blond television reporter said. "It is still unclear exactly what happened and the police are continuing to investigate. This is Doris Norris reporting."

Just then, the bishop came in, accompanied by Marks rector. Jason stood up for them as Mark punched buttons on his bedside controls and turned off the television.

"How are you feeling?" The rector asked.

"Well enough," Mark replied, "I've been here before."

"Let's hope it's the last time," the bishop replied, smiling slightly. Then he went on, "How are you holding up?" he asked Jason.

"Pretty good," was Jason's sturdy reply.

The bishop looked at him shrewdly for a moment. "Have you been here all night?"

"Yes," Jason said, "ever since Mark came to rescue me and got himself shot."

The next pause was longer. "Do you love him?" the bishop asked.

"Yes, sir, I do," Jason said firmly.

"Love's always a good thing," the bishop said. His smile included both of them.

Then the rector gave them both the sanctified Communion bread and wine he had brought with him from All Saints. The bishop anointed Mark for healing with *olium infirmium* and gave them both his blessing. The door closed behind him.

"OK," Jason said, placing emphasis on each letter.

Mark just smiled. Relaxed, content, and still feeling the drugs, he began to drift off to sleep again.

Jason quietly switched on the television as he took up his watching and waiting.

Chapter Twenty-Seven

Atlanta, 1997

Next day, when the pain medications were being reduced and Mark was no longer under the influence, it was the cops' turn to visit. He was accompanied by a couple of very senior police officials.

They asked Jason to take a break and get something to eat. He left reluctantly and they began to ask their questions.

Mark could honestly answer that he had no idea that anybody employed by Jack Johns was anywhere near Atlanta, let alone in the churchyard. To some of the other questions, he fudged and said that it was privileged, confessional information and could not be shared with them.

On the other hand, the police told him a good deal. Two shots had been fired, which Mark knew. The first one, intended for Jason, had missed its mark because Mark had grabbed the assailant's wrist. It had struck a bronze statue of Jesus in the cemetery and ricocheted, hitting the man called Third in the head and fatally wounding him.

Had Mark ever met anyone connected with Johns, they wanted to know.

Again, an honest "no" from Mark.

Throughout the interview, Mark was worrying desperately about two things: What had happened to his assailant after Mark had been shot, and most importantly, where were the papers? Nothing had been said about them at all.

He tired quickly, and the police, realizing that he knew little more that he could or would talk about, left him in peace.

Jason returned shortly after the police left.

"Jason," Mark said. "What did you tell the police? What happened after I was shot? What became of the guy with the gun? I need details!"

"Oh," Jason said brightly, "I just told 'em the truth. These two guys grabbed me and called you because they thought you'd pay them off to get me back. So, you showed up, and there was a struggle and the gun went off. They tried to shoot me and did shoot you."

"What about the guy with the gun?"

"Oh, he ran up to near where I was hiding, took one look, said "Oh, shit," and took off. I think he dropped the gun up there, too, cause I heard it hit something."

"And what about the files I had?" Mark asked.

"Oh, those," Jason said, "That's easy. I got the papers right here under my sweater."

"What?" Mark said. "Do you really?" Relief flooded over him like an incoming tide.

"Well," Jason said, "It's like this: they've been going to an awful lot of trouble to get their hands on this stuff. So I decided I shouldn't tell the cops about it till I talked to you. So I didn't. And I didn't want to bother you with it yesterday. I figured you needed to rest up."

So, there it was. Jason had the file. The cop's earlier dismissal of Jason as a hustler, coupled with his old street-smart ways, had kept him completely silent until Mark asked.

"Thanks, Jason," was all that Mark could muster. "Thanks a lot." Then: "You're right, too. It is secret and it's important. Maybe I can tell you about it someday and maybe I can't. Can you trust me on that?"

"I guess so," Jason said, grinned, "seeing as how I've already trusted you with my life. I knew you'd come for me," Jason went on, "I knew you'd do best for me you could."

Mark had tears in his eyes and Jason kissed them away.

"Don't cry, silly," he said, "don't do that."

"I can't help it," Mark responded. "I love you, you know. I could never let any-body harm you if I could help it."

"Well," Jason said, "you don't have to go all mushy about it."

"Now," Mark said, business-like again, "about that file. Sorry, I've got to take care of the loose ends."

"O.K.," Jason said, grinning a wicked smile, "what do you want me to do, now that I'm not a lose end any more?"

Mark laughed hard. It hurt and he didn't care. "Just let me check through the file, please."

Jason handed over the water-stained file folder. Mark looked through the contents.

"It looks like everything's here, as well as I can remember. But I thought there were five of these discs. There are only four. You sure you got everything?"

"Everything I saw."

"Then I must have counted wrong."

Next, Mark called the cathedral and asked for the bishop, who answered after only a brief pause. "Mark, are you alright?" was his first question.

"Oh, yes, sir, I am feeling much better than I have for some time." Mark replied, winking a Jason. "However, it's not the gunshot, but other matters that are now at hand."

"I don't follow you," the bishop said, puzzled.

"It's something of a personal nature," Mark said, "so I'd appreciate it if you'd make another hospital call as soon as it's convenient."

"Let me rearrange a couple of things on my calendar, and I'll get to the hospital as soon as I can," was the bishop's response. "It will probably be late afternoon."

Mark said, "Thank you," and broke the connection.

Late that afternoon, as promised, the bishop arrived. As Mark and Jason had arranged, Jason excused himself, saying "I guess you're in good hands, Mark, so I'll take a break and get a Coke or something."

"Now," said the Bishop, "What's this all about?"

"Please allow me to explain, sir," was Mark's response. "While I was going through Paul Thomas' belongings I found a the combination to a file drawer in his study. It had the usual important papers that one would expect, and some unexpected files that concerned Paul Thomas' earlier years and some other connections."

Mark paused, trying to figure out how to put what he was going to say in the most charitable way.

"Go on," said the bishop.

"Well," said Mark, "the papers show that there was a tie-in between Paul Thomas and Jack Johns. What began as a very close relationship later became adversarial. What happened is not clear to me, but making any of this public would not be helpful."

"I see," said the Bishop. "And where is this file now?"

"I have it here in the bedside stand. Jason picked it up in the confusion right after the police arrived. He kept it for me."

"But you didn't tell me about this earlier. Why not?"

"I had intended to bring all of Paul Thomas" papers to you, once I had found them. I had hoped, at that time, that we could discuss this particular matter. I was going to call you the next day. But, before I could do that, Jason was kidnapped."

"I begin to see," said the Bishop. "The ransom was to be the papers. And that was why Jack Johns sent his bodyguard to the churchyard."

"Exactly."

"And your heart said that Jason's life was the more important thing."

"Yes. An easy choice."

"Yes, easy. As you say," the bishop observed, "Paul Thomas is dead, and could not be harmed, but Jason is alive and needed rescuing. And you couldn't call the police without risking exposure of the whole sorry business, whatever it is, so you took the rescue upon yourself."

"Yes."

"And what is to be done with this mysterious file?" the bishop continued.

"My recommendation?" Mark said. "Destroy it without reading it."

"Then that is what I shall do. Did Jason read it, do you think?"

"He said he didn't," Mark said

"Then," the Bishop continued, "I'm quite sure he didn't. The secret, is seems, is to be yours alone."

"Yes. And, like any good confessor, I have forgotten it already." Mark replied.

Rolling over on his side, and groaning slightly with the effort, Mark removed the file folder from the drawer and handed it to the bishop.

The Bishop had just placed it in his briefcase when there was a knock at the door and in walked Jason.

"Come along, Jason," the Bishop said, "I'm starving. How does pizza and beer sound to you?"

"Great," Jason said. And then, grinning, "I guess we'll just have to leave the invalid here"

"Mark," said the Bishop, "you might just look up a verse of scripture while you're waiting for your dinner tray. Take a look at John 15: 12."

Mark smiled back at the Bishop as he and Jason went out the door together. Mark didn't have to look the verse up to know that it said:

"A new commandment I give to you, that you love one another."

After pizza and beer, the bishop dropped Jason back at the hospital. Then that Right Reverend gentleman went home and lit a fire in his fireplace.

Chapter Twenty-Eight

Atlanta, 1997

Doris Norris hated her name. She had been named for a wealthy aunt. Unfortunately, when the aunt died, it became evident that the ploy had not worked. Doris had not been remembered in the will. She had, however, been saddled her entire childhood with classmates who chanted,

> *"Doris Norris,*
> *you're a horse-ass,*
> *Nah! Nah! Nah!"*

She grew into an ungainly girl with pimples before anybody else had them and had obvious breasts by age 10. To make matters worse, she was smart, studied hard, and read a lot. She had no really close girlfriends, and the boys ignored her. Throughout her teenage years, she hoped for a way to escape her unhappiness.

College offered her that chance. She studied creative writing and spent her free time writing for the college newspaper. Near the end of her sophomore year, a Senior girl, which whom Doris had seldom spoken, and who lived down the hall from her, stopped by. Doris was a bit surprised by the unexpected visit.

"Doris," the girl said, "I want to talk to you."

"About what?" Doris wanted to know.

"Look, Doris, do you even know who my little brother is?"

"Yeah, sure. He's the quarterback on the football team. I've interviewed him often enough."

"He likes you."

"Uh, oh," Doris said, "I don't think so."

"What? He lies to his sister about something like this?"

"Oh, no, Marylyn, I didn't mean that. It's just that boys have never been very interested in me."

"Look, Doris, you're really a good-looking young woman. Only you don't seem to know it. Or, if you do, you don't know what to do about it. Come over here to the mirror."

Reluctantly, Doris obeyed the older girl.

"Now, pull your hair back," Marylyn said, "and lose those glasses."

Doris did so. But when she looked at herself objectively in the mirror, she was more than a bit surprised. She had changed; she had grown up; she looked, well, womanly. She rather liked this.

"Now," Marylyn announced, "Gary is going to ask you to a dance. And you're going. And you're going to look the part. You are and are spending Saturday at the beauty salon and going shopping."

Doris started to object.

"Hush," Marylyn said. "My treat."

By the time that Saturday was over, Doris had been easily transformed into the proverbial swan. She was asked to the ball. She went. She was overwhelmed by the sudden discovery that she was beautiful.

Doris's elective studies included courses in television broadcasting. Her intelligence and natural sense of the dramatic made her a good location reporter. An Atlanta station snapped her up as soon as she had graduated.

She spent the next three years covering house fires, automobile wrecks, convenience store robberies, shootings, and storm damage. And she waited for that moment that all young reporters wait for: her big break.

She was on duty when the police radio band announced a shooting in the churchyard at All Saints. She and Bud, her cameraman, grabbed a production van and hit the street. They got there second, and only seconds behind the first arrival. The police wouldn't let them any nearer than across the street, but they got some reasonably good shots anyway. Pretty soon all of the competition packed up and drove away.

But Doris wanted to stay. "It's a slow night, Bud," she said to her cameraman. "Let's get some closer shots around the church after the police finish."

In a few minutes, the yellow crime scene tape began to come down.

"Is it alright if I go in now?" she smiled breathily at the first officer she met.

He melted in his tracks and stuttered, "Sure."

The churchyard was dimly lit, but she looked around anyway, planning some shots that they could get as soon as Bud brought the equipment. Then she saw it. As she turned away from looking at the bronze statue of Jesus in the Garden, a small, bright silver reflection caught her eye. When she looked again it was gone. She took a step back, and saw it again. A glimmer of silver under the clustered leaves of an azalea bush.

What she called "the angel on my shoulder" seemed to prompt her into action at just the right moments. This was one of those. From beneath the azalea bush, Doris Norris retrieved an unmarked, silver compact disc. She looked at both sides. It was quite clean and therefore dropped only recently. She dropped it into her capacious handbag.

As soon as Bud brought things they needed from the production van, Doris concentrated on getting the additional shots she needed, did a little more on-camera reporting. She worked quickly and cleverly. Back at the station, she worked on the rest of the script for her story, and helped to edit the bits together. It was good. Her boss congratulated her (not for the first time) and sent her home.

As soon as she got there, she poured herself a large glass of Piesporter, kicked off her shoes, and turned on her computer. When she inserted the disc, the computer didn't recognize it. Next she tried it in her DVD player. That worked just fine.

Doris leaned forward and watched intently. It was immediately clear who the people were, and each of them was famous: the famous television evangelist and his wife, Senator Nicholas Hutton, a possible candidate for the White House, and the chief strategist of the nation's Conservative Party.

>*"Refreshments, anyone?" Martha Johns asked, playing hostess. She gestured carelessly towards the sideboard where the butler was standing. Getting no response, she nodded to him, saying "We'll wait on ourselves if we want anything later."*
>
>*The butler closed the door silently behind him and Martha rose and crossed to the bar. There, with expert ease, she mixed Jack his favorite dry Martini and pour three stiff Scotches over the rocks for the rest of them. Clearly, she knew the drinking habits of her guests.*
>
>*Senator Nick Hutton raised his glass. "To continued success," he said.*
>
>*"We were certainly very successful after our last national campaign," bob, the strategist, interjected, "your speech to the convention was very helpful in that regard."*
>
>*"Naturally," Jack said, "we're always glad to help our friends in any way we can."*
>
>*"Let's get down to brass tacks," Bob said in response. "As you know, I don't believe that politics has any rules. I think it should be winner take all. We intend to put the opposition out of business. The idea of a loyal minority, a loyal opposition, is an outmoded and useless idea. Our nation has outgrown that. The time has come for us to establish a new worldwide empire. We do not intend to let anybody keep us from doing that."*
>
>*Nick added, "The world is changing very rapidly. It's currently in a renaissance that's affecting the whole world. We have increased communication, travel and trade. We have increased movement of populations. We have challenges to the authority and stability of established governmental and religious institutions."*

"It's the same kind of thing that the Western hemisphere went through beginning in the fourteenth century, only it's worldwide."

"I'm no student of history," Jack said, "but I understand what you're saying. We do talk about living in new times, don't we?"

"We do. And these new times present real challenges to those of us who, in one way or another, are world leaders." Bob's gesture took in the whole room.

"We come now to the delicate part of tonight's business," Nick said. "You have kindly assured us of the security and privacy of your home. I mention that because the heart of the matter is so sensitive that I must extract a promise from the two of you. You may not reveal any part of what we discuss next to anybody else, ever. The knowledge that I am about to reveal to you presents certain dangers. It will become equally dangerous to you as well."

"Please continue," Martha said.

"Yes, please do," said Jack, clasping his hands.

"Our world wide renaissance is going to be short lived, I'm afraid. Irreversible cataclysmic changes are going to cut it short."

Bob chuckled. "Indeed. This is a once in millennium opportunity, because what the Reverend here would call the Apocalypse has already begun. The four horsemen are already on the move. Or, to put it in modern terms: our world, as we know it, will shortly come to an end."

"What are you talking about!" Martha said. "The Apocalypse, and the end of the world, and all that guff. You don't believe any of that stuff any more than I do."

Nick replied somewhat stiffly, "Unfortunately, Martha, it is fact not fancy. Neither Bob nor I are speaking metaphorically. You have undoubtedly heard about global warming, have you not?"

Martha pursed her lips at his change in tone. "Certainly I have," she said coolly. What about it?"

"What we know, with great certainty, it this: Isaac Newton was right. The world as we know it will end by 2060. Of course, that's coincidence; Newton didn't have a clue.

"The flow of the major sea currents is already being slowed. It has to do with the melting of the polar ice caps, as you may have heard. The water is getting less salty and doesn't sink as well at the poles as it once did. When that flow stops, temperatures in the northern and southern regions will no longer be tempered by warm water. And they will begin to freeze. Rapidly. Once the freezing starts it will take ten to fifteen years for the entire globe to be enveloped in another ice age."

"So, the Earth's going to turn into a snowball," Martha said, "and it's being kept secret? How can that possibly be?"

"It's simple. The leading climatologists work for us."

Jack had been listening intently, saying nothing, but taking it all in. "Just who is 'us?'" Bob nodded for Nick to say it: "The Fourth Reich."

"What?" Jack and Martha exclaimed simultaneously. "What!"

"That's right. The impending global crisis gives us the perfect opportunity, our dream for a better world," Bob explained, "A world that is much better than this one."

Jack Johns started to say something, but Bob interrupted him. "Before you say anything, Jack, let me read this to you:

"The national government will maintain and defend the foundations on which the power of our nation rests. It will offer strong protection to Christianity as the very basis of our collective morality. Today Christians stand at the head of our country. We want to fill our culture again with the Christian spirit. We want to burn out all the recent immoral developments in literature, in the theater, and in the press — in short, we want to burn out the poison of immorality which has entered into our whole life and culture as a result of liberal excess during the past years."

You've got to admit it sounds an awful lot like what you believe, doesn't it?"
"It does."

"That is our objective, too," Nick said, pressing his point. "We want a strong moral nation with strong leadership. Within the next thirty years or so, civilization as we know it is going to be on the verge of collapse. First the seas will rise and drown the low-lying land. Millions of people will be on the move, looking for food and shelter."

"The United States must be able to repulse these migratory hoards," Bob said. "It will be possible for us to thin our own population and relocate the rest, but if we are overwhelmed by an influx the other races, our battle to save civilization will be lost. The whole world will sink into another dark age."

"Annihilating these hoards is essential to controlling the situation. Their numbers are vast and many have already begun to migrate into the more developed parts of the world. They are undermining the world's labor market and causing civil unrest in various parts of the world. That has to be stopped."

"I recognize that civil unrest is undesirable," Jack said, "but how do you stop it on a worldwide scale."

"By keeping it from happening in the first place. We do it by greatly reducing their numbers."

"The plague of AIDS is spreading. Famine persists in many parts of the world and an increasing death rate in much of it, too. Nature has already started the process for us. We just stand by and let nature take its course. AIDS is but one of the weapons in natures arsenal. Infectious diseases of all sorts take their toll almost entirely among the lest desirable among us."

Jack looked at him, intrigued. "Are you telling us that thinning will come about through using disease?"

"It's already happening. Fortunately, that idiot actor Reagan was easily manipulated into doing nothing about the AIDS epidemic until it was too late to stop its spread. A vaccine could probably have been developed then, if we hadn't stopped it. It could still be developed now, but we are making sure it won't be."

"I like it," Nick said, "The brown and black races, and the queers, are screwing themselves into extinction."

"And the drugs that are developed will remain expensive, I suppose," said Jack.

"Exactly," Tom replied, "That will keep them out of the hands of the poor. The overall result will be many fewer of the dark skinned races, leaving Aryan Christians able to maintain control over the world."

"All of this will take time, of course," Nick said. "Natural processes take time, even when inaction helps them along. Sometimes benign neglect is our best tool."

"I don't see how that's going to help us govern on a world wide basis. I can't see how you can go running roughshod over the territories that belong to other countries," Martha objected.

"Dear lady," the Tom responded, "you have put your very intelligent finger squarely on the second part of the strategic plan. That is the purpose of the new War on Terror. Terrorism gives us the perfect opportunity to invade any country we like. We can start a war anywhere we like on the pretext that we're going after the terrorists."

"Arms and manpower; I'm not sure the American people will stand for that, at least in the long term," Martha said.

"The answer is a "guns and butter" economy. As long as the American middle class has its comforts: a decent house, a couple of cars, leisure time and plenty of cheap food they won't complain," Nick explained. But, we also have to keep them afraid. As we've said, the shadowy army of terrorists can be anywhere, anytime. They are our foreign threat. We will also need an enemy within, and that is the queers. If the American population is well-fed and has enemies to hate, they will remain passive."

"Things will get pretty bad here at home, too, won't they?" Jack said.

"Yes. Your most important role will be to explain that all of this as the will of God. That the climatic changes are an act of God. So you see, Armageddon really is upon us."

Jack had listened, but said little. Now he spoke in his most prophetic way. "It is our Christian duty to cooperate with the four horsemen as they cleanse the world and prepare it for the coming thousand years of peace."

The others said nothing. The bargain had been sealed.

Doris didn't wait for more. She grabbed the phone and made a reservation for New York. Next she called a contact at American Broadcasting and said she needed to speak urgently to the head of the news department. She left her home number, emphasizing that it was critical that the call be returned there. Next she called her own station and said she had become suddenly ill. Probably a stomach flu bug, she suggested.

She packed a bag for three days. While she waited for the phone to ring, she called a livery service, said to send a car and have it stand by outside her apartment building. She gave them a credit card number.

Just as she hung up, the phone rang returning her call. She said "thanks" for calling her right back, then: "According to every ethical principal I learned in journalism school, I shouldn't be doing this. I'll probably be fired before I ever get back to Atlanta. And I don't care. This is a case of national security, and I want you to break the story. It's a plot to take over the government."

"Are you serious?" he asked.

"You bet I am. I have hour and one-half hours of uninterrupted video recording of the entire thing. Senator Nick Hutton, that television evangelist, Jack Johns; it's dynamite."

"Get here as quick as you can."

"I have a car waiting." Doris said. She gave him her flight number and time of arrival. She knew she wouldn't have to ask about transportation when she arrived. There would be a car waiting for her at the other end, she was certain. She was right about that, too.

The next day, the body of a young woman, later identified as Doris Norris was found floating in the East River. There was never any explanation of what he had been doing in New York.

Shortly after the resolution of this serious security failure was reported to Buenos Aires, Senator Nick Hutton and the leaders of The Foundation for Religious Truth in America were summoned to Argentina. The meeting was at once hurried and unusual. The leaders of ODESSA preferred to keep their distance from ODESSA's operatives. But the leadership was very seriously displeased. Operation Aurum, they said, had suffered a severe setback. They expressed their unhappiness clearly and at length.

Certain steps would be taken.

Epilogue

Atlanta, Springtime, 1997

The unexpected and tragic death of Doris Norris remained news in Atlanta for a few days, only to be supplanted by more exciting national events.

The Foundation for Religious Truth in America announced that it had suspended financial support of the JJWWM television network, pending the outcome of an IRS investigation into Jack and Martha John's finances.

All aboard had apparently died when a private Pan-American Oil and Gas jet disappeared from the skies over the Gulf of Mexico. On board was the popular junior Senator from Oklahoma, Nick Hutton. The Coast Guard found a debris field, but no bodies were recovered.

The news failed to cover a service in tiny Mikell Chapel at St. Philips Cathedral. Only Mark's rector and his wife, the bishop and his wife, and a few close friends attended the ceremony. Jason was as nervous as a cat and so was Mark. But everything went smoothly as the bishop solemnly blessed their relationship.

Afterwards, there was a reception in Jason and Mark's Buckhead condo. Sun poured in through the French windows that were open to the balcony and the welcome spring breeze. The buffet luncheon was excellent and the Champaign, brought by Talbot Smith, was superb.

As he was leaving, the bishop dropped his bombshell. He had followed up on Paul Thomas' savings account in Tulsa. There was almost a million Dollars in it. As Thomas' heir, Jason would get it all.

Later that night, together in their new big bed, Jason snuggled closer to Mark as they slept.

Amor Vincit Omnia

444

978-0-595-45190-6
0-595-45190-X

Printed in the United States
85876LV00005B/81/A